SAVOUR

SAVOUR

JACKIE BATEMAN

anvil press / vancouver

Anvil Press Publishers Inc.
P.O. Box 3008, Main Post Office
Vancouver, B.C. V6B 3X5 CANADA
www.anvilpress.com

Library and Archives Canada Cataloguing in Publication
Bateman, Jackie, 1970-, author
    Savour / Jackie Bateman.
ISBN 978-1-77214-000-2 (pbk.)
    I. Title.
PS8603.A8385S28 2014   C813'.6   C2014-905235-9

Printed and bound in Canada
Cover design by Rayola Graphic Design
Cover photo by Peeter Viisimaa
Interior by Vancouver Desktop Centre
Represented in Canada by Publishers Group Canada
Distributed by Raincoast Books

The publisher gratefully acknowledges the financial assistance of the
Canada Council for the Arts, the Canada Book Fund, and the Province
of British Columbia through the B.C. Arts Council and the Book
Publishing Tax Credit.

To James

ACKNOWLEDGEMENTS

A special thanks to my mighty agent, Joanna Swainson, for her invaluable support and guidance. A heartfelt thanks to Brian Kaufman and the team at Anvil Press. Thank you to Jenn Farrell, my editor, for her unflinching brilliance and unicorn-riding imagination. And finally, to my family, for putting up with me writing all the time. It's been emotional.

ONE

Banana Dave's Fruit Stall, Soho

Lizzy peered around one of the posts, trying to see the new girl on Keith's stall. The girl looked even younger than her, from there anyway—maybe fourteen or fifteen. She was wearing a Hello Kitty T-shirt. Talk about babyish, unless she was wearing it in an ironic way. It was hard to tell.

"All right, Lizzy, you working all this week, then?" Keith caught her staring and waved at her.

"Aye, I'm full time now. I'll be here all the way 'til Friday," she called over.

"Aye, aye. You sounded well Scottish then."

"Shut it, you." She had sounded a bit off, and knew it as soon as she'd opened her mouth. Keith liked to tease her, and she didn't mind that. But she should be more careful. You never knew who was listening, and there was no use standing out from the crowd when she didn't want to be found. She'd been trying to shake off her old accent for the last three years, but sometimes, when she was caught off-guard, she lapsed back into it.

Lizzy turned back to her own stall and shifted some fruit around so the best bits were at the front and the rotten bits were hidden. Dave had taught her to do that. Whenever she served someone she didn't like, she put the bad fruit at the bottom of the bag to bulk up the weight. Like Spinner, the pimp guy, who was always sniffing around like a big rat. Not that he bought anything very often. Too tight. She knew someone else just like him back in Scotland and had hated him on sight as well.

She yawned. It had been a bad night at the hostel. A ruck had kicked off in one of the rooms across the landing in the early hours and she hadn't been able to get back to sleep. There was a lot of shouting, and what sounded like someone's head being cracked against the wall. She'd been curious to see what was going on, but resisted in the end, too scared to leave her room. She didn't want to get hurt, or even get involved with anything. The less exposure she had with the police, the better. In any case, the last time she helped the Indian woman down the hallway, she'd got a boot in the leg and a bruise that lasted about a month to show for it. That woman had some nasty boyfriends.

She wiped her hands on a corner of the apron that Dave had given her to wear. It had a big pocket for loose change, and wearing it made her feel like she had a proper job. She was in charge when Dave wasn't around. Underneath the apron she wore a pouch around her waist where she put all the notes and the bigger coins, so no one could dip into the earnings.

One of the early morning oldies appeared then, holding out his crumpled carrier bag. "Mornin', my love. Six bananas and one of them peaches, please. I'll have that one at the front." His hands shook as he touched his flat cap to her.

"There you go." She put the fruit in his bag for him, and handed it over.

He put it on the ground between his legs, then straightened up and raised his palms up to the sky. "Thanks, love. Let's have a smile, shall we? The sun's nearly out."

She gave him her best smile. He was a regular, and dead sweet, really. She remembered her mum saying she enjoyed serving all the oldies first thing in the morning when she worked in the newsagents back home. When she was alive.

As the man hobbled away, she felt the smile on her face break down. Anything that reminded her of Mum made her stomach hurt, and it was a special day as well. She stared at the ground, nudging her foot against a sweetie wrapper and some stalks and leaves that had fallen from the fruit punnets. They rolled towards the gutter as she kicked at the memories.

A hard voice pulled her back. "There she is, Banana Dave's glamorous assistant."

It was Spinner. A cold streak found its way through her, bringing up the hairs on her arms. She looked up at his sneering face, the gold tooth. He was wearing those tight jeans with designer creases in the crotch. *Gross.*

He took a few steps closer, and lowered his voice. "What's up, Blondie? Down in the dumps, are we? Need some extra cash?"

"Not from you." She caught a waft of his cheap aftershave and screwed up her nose.

"You will, darlin'. You will. All the market girls need the Spinner sometime or other."

"I won't." She looked around the market. Where was Dave or Keith when she needed them?

"I could give you some extra pocket money to buy new headscarves. Why'd you hide away that lovely hair of yours, anyway? Natural, is it?" He looked at her crotch as he spoke.

Lizzy gave him the most disgusted look she could.

He picked up an apple, threw it in the air and caught it with one hand. Polishing it on his thigh, he cocked his head to one side. "You're a tough nut to crack, you are, but it won't be long before you'll be giving the Spinner that smile of yours, and not just saving it for the old gits 'round here."

"You going to pay for that apple?"

"Nah." Spinner pushed it into the inside pocket of his leather jacket and held his arms out. "You going to come and get it back?"

"Nah." Lizzy turned away, busying herself with unpacking some pears. She felt his eyes shift over her before he dragged his revolting self away. She knew when he had gone, didn't have to turn around to see. The smell of him, the feel of him, had lifted. Cheeky bastard, talking about money for scarves. If only he knew. The only reason she wore them was to hide her signature blonde hair. With what she got paid, she couldn't afford to keep dyeing it.

Berwick Street was busying up already. This was Lizzy's favourite time of day because she got to see all the posh folk on their way to work. There were advertising agencies and film companies and model agents all about Soho, scattered among the clothes stores she couldn't afford to shop in and restaurants she dreamed of eating in. The only places she got to see inside were the grimy street cafés and newsagents that lined the market. Mostly it was the same people that walked through during rush hour, regular as clockwork. Black coats, high-heeled boots, guys in tight skinnies and combat jackets. She wondered what they thought of the market, or of her working the stall. That's if they thought about it at all, or even noticed her shabby jeans and worn-out Doc Martens. She studied her fingerless gloves, showing grubby, bitten nails. Sometimes she painted them black, but it soon chipped and made them look even worse. The street was just a route, a shortcut to where everyone had to get to by nine o'clock. No one really looked at anything or anyone, least of all her.

Here was that tall girl, the one carrying the gold leather hand-bag with metallic straps, tight under her arm. She had shiny long hair like Pocahontas, always immaculate, and wore big sunglasses whatever the weather. Lizzy wished she could go with her, follow her to some sophisticated office full of suits and fancy carpets. The girl was gone in an instant, rounding the corner in the direction of Carnaby Street before disappearing into the crowd. Lizzy kept looking that way, as if she'd come back at any minute, beckon to her. But it didn't happen. She could be that girl, strutting her way to some glam job in advertising or filmmaking, getting tea made for her and drinking cocktails after work in one of those bars on Old Compton Street.

Maybe one day.

Spinner was talking to the new girl. Of course he was. She watched as he waved his hairy hands around, showing off, and grinning like the charmer he thought he was. The girl was smiling a bit. Keith must have gone off to get change. Normally he'd never let Spinner near his stall. She'd have to warn the girl. From what she'd heard, once Spinner got hold of you, it was difficult to break free. There was a rumour that the redhead who used to work on the flower stall became one of his prostitutes. Anything was possible with that creep.

The morning had disappeared, and Dave showed up just as Lizzy was nearly dribbling from hunger. He always let her take from the "very ripe" piles, but there was only so much fruit she could eat.

"All right, Lizzy darlin', how's the morning been?" He clapped his hands together and grinned, showing some rotten teeth.

"Good. Quite a bit sold, if you must know. Here's your pouch thing and the apron. I'm off for my break then, if that's okay."

He took them from her, lifted the pouch up and down and whistled. "Nice one. Tons of dosh in there. I better take it all to the bank when you get back. Here's something for your lunch. Treat yourself in the café. You look like you need a good feed. Turn sideways and you'd disappear, you would."

She took the five-pound note from him. "Cheers, Dave. Won't be too long."

"You get down to Dina's and get something hot down your neck." He turned away to serve a customer, wrapping the apron string around his waist.

He was okay, Banana Dave. He looked after her. Lizzy had told him a bit about where she was from, who she needed to hide from, and he'd accepted it, not asked many questions. In the beginning, he'd said he wouldn't give her any work, that he could tell she was a runaway. After a bit of persuading, he agreed to take her on for a trial, cash in hand, but only because he was knackered that day. She might have been a street kid back then, but she knew how to work hard, and she soon showed Dave that he needed her. Lizzy liked being on Banana Dave's stall because no one messed with him, not even Spinner. He wasn't a big guy, but he had that wiry, unstable look about him that kept trouble away. Once, some dodgy bloke tried to give him a fake twenty, and he went mental, shouted at him until the veins on his neck throbbed, and his eyes flashed fireworks. He was on her side, and that had to be a good thing. So was his mate Keith on the veg stall. She wandered over there and nodded at the new girl. "I'm off to the greasy old café, if you want to come." She pointed in the direction of Dina's Diner.

The girl looked at Keith and raised her eyebrows.

He pulled out a roll of notes. "You should go with Lizzy. She'll show you around a bit. Here's a fiver, love, go and have egg and chips." He pushed her shoulders gently and grinned at Lizzy. "This here is Natalie. She's my most favourite niece, aren't you, darlin'?"

Natalie finally spoke. "Yeah."

"You coming, then?" Lizzy started to walk.

"Yeah, I'm starving." Natalie followed behind.

Lizzy led Natalie through the market to the end of the street. "This is the café where most people get chips and that. It's dead cheap. Otherwise, it's Maccy D's on Oxford Street, but it's always packed in there. Or sometimes I just get a Twix and a Coke in the shop." She opened the door and waved at Dina, who was in the back frying up.

The two girls took stools at the window. There were a few empty tables, the morning late-breakfast rush over, a cloud of burning fat settling in the air. The strong smell of chips mixed with the tang of ketchup was making Lizzy's mouth water. She studied Natalie's green trainers, which looked good with her dark jeans. The girl had good taste. Even her T-shirt looked okay, although Lizzy wouldn't have worn it herself. All her clothes were black or grey, best for sinking into the background.

Lizzy looked up at the chalkboard. "I'm having a bacon sandwich and a Coke. What do you want? I don't think Missy's here today, the girl who takes the orders, so I'll shout out what we're having." She waited for an answer, drumming her fingertips on her leg.

"Same," said Natalie.

Lizzy shouted over to Dina. "Two bacon sarnies and I'll grab two Cokes out the fridge—thanks, Dina!"

"Got it!" Dina didn't even look up, busy flipping fried eggs.

14

Lizzy put the cans down and cracked one open. "So, how old are you, Natalie?"

"Sixteen." Natalie picked at some dried sauce on the table.

"Really? Same as me?"

Natalie looked out the window. "I will be in September. Uncle Keith said I have to be sixteen to work the stall, officially. Don't say nothing, will you?"

"Course not. I'm nearly seventeen now, but I've been working for Dave on and off for a couple of years. So I've been there and done it with the underage thing, and don't worry, I won't say nothing. The inspector never speaks to me, anyway."

"Thanks. I was trying to get a job in a shop nearer to home, but there was nothing going. Mum and Dad didn't want me to work around here, but Uncle Keith's a right laugh and I told them it was this or nothing. They don't half make a fuss sometimes. It's all right, the market, not as boring as I thought it was going to be. There's a boy on the flower stall that looks well fit." Natalie giggled, put her hand over her mouth.

"He's not bad looking. Got a girlfriend, though, I've seen her hanging around him. She wears these terrible hats, and thinks she's a film star."

"Maybe she'll go off with Brad Pitt and leave him to me." Natalie put one hand on her heart and fluttered her eyelashes.

They smiled at each other.

"Here's your sarnies, love," Dina called out, slamming two plates down on the counter behind her.

"I'll grab the food, be right back." Lizzy sprung up. "Cheers, Dina. Where's Missy, then?"

"Got a cold. That's what she's saying, anyway." Dina shook her head. She had splatters of egg down her apron and a plaster wrapped around her thumb, like she'd had a fight with the frying pan.

Lizzy leaned in towards Natalie as she put the food down between them. "There you go, get that down you. And before I forget, I've got to warn you about Spinner, the arsehole who was showing off to you earlier."

15

"The bloke with the gold tooth?"

"Aye, him. He's bad news. Don't listen to him or go with him any-where, right?"

"Right. Did he do something bad to you, then?" Natalie took a big bite of her sandwich, and ketchup oozed down the sides.

"No, not to me. But I've heard terrible things about what he's done to other girls, like he's given them bad drugs, made them into pros-titutes, and taken them away from their families and stuff. Just be careful—he's a scumbag."

"I will. Where you from, then? Not from London."

Lizzy slapped her forehead. "Oh yeah, I said 'aye' again didn't I? I'm from Scotland, but I'm trying to fit in. Sometimes I say words by mistake, like they're stuck inside me and won't go away."

"Why are you trying not to sound Scottish? You embarrassed, then?"

"Look, I ran away from Scotland three years ago and I don't want anyone to find out. I just want to be like everyone else, blend in. You know? I can tell you, seeing as you're Keith's family and Keith is Dave's best mate."

"Did you run off by yourself?"

"Nah, I came with my boyfriend Simon. It was good at first, but then it went really bad. He liked his drugs a bit too much and I didn't want to go that far in, if you know what I mean."

"Yeah, my cousin Mitch got into crack and went a bit mental. What about your mum and dad?"

"Mum's dead. My dad might as well be."

"Shit, sorry." Natalie held her sandwich mid-air.

"It's okay. Well, now I've got a secret of yours, and you've got one of mine. So we're quits." Lizzy held up her Coke can and they banged them together.

"Cheers, big ears." Natalie drank, her eyes fixed on Lizzy's. "Call me Nat, if you like."

"Okay." Lizzy ate slowly, the taste of fried bacon, grease, and ketchup on white bread so delicious after the long morning. Their sudden silence seemed right, as though they had an understanding already. It felt like the beginning of something, a true friendship that she hadn't had since she was at school. It cheered her up a bit, because today she missed her old life more than ever. She usually came to this place alone, watching folk at the other tables, always chatting in pairs or fours, sometimes whole families sharing the vinegar bottle. It made her yearn for home, even though she knew she'd never go back. She had nothing to go back to.

After a few minutes, Spinner walked past the café and spotted them in the window. He paused his swagger and lifted a hand at them both. The two girls looked away.

"Bad jeans," said Natalie.

"On a right eejit."

"What's an eejit? That's well funny."

"A wally, a jerk. Where I'm from, he's an eejit—or worse. I think a lot worse, actually." Lizzy snorted.

"Yeah. Total scum."

They finished their food, dabbing their fingers on their plates to pick up the last crumbs. Spinner skulked away, tapping his mobile and nodding, like it was talking to him. Lizzy thought of all the things he probably did, bad stuff she'd seen before back in her hometown of Dalbegie. She wondered if it was possible to live in a world without drug deals and violence and dead eyes all around. It didn't seem to matter where you thought you were escaping to, some things never changed. The world was full of guys like Spinner, and there wasn't much you could do about it except keep your distance. If you let them in, or even close, your life became theirs. She knew that from experience, from all the mistakes she'd made before, but she was old enough to know exactly what she was doing now. Sweet sixteen.

Her bed was freezing, even with an extra blanket. The room at the hostel had always smelled of damp, but it was hers, and it had to be better than sleeping in a cardboard box surrounded by druggies. It would warm up in a bit, once the heat from her body had radiated under there. She had two pairs of leggings on, and her coat. She shifted onto her side so that she could look at the flowers she'd bought from Mary's stall at packing-up time. Purple irises, in season already, Mary had said proudly. But Lizzy knew that. They were always her mum's favourites, around at this time of year. She'd put them in water in a tall plastic cup, the one that wasn't too mouldy. The flowers were bright and cheerful against the dirty cream wall and the washed-out Formica. They'd make a good still life painting, she thought, a change from the usual pristine glass vase and the carefully placed dewdrops that she'd seen all over the place. Real life wasn't perfect like that.

I wish I had that fake fur hat I used to borrow off you…so warm. I wish I had you.

I met a new friend, today, Mum. She's called Natalie, and she's dead sweet and likes a laugh. She reminds me a bit of Molly from home, in that innocent way, but at the same time she's into trendy clothes and wears make-up. I thought at first she was just a kid, but she's not that much younger than me. Even so, I'll need to watch out for her a bit, especially with that Spinner guy sniffing around where he's not wanted. He's a total creep. You'd hate him. I know you would. You'd say he was a choob, a waster.

As if I haven't got enough to worry about, without Spinner giving me the shivers. I'm still terrified that Roy's going to find me, and I'm still seeing his ugly face everywhere: at the bus stop, in the market crowd, sitting in Dina's. I know London's a big place, but if he decided to come looking, he'd find me eventually. I'm trying so hard to blend in, I really am, and I'm sorry if it hurts your feelings that I'm trying not to be Scottish any more. I know where I'm from, but right now I need to live a few lies.

If I shut my eyes and concentrate, I can feel you lying beside me. I can hear your breath, warm and alive, and you're listening to everything I'm telling you. It's good while it lasts, but in the end I know it's not really true.

Sleep tight, Mum, my wee angel in the sky. Happy Birthday.

TWO

Helen's Hovel, South London

Helen's street was clean, except for all the dark grey chewing-gum marks dotted around the pockmarked paving. Cars didn't get broken into here. There was no trouble, not really. She closed the front door behind her and stood on the pavement for a moment, inhaling the damp and petrol fumes. She had left the house with a loose plan and needed to collect her thoughts, decide where and how she would be able to feel something. This numbness she couldn't stand, and she knew exactly what would remedy it: a clandestine visit to The Audacious.

Two teenage boys lumbered around the corner, one of them bouncing a ball, all feet and skinny legs, the smell of spray deodorant contaminating the air.

"So your bird is well fit, mate. She got a sister?" One of them slammed the ball into the other's chest.

"If she has, I ain't seen her."

"Well, ask her if she's got one, you plum."

"All right, keep your nob on."

They jostled, almost bumping into Helen, not seeming to notice her standing right there. Maybe it was the grey coat, or her shortness. Or perhaps someone approaching their fortieth birthday simply became invisible to teenage boys. Either way, it didn't matter to her.

Helen began to walk towards the park, surveying the way ahead. It was a little early to go anywhere near The Audacious, so she decided on a visit to the duck pond followed by a late breakfast at Dina's Diner, which was quiet on Mondays. Her eyes strayed to the tops of the terraced houses. This was a typical pocket of London, net curtains yellowing the windows, and everything covered in a thin film of traffic grime. There were no trees on this street, just sparse patches of grass covered in dog shit. Helen had moved into number 18 many years ago and had so far managed to avoid talking to the neighbours, or anyone else in the area. People came and went and she couldn't care less about any of them. It was crowded, but it was private.

. The two teenage lads had already reached the next road and she was far behind them, her legs stiff from lying in bed for almost two days. Weekends were difficult to deal with outside of the house, with everyone busying around, and so she'd stayed in. Helen had got up only for the bathroom and to get food and water, eating and drinking under the duvet, propped up by pillows. She had watched daytime television, reality shows, celebrities dancing and singing and talking. It had all blurred into one. At weekends she was never sure when day turned into night, when she should feel tired.

The park was only a ten-minute walk away. She would sit on a bench and watch the ducks. She liked the mallards, their green heads and yellow beaks bright and cheerful against the drab concrete edge of the pond and all those dark railings. There was a chill in the air, but she was wearing the coat and a wool scarf wrapped twice around her neck. She should have brought some of the stale bread from home. It was covered with speckled mould now, a whole-wheat loaf that she had bought last week, but didn't like. She wouldn't eat it, so the ducks might as well. It wasn't a good idea to go back for it though, now she had actually managed to get out. The crumpled sheets, the pillows, and the warmth of home would pull her back in.

As she crossed the road, a black cab screeched to a halt. The driver rolled down his window, incredulous. "You awake, darlin'? Watch where you're going, will you?"

Helen stopped in front of the cab, and turned to look at him.

"Move then, you daft cow." He honked his horn.

She stared for a moment longer, at the eagle tattoo on his thick, pale arms, then meandered to the other side. In the depths of her consciousness she could hear shouting, but didn't listen. What others thought of her wasn't important.

There were a few other people on the street now and she stared at the cracks in the pavement to make sure she didn't meet any questioning eyes. *What was she doing, walking into the road like that? Was there something wrong with her? Why didn't she say anything? Is she deaf?* She could hear them—their questions—floating all around her. They would never be answered, of course, and so they would drift away into nothing where they belonged.

The ducks were swimming, scattered around, paddling in different directions. There were two mallards and several of the other brown-feathered variety occasionally splashing their wings and dipping their beaks in the water. Helen sat on a bench and watched as a young woman at the edge of the pond held out a plastic bag full of bread. Her daughter was throwing handfuls of crumbs into the water, along with some lumps big enough to sink. The ducks were ignoring them, as if the bread was inedible. It would have been comical if it weren't such an irritating, self-serving spectacle. Helen sunk her hands into her coat pockets and made them into fists. This mother was pursuing a clichéd activity for her toddler, purely for selfish gratification, to be able to proclaim her romantic notion of an early morning jaunt. "We fed the ducks their breakfast." Helen shook her head. *Good for you. Award yourself a mother medal.*

The mother emptied the remaining contents of the bag into the water and started back up the path towards Helen's bench. Her daughter wailed and stamped her feet. Helen hoped they wouldn't talk to her, wished them gone so she could have the place to herself for at least a little while.

"Come on, Kylie, we got to go down the shops, haven't we?" The mother stood with her hands on her hips.

"No. I want the ducks."

"I'll get you a bag of crisps."

"No."

"And one of them strawberry things, the chewy ones."

The child was quiet for a moment, then decided to follow her mother. The two of them were close to Helen now. She dug her fingernails into the palms of her hands and looked hard into the distance.

"All the same, ain't they?"

The mother was talking to her. She wouldn't look.

"Kids." The mother stopped in front of the bench. When she got no response, she snorted. "Suit yourself."

As the sounds of the child grew fainter, Helen began to relax, her jaw unclenching. The day could finally begin.

The park gradually came into focus. Hands rigid from the cold, her eyes watering, Helen stood up and shook her legs. How long had she been sitting there? There was a discarded sandwich bag on one of the other benches, and a crushed can. Someone else had been here. Her knees were sore and she bent to rub them before walking around the pond. She picked up the sandwich bag to see if there was anything inside; she was hungry now. There was only a discarded crust, which she tossed into the water for the birds.

Dina's. She would have her usual bacon, two eggs sunny-side up and buttered toast. It was a fair way to Soho, but nothing else would do. She hurried, head down, to the bus stop, her stride broken only when some pigeons fluttered towards her as she turned a corner. They were like rats, vermin with wings. She'd never understood people who wanted to feed them seeds in Trafalgar Square, encouraging disease and excrement. She didn't understand a lot of things other people did.

After a short bus ride, she got to Berwick Street. The market gave the place some colour, with its apples and bananas and cheap cotton, traders shouting and dealing. She slowed, calm now, and made her way to the café. This was one of the places the market workers went for lunch. It was inexpensive, with the smell of hard graft and real life, and she felt comfortable in there, no reason to behave in any particular way. The sign above the door was scratched and faded, hanging from two nails. It had been there forever. As she pushed the door open, familiarity wrapped itself around her.

"Want your usual?" Missy, the owner's daughter, was taking the orders.

"Yes." Helen sat in the corner, facing in.

"Cup of tea with it?"

"Please."

Missy wiped the table down, flicking some crumbs on the floor, then scribbled the order on a crumpled pad. "I've had a right sodding morning; mad it's been in here for some reason. Calmed down now, though."

"Your mum not in, then?" Helen liked seeing Dina.

"No, she's got a stinking cold. Thought it was best she kept away from people's food in case she sneezed on their eggs. We got her brother cooking up today."

Helen had come at the right time and missed the rush. The street cleaners were at their usual table by the window, plates piled high. On the other side was a family that looked like they didn't belong. Granny had a bacon sandwich, and the young guy and his two kids were all eating egg and chips. Helen wondered where they'd come from and guessed they were passing through, with somewhere touristy to go. The granny was smiling at her now; perhaps she'd been staring too long. She turned away and studied the chipped Formica table, pulled some paper napkins from the plastic holder, then fixed her gaze out the window. Less than fifteen minutes away from here was The Audacious, the very thought of it peeling the numbness from her skin and setting it alight. She'd go after she'd eaten, just to look, to be there. It was too early in the day for anything to kick off, but she could soak up the anticipation.

The food came at last.

"Double egg and bacon," Missy announced as she crashed the plate down.

The eggs wobbled and a piece of toast slipped off the plate and onto the table. She would eat it anyway. It was her first proper meal in days. Helen cut into the yolk, let it run.

Anything could happen here. The alley was riddled with discarded needles, litter spilling from commercial dumpsters, empty takeaway cartons on the ground. Along with the rotting, damp smell was the unmistakable stench of human shit. This was the entranceway, of sorts, to The Audacious. It was a narrow in-between passageway in London that any normal resident would avoid, where any tourist gone the wrong way would turn back. Helen stepped in. She was used to the wrongness of it.

She walked about halfway down. On one side of the building there were three metal doorways evenly spaced, the middle one being the important one, the one that led to The Audacious. It was the only way in, and the only way out of the place. All three doors were covered with graffiti, filth and rust. There were no signs, nothing to suggest they were anything but some backstreet emergency exits.

There was a noise, she was sure of it.

Someone was banging on the inside of the middle door. Perhaps they were trying to get out. She stood quite still and listened. The insulation was well designed in there, so that nothing significant could be heard from outside, but still, there was a faint but unmistakable thump just inside that door.

She stood behind a dumpster and waited, pulling her scarf up with one hand to cover her nose, her other hand in her coat pocket holding her emergency penknife. What was she waiting for? Anything. It didn't matter.

The door burst open moments later and a man fell face down on the concrete. He was holding onto his nose, blood dripping through his fingers.

"You're finished—don't come back," a man's voice said from inside.

"What about my money? Give me my fucking money," the bloodied man cried.

"You didn't complete the job. You don't get nothing if you don't deliver."

The door slammed shut and Helen held her breath.

"You fucking bastards." The man on the ground was wailing, sobbing.

He must have let them down. The man got up and kicked the door, just once, still holding his face. Then he turned and staggered to the main street, towards Helen. She shuffled back until her coat was sticking to the brick wall, but he would still be able to see her there if he looked 'round. He went past, hadn't noticed her.

Helen hurried through to the other side of the alley, her heart pumping. She felt alive. Her footsteps resounded on the paving, the splash of a shallow puddle muddying her ankles. Were footsteps coming after her? She couldn't tell, didn't want to turn around to find out. She had to get to the end of the alley.

"Hey!"

He was shouting at her now, the man. She quickened her pace, breath coming in short bursts, and looked forward at the black cabs, busy people, and the bicycles drifting past the opening.

"Hey, you! Who are you?"

She reached the road, turned the corner and saw a double-decker pulling away from the bus stop a few yards down, one of the old-fashioned ones with an open back. She ran, grabbed the bar and pulled herself onto the deck just as it picked up speed. She looked back and saw the man turning the corner, looking left and right, bewildered at her disappearance.

The conductor tutted his disapproval. "Could have hurt yourself there, love. Go and sit down, will you? There's plenty of room up top."

She climbed the steps, the bus jolting her from side to side. She'd forgotten to ask where it was going, but it didn't really matter. It was invigorating, to go somewhere, her insufferable itch scratched. When the next viewing was scheduled at The Audacious, she would be on the other side of that middle door. It had become her only reason for living.

THREE

The Porty, Edinburgh

The pub door crashed open and everyone jumped, even the beefed-up dockers at the bar. Steve was about to get up and get another pint, but changed his mind quick. A stocky man in denim looked around the room at the sorry sights it held. His hair was wild and tangled, his fists clenched. It was D, and he didn't look happy.

Steve let go of his glass and tensed, waiting to be spotted through the dense clouds of cigarette smoke. D was probably after him. Scrap that, he thought, D was definitely after his guts. Who was he kidding?

D bounded over and scraped a chair through the sawdust, damp now from the spillages of the night. "Ah, there you are, Stevie-boy." He sat opposite, put his elbows on the table with a bang, and leaned in so close that Steve could feel his rancid breath, warm on his face.

"D. Good to see you, pal."

D didn't flinch, his gaze level, bloodshot eyes unwavering. Red veins bulged on his nose. "Got something for me?"

There were a dozen or so men left drinking in The Porty, the die-hards. Steve might have described them as the dregs. Long after closing time for most, this was one of the few remaining pubs in Edinburgh that was a twenty-four-hour host to the drunk. Most of them were deep in their stupors, aware that D wasn't happy but not appreciating that he might actually murder Steve with his bare hands. Steve was drinking with his best pals, Ed and Jake, and somehow, because it was his birthday, he thought he'd be safe. But here was D in front of him, giving him the stare, and he didn't feel exactly immune to his wrath.

Steve glanced at the bar and wondered if the head barmaid still had that crowbar under the counter. Evelyn didn't stand for any trouble and all the guys knew it. She had arms as thick as your leg and a face set into a scowl even when she was being friendly. He'd seen Evelyn use the crowbar a good few times in the ten years he'd been drinking down there. She'd always said she hated doing the midnight to sunrise shift because if something kicked off, it would be then. But from where he was sitting, she didn't seem to mind getting stuck in. There would be vomit, there would be blood, smashed glass, and when she was on form, broken limbs as well.

In the few seconds D was sat waiting for him to speak, Steve had scanned the room and spotted Hamish, the landlord, in the far corner. Looked like he'd had quite a few pints and probably wouldn't be much help. He had a lit cigarette permanently planted in his lips, his eyes squinting with the smoke.

I am fucked.

He looked D in the eye, or thereabouts. "I've no' got the money with me. Just here with my pals having a few bevs and that. It's my birthday tomorrow." Steve cringed as he said it. As if D would give a shite.

"Your birthday, is it? Well, congratulations," D said, widening his eyes.

Steve's pal Ed had been sitting next to him, but now he shuffled over to the next table, leaving him alone with D. This wasn't going to be pretty. Everyone was looking, in one way or another, but luckily not all of them could hear, what with the music. Evelyn had her favourite on loud, the seventies compilation with Odyssey, Earth, Wind & Fire, the Bee Gees. The later it got, the dimmer the lights, and the louder the music. That was how it went.

He drained the dregs from his glass. "Will I get you a drink? A pint of Tennent's, is it?"

D stared at him for a moment. Eventually he nodded. "Aye, that would be a start."

Steve hoped a pint would calm D down, but at the same time he was worried it might antagonize him. It was worth the risk. What else could he do?

He staggered up to the bar and leaned towards Evelyn. "Couple of drinks over here, please, doll."

Evelyn grabbed his glass. "Another pint of the same, Stevie? I'll stick it in here. No point getting you a fresh mug when you wouldn't know the difference."

"Aye, give us Tennent's lager this time. I think your pale ale is off."

"It's no' off, you've drank too much of it, you numpty, and it's rotting in your guts. You wouldn't know cat's pee if I gave it you."

Steve managed a smile. "That'd be right."

"You off home soon? Your friend doesn't look very happy." Evelyn handed him his pint, beer slopping over the sides.

"Aye, I'll be off as soon as I've drunk this beauty." He held his drink up to the light and kissed the side of the glass.

Evelyn rolled her eyes. "Aye, right."

While she was pouring the second pint, Steve looked across at Ed and Jake. They were steaming, even by his standards. Ed got up and came over, eyes red and bleary. "All right, Stevie-boy? I think I'm done. Need to get back to the woman or she'll kill me." He looked at his watch up close. "Fuck, she'll kill me anyways. Why don't you come just now?"

"One more and I'll come with you down Leith Walk. One more, eh? I've just got one in, and one for D."

Ed stubbed out his cigarette in the ashtray that was spilling out onto the bar. He looked down at his glass and studied the two inches of dark brown liquid, warm and viscous. He heaved slightly, like the thought of it was going to make him sick. "I'll just finish this. I'm done in. We should go."

Ed was always the first to go because he drank so fast. He'd get more stick for being a lightweight if he wasn't so hard looking, what with the shaved head and all the tattoos. Jake was also downing his dregs. His glasses were askew on his face, a dribble of ale down his chin. Steve wondered if anyone had ever told him he looked like the Swedish Chef from the Muppets.

Evelyn slapped down the pint. "There you go, Stevie. Give it to your friend, drink up and get to fuck home wi' Ed."

"Oh, charming. Thanks, doll." He made his way back to the table and put the drinks down. D grabbed his, put it to his whiskery mouth, and downed it in two, long gulps. He wiped his lips with the back of his hand and glared.

Steve sat down on the edge of his chair. "I can get you half on Tuesday, which is pay day."

"I don't want half. I want it all. Now."

Steve took a gulp of his lager, for courage. "As I said, I've no' got it just now. Sorry, D."

"I've been hearing it for weeks, your shite. I've had enough of it the now." As he stood, D swiped Steve's pint, knocking it to the floor. Glass smashed and beer splashed up the wall.

Steve held up his hands in surrender.

"Take it outside!" Evelyn was shouting, already holding up the famous crowbar.

There it was. That fuckin' thing. Steve made an alcohol-hazed decision and decided to run for it. His legs usually worked, even when his head didn't. It was a talent, like they had a brain of their own. He made for the door, saw that neither Ed nor Jake jumped in to help slow D down, mind, but he didn't really blame them. You didn't want D for an enemy if you could help it.

Outside, the cold rushed into his lungs, sobering him, keeping him moving. The dim light coming from The Porty window lit a few yards of pavement, but beyond was gloom. Even Constitution Street and Leith Links were thick in darkness, save for a few streetlamps to guide folk home. He sprinted towards Leith Walk, to its doorways and side streets and places a man could duck in and not be found. He knew these streets like he knew his own ma's face and they were dark, on his side. He'd go the winding, long way that seemed to go north but ended up south.

"Get back here, you fucking wee shitebag," D was shouting behind, his words getting farther, then nearer, then farther again.

If D caught up with him, he was dead, or as good as. There was no way he could go home, as D knew where he lived. He'd be up those tenement stairs and into his flat like a shot, easy target. No, he'd go to his ma's on the other side of town, but only if he could shake him off.

First Chapel Lane then down Water Street to Tolbooth Wynd. He ran past the poncey gallery with the floor-to-ceiling glass front, and the new wine bar usually full of posh shites if it was still open, which it wasn't. He didn't stop, could hear heavy feet behind, and a lot of swearing. D must be getting fit with all his chasing. Down Henderson Gardens, in and out of tenements. There were lots of wee places to dart in and out of, quiet alleys where no folk walked after dark. Some of the streets were cobbled and he worried he might twist his ankle, but was too terrified to slow down.

His breathing had settled into a rhythm, deep and full, as if the longer he ran the easier it became. Ed always said Steve should be a marathon runner, couldn't believe how far he could go without passing out. Ed couldn't run for a bus without needing oxygen.

The footsteps behind were gone. He was sure of it.

Steve ran a bit farther, wanted to get partway down Leith Walk and off again towards his ma's. He'd done it, for now anyway. He slowed down, walked a bit, stopped in a doorway and listened. Everywhere was quiet, save for an inebriated singsong kicking off in one of the tenement flats above. He leaned against the grey stone wall and sighed with relief. He was safe, for now.

Ma came into the living room as soon as the birds starting singing, baffies on, a mug of tea in her hand. "I didn't hear you last night there, Stevie. Are you all right, darlin'? Do you want a cup of tea? Did you have a good time with Ed and Jake? Did you lose the key to your place?"

"No questions just now, Ma."

"Oh, you've a sore head I bet. I'll away and get you a drink of water and a tablet. Happy birthday, son."

The sofa had been there since the seventies and it felt like it as well, all lumps and smells. Steve winced as he tried to lift his head from the nylon cushion, reaching to scratch his leg. Then he remembered the chase. Edinburgh was a small city, a place you couldn't run and hide for long. Of course he could get a plane to America, but that would cost just as much as he owed D. He had to do something about the cash he owed him, scrape it together. But not now. His head felt like it was going to fall off, so heavy and hot and damp.

"There you go." Ma sat on the edge of the sofa, smoking a Regal and waving at it, like the smoke wouldn't smell if it was going in the other direction. But she was just doing her best for him, like she always did. She offered him a glass of water and a headache tablet, leaving the cigarette between her lips.

"Aw, thanks, Ma. I'm feeling a bit tender, you know?"

"My wee boy. Forty. I can't believe it, so I can't. Forty years, gone just like that, and your father not even around to see you grown into a man."

"Don't cry, will you, Ma. I don't think I could take it this morning."

"I will cry, so I will. I always go daft on your birthday, eh?"

"Aye, you do as well. You could always take your mind off it and make me a bacon roll."

"Bacon roll, listen to it. You need yourself a woman of your own to make you the bacon rolls. I'm too old for all that. A piece and jam does me, unless you're here. When are you going to get yourself another woman, Stevie? I'm talking about one you could keep."

"Ma, for god's sake don't start that again." Steve sat up slowly and pinched the top of his nose. "That's the last thing I need the now."

"Well. Forty years old and wasting yourself on nothing. You should get together with that Cynthia in Marks and Spencer's, a lovely girl she is. Divorced now, the kids all at school. It's not right, you being on your own. That Sandra, she was never right for you. But it's not to say you don't deserve someone." She tapped her cigarette ash into her cupped hand and sighed heavily. "I'll make you a bacon roll, of course I will. It's your birthday and you're my wee boy. You're always welcome to that sofa, you know. Any night you like."

"Aw, thanks, Ma."

"I've got a wee present for you as well; I'll give it you after. Nothing much, mind."

Steve held onto his head and shut his eyes. Ma drifted off into the kitchen and before long he could hear sizzling. The most delicious smell that could possibly hit a hungover nose wafted through and settled around him. Bacon. When he'd eaten he'd get a hit off Ed down the Shore. He really needed it today. He could owe Ed the money. He lay back and heard Ma sniffling, trying to hide the noise with the clang of the frying pan.

"Are you greetin', Ma?"

"Aye. Don't mind me, it's always the same on your birthday."

He lay back. She was right; there had always been a few tears on this day, ever since he could remember, even when he was a bairn. She claimed to be emotional, but she never cried any other time, not even during the soppiest film. There was something else that bothered her about his birthday, but she'd never say. And he'd never asked.

The clang of hammers and the constant whir of drills and circular saws wasn't doing Steve's headache much good, but him and Ed worked the docks development and this was where he was going to get a hit. It was a crime to have to traipse down there on his day off, but that was just tough shite. It would be worth it, if he could get the day started right.

Ed was in one of the new buildings, putting down some flooring. They'd been working together on the job for a week or so, banging and sawing and getting covered in wood chips. Ed looked like he was struggling a bit to focus, his eyes even smaller and redder than usual.

As Steve stepped over the pile of timber, his pal looked up and grinned. "What's that on your head? Did you get it free at the barbers when they scalped you?"

"This is a birthday present from Ma, shut it, you." Steve touched the knitted beanie. It was bright yellow and made from the finest wool out of that bird's nest of a knitting basket that his ma had filled over the years.

Ed wiped some sawdust out of his eyes. "You look like a walking lemon."

"Aye, I know. Does it suit me?"

"Aye. I take it D didn't kill you, then. Did you get away on those super legs of yours?"

"It took a while to shake him, but I got away. He's getting faster, mind."

"He's after you big time. Jesus, I feel like shite after last night. I don't even remember getting home. What you doing here, anyway? I thought it was your day off."

"I need a hit, Ed. It's payday tomorrow. I can give you the money then." Steve pressed his palms together in a begging way.

"Is that a joke?" Ed turned away, pushed down on his hard hat. "I've nothing on me, anyway."

"You've always got something on you. Come on."

"No way. Save your cash, all of it, for D. You better get hold of the money, especially if you're going to dance about in that hat. He's going to find you, easy, and fucking kill you, Stevie-boy."

"I'll be okay. Just one hit. It's my birthday the day."

Ed dug deep into his trouser pocket and pulled out a plastic wrap. "Oh, aye, so it is. I must be some sort of mug. This is a small one, you can just give me a five tomorrow."

"Cheers, Ed, you're a pal. I'll see you in the morning."

Steve took it and left before Ed changed his mind. The foreman saw him crossing the site and waved. He waved back, and muttered under his breath, "See yers tomorrow, thanks for the score."

He made for the Links. He would sit on the grass and smoke a fag, then have a wee hit, maybe two. He could always pop in The Porty for a quick half, just to get rid of the hangover, but then again, that might not be wise after last night. It was hard to keep away though, when all that alcohol was sat there, calling out to be drunk. He remembered the yellow hat then, and stuffed it in his trouser pocket. No point drawing attention to himself by being the walking lemon.

One of the trees on the far east side was bigger than some of the others, with a good trunk to lean on. He brushed the earth free of twigs and sat down facing the old jam factory, now some posh twats' offices. It made him laugh, to think of folk inside, wearing Armani suits and sipping herbal tea at their desks, not aware of the proper work that had gone on before. He got out the plastic and unwrapped it, rolling a note with one hand like the expert that he was. Sniffing long and hard, he clenched the packet and banged his head back against the tree. This was what it was all about.

Above the rush of blood to his head, he could hear footsteps coming towards him, heavy and urgent. He opened his eyes and tried to focus, but everything was slowing down.

Two thick-set legs were in front of him, in silhouette against the falling sun. There was a vague outline of a wild head, hair straggling out at all angles. They could only belong to one person. *Shite.* It couldn't be him, not now.

FOUR
Lizzy Finds a Web

Lizzy's stomach was rumbling. It had been a long morning working the stall, busy as well, even more than usual for a Friday. The market had become even livelier as it got close to lunchtime.

A woman in a black, fitted suit took the last of the yellow plums. "Thanks, my dear," she said, her smile brilliant white.

"Here's your change, love. You have a good weekend," said Lizzy.

"You too." The woman smiled at her, as if surprised by the sentiment.

Lizzy was good with the gab, as Dave would call it. He'd be dead pleased with her, said he wasn't sure the yellow plums would sell. Lizzy watched the woman stride away from the bustle of the market towards Wardour Street, a green recycled shopping bag over her expensive shoulder, along with a leather designer handbag. She was too thin, probably only ate fruit. Some kind of life people had around here, with their clothes, the teeth, all that healthy eating. She wasn't jealous, exactly, but it did seem unfair that some folk had everything and some had nothing.

"Do you fancy the chippy?" Natalie called over.

"Yeah, I could murder a bag of chips," she shouted back, "soon as Dave gets here."

She'd been hanging out at lunch break with Nat every day that week. On Monday they got chocolate bars from the shop and went

34

for a walk down Carnaby Street, looked in all the windows at things they couldn't afford. They had a bit of a laugh, especially at some of the folk that worked around there, all thinking they were dead trendy. She used to do stuff like that with her friend Molly back home. She wondered what Molly was doing now, and if she ever thought about her, or wondered where she was. Before Lizzy ran away down South they had drifted apart a bit, but Molly had been a good pal since they were in nursery. You can move away from a place, but you don't forget old friends in a hurry.

"There she is, my best girl." Dave turned the corner and put his hands out for the apron.

"All right, Dave, I'm dead pleased to see you. I could eat my hand."

"You mean I'm *well* pleased."

"Yeah, *well* pleased to see you. I can never remember that one, it seems weird to me."

Dave shrugged, tied on the apron and went about serving a middle-aged couple who were attempting to pick through the strawberries for the best ones. "If you touch 'em you got to buy 'em," he said, but not in an unkind way.

Lizzy looked over at Natalie's stall to see if she was ready to go, and her heart went cold. Spinner was there again, whispering to her friend. Keith wasn't paying attention, busy sorting out some of his stock, sifting through boxes of green this and orange that, exotic vegetables that Lizzy didn't know the names of. Natalie was giggling, like Spinner had tickled her ear.

"You ready, Nat?" Lizzy shouted over.

Natalie looked up and Spinner scowled at the distraction. He started to back away as Keith had seen him now, and had raised his fist. Lizzy skipped over, feeling pleased for drawing attention to Spinner's flirting. He was always after something, and she was worried that his whispering could be his sinister way of drawing Nat in.

"Get lost, you scumbag," Keith growled.

"Calm down, I'm not doing anything," Spinner said, holding up his hands.

"You leave her alone."

"Yeah, yeah," Spinner mumbled as he skulked away, sucking on a cigarette.

Keith watched Spinner go, hands on hips. "Right, girls, he's slung his hook. Nat, he's bad news. Don't talk to him, okay? Are you two off to get something to eat? I'll treat you both today. I've done well."

"Thanks, Uncle Keith, we're off to the chippy." Natalie looked guilty. "Spinner was just having a laugh, I think."

"He's never just having a laugh, darlin'. Don't trust him." Keith handed her a note and rubbed the top of her head.

"All right, I won't." Natalie pocketed the money and nodded her head towards the chip shop. "Come on then, Lizzy, what you waiting for?"

They linked arms and made their way through all the people hurrying along the backstreets of Soho. Nat went quiet, and Lizzy wondered if she was embarrassed about the scene with Spinner.

"Smell that salt 'n' vinegar. It's making me even more hungry. Will we sit in there or eat them on the bench outside?" Lizzy squeezed her friend's arm.

Natalie sniffed the air. "Let's sit on the stools by the window, watch all the people."

"Yeah, we can play the marry-or-shag game. What did Spinner say to you? Was he being creepy?"

"He was just mucking around, said my hair smelled nice."

"Gross."

"Yeah."

They got the chips and sat up in the window overlooking Market Street. Lizzy squirted a generous helping of ketchup on her plate and ate quickly.

They played the game.

"Shag." Natalie grinned, as a hipster walked past, dressed in black, a rolled-up newspaper in his back pocket.

"Marry," said Lizzy. "I've always wanted to end up with a guy who looks good in black skinnies."

"What about him over there, the one with the pin-striped suit and brogues?" Natalie pointed with a greasy finger and giggled.

They looked at each other. "Chuck off a cliff!" they said in unison.

"I wish someone would chuck Spinner off a cliff," said Lizzy. "He really shouldn't be creeping around the market like a filthy rat all the time."

Natalie shrugged. "Just ignore him."

The hostel was usually full, but Lizzy had an agreement with the manager, Mike. She'd been staying there for eight months now, paid her dues on time every week, and he trusted her. She got the single room with the double lock for cheap, and in return Mike got his money, prompt. She could leave her stuff there, no problem, and knew it wouldn't get nicked. Not that any of it was worth stealing.

Lizzy slammed the door behind her, turned the deadlock and slumped to the floor, exhausted from being on her feet all day. She kicked off her boots, the black leather worn and cracked, a faint smell of rotten fruit encrusted in the grooves of the soles. She groaned, rubbed her toes, and looked around the sparse room. One day she'd have her own place, with a shower, no sharing, and a walk-in wardrobe like they have in the magazines. But for now, a sink and a squashy bed would have to do. Shivering, she decided to leave her coat on as she leaned back against the wall and shut her eyes for a moment.

One of the other bedroom doors in the corridor opened and shut, twice, like someone was trying to make a point.

"You happy now, you fucking whore?"

That woman was shouting, the Indian one with the tattoo on the side of her face. She was always quite nice to Lizzy, but looked like she could give it hard if she wanted to.

"Why don't you mind your own business and piss off back to where you came from, you stupid slag."

That sounded like Janice, the street cleaner, who stayed there sometimes. Lizzy and Natalie once saw her spitting phlegm into the gutter. She was rank, Nat had said. The two women carried on shouting at each other and Lizzy pulled out the portable stereo from her cardboard box, turning it on loud to drown them out. Not too loud though, Mike wouldn't like it. She had a CD in there of The Smiths, *The Best Of*, given to her by Banana Dave because he said she probably missed out on them and he didn't think anyone should be deprived. All the music from the eighties still seemed exciting to her, better than anything. Morrissey sang to her about comas and the streets of London while she made herself a piece and jam for her tea. No butter on it though, as butter would go off without a fridge, but lots of jam on thick white bread. It would do. If Granny Mac could see this, she'd think it was a bit sad, but she'd been having it that way for three years now and had got used to it without the butter. In fact, she didn't even want it now, that layer of fat. Cracking a can of Coke, she sat on the bed, cross-legged, as happy as she could be when alone and a little bit afraid. If only she had a telly, then it wouldn't be so bad.

Tomorrow, Lizzy would ask Nat if she wanted to hang out one night, maybe at the weekend. She lived in Kidbrooke or nearabouts, and there were loads of night buses that went that direction, or if her mum didn't want her to do that, she could even sleep on the floor at the hostel or top-to-toe in the bed. Nat had said her mum didn't let her go out much, said she was too young, and they were always rowing about it. Nat said she kept telling her she wasn't a kid any more, and to back off. They'd have such a laugh, get some beers and drink them in one of the parks. Lizzy needed someone close to her again, seeing as she'd left everyone else behind. She whispered into the room.

Miss you, Mum.

She liked to imagine a tiny flutter of a touch to her cheek when she spoke to her. She could feel it now, warm and comforting. There it was. She was still around.

It was seven-thirty and the sun was trying to come out, but it wasn't getting any warmer in the shadows of Berwick Street. Lizzy slapped her hands together, the fingerless gloves not cutting it this morning.

"Help me with some of these boxes, will you, darlin'?" Dave said, heaving crates of fruit from the back of his van over to the stall.

"I'll take the smaller ones from the back," she said, testing the weight of them. The bigger ones she couldn't even lift up. "What's in the big ones, anyway? Dead bodies?"

"Watermelons. Although I could think of a few dead bodies I'd like to be in there." Dave bared his gums.

"Let me guess. Your mother-in-law, the bank manager, and Spinner?" Lizzy hauled a box over to the stall and set it down carefully on the floor tarp.

"Got it in one. You're a fast learner, girl."

"*Well* fast," she said.

"Thanks for coming down early, Lizzy. I couldn't do all this without you. I'll make it worth your while, okay?"

"I know you will, Dave."

Lizzy finished the job, and when Dave drove the truck away to park it, she started to unpack the fruit and put it all in the right places. She kept looking over at Keith's stall, but no Natalie yet. Keith was sweating in his wooly hat, shifting his own crates and attempting to put out all his prize vegetables himself. Nat worked all week usually, unless she was sick. Lizzy thought she looked fine when they went to the chippy together yesterday—full of it in fact.

Dave reappeared to help set up, but Lizzy had nearly finished by then.

"Christ, you're fast. Nice one, Lizzy." He stood at the front of the stall, hand on his forehead. "Do you need me, or shall I just get going and come back at lunch?"

"Could do. Or should I help Keith over there for a bit? Looks like he's struggling on his own."

Dave looked over and then frowned. "I'll go and see what's going on."

He went off to talk to his friend while Lizzy served a couple of customers on their way to work, buying an apple here and a couple of bananas there, nothing much. She was distracted, kept looking over at Dave and Keith. Keith had got on his mobile, pacing up and down, while Dave watched his stall.

After a few minutes, Dave came back, looking worried. "Can you go and give Keith a hand? I'll stick around here. Natalie's gone AWOL; she never came home last night. He just called her house and spoke to her dad. They're all in a right state. Did you see her last night or anything, darlin'? I know you two are mates."

Lizzy felt her blood burn at the base of her neck, a familiar sick feeling in her stomach that she got when her mum disappeared. "No, I left when you did yesterday. She was still packing up with Keith."

"She gets the bus home," Dave said, looking off into the distance.

"I know she has a mobile, so she can call her mum in emergencies. I can't afford one myself, otherwise I'd call her."

"Well, she never phoned either. They've tried to call her, but it rings through to voicemail."

"Shit." Lizzy traipsed over to Keith's stall and silently started to help him set up.

Keith looked up and nodded at her. "Thanks, Lizzy. You don't have any idea where she is, do you?"

"I don't, Keith. Sorry."

They finished setting everything out, Keith occasionally checking his phone, making sure he hadn't missed any calls. His fingernails were black from working the stall, but everything else about him was immaculate. Lizzy could smell the washing powder on his clothes, and some kind of deodorant or aftershave. She wished she had an uncle who cared about her as much as he did about Natalie. Some chance.

Lizzy focussed part way up the street. There was that leather jacket, the tight jeans. Spinner was passing something to one of the traders. He was walking towards them now; she would know that cocky stride anywhere. She tensed, almost crushing an aubergine in her hand. There was something about him; she could sense he was entrenched in the same kind of shady deals as Roy back home. When Spinner was around, it was like he was so much a part of Roy's world that Roy himself could turn up at any moment. The thought of his face gave her goosebumps. She'd spent the last three years in London looking over her shoulder, hoping he'd never find her. But you could never be sure with Roy, who he knew, or where he'd be.

Spinner passed the stall. Keith was serving a customer and didn't see him, but Lizzy was onto him. She looked him in the eye, unsmiling, and he gave her a hint of a smirk, she was sure of it. He better not have anything to do with Natalie. There was a kind of triumphant look in his face, and it made her wonder. Did he know something?

She slammed down the tomato she was holding and stomped a few paces towards him. "You look guilty."

He turned to face her. "What you talking about, Blondie? Just want an excuse to chat to old Spinner, eh?"

"You better not have something to do with Nat."

He looked off to the side. "Why, she get hurt, did she?"

"She ain't here; she's gone. Where is she?"

Keith had seen her talking to Spinner and he was coming over now, his face bright red. "What's going on over here? What've you done, you fuckin' little shit?"

"I've done nothing. Tell the little princess here to back off or she'll be sorry." Spinner started to walk away, pulling out his mobile and tapping on it.

"Fuck off—you're scum," Keith called after him. "You all right, Lizzy? What was he saying, then?"

"Nothing much. I should've left it, but he looked at me funny and I got this bad feeling about him."

Keith put his hand on her shoulder and led her back to the stall. "Best leave that kind of thing to me and Dave, or the police. Don't get involved, darlin'. He's too dangerous."

Lizzy shrugged. She hoped Natalie would show up later that day, but at the same time dreaded to hear where she'd been. Yesterday she'd given no hint that she was going to be doing anything bad that night, and Lizzy was certain that it was because Nat hadn't even known it herself. She looked over at Dave, to see if he'd been watching. His face was set in a scowl, his eyes following the back of Spinner, fists clenched. Between them they'd figure this out and if Spinner was the one who took Natalie, he'd pay for it.

FIVE

·Helen at The Audacious

Her head itched. Helen stared at the television, at the toothy presenters talking about nothing, and scratched at the base of her scalp. She tried to remember the last time she'd washed her hair. It was one of those arduous little tasks that should be done, but sometimes even thinking about simple things sapped her energy. It was so warm there in bed, so comfortable, like lying on a cloud and floating through time.

Nothing was going on. In fact, nothing had happened for over a month now, which wasn't unusual, but still, it was hard to wait. Everyone in The Circle was in agreement that irregular and infrequent showings were vital to the secrecy and exclusivity of The Audacious. And so it must be.

A documentary was in full swing. Helen had missed the beginning as she'd been thinking about everyone in The Circle, daydreaming about what would happen at the next session. Each one seemed to step up a notch. But here, on screen, a middle-aged woman was talking about her childhood, blaming her father's absence for all the failed relationships in her adult life.

"Deal with it!" Helen screwed up the bedcovers in her hands as she shouted at the television, felt the burning rise up her neck to her face.

Bloody woman. She kicked her legs out of the covers. It was too hot, too sticky all of a sudden. Thoughts of her own life as a young girl were rising up from nowhere and taking over. Never mind not having a father; what about not having any family at all? The woman on the screen was crying now. *Boo-hoo, my dad ran away.* Helen jabbed at the remote control to turn her off, to make her self-indulgence disappear. She put her fingertips to her forehead, as if she could jab at the memories to go away, but unfortunately it didn't work like that. There was a time when she realized she wasn't wanted much of anywhere. It wasn't anything to do with folk around her, or the absence of anyone in particular, but a part of life as it had always been.

Her foster mother was smoking vigorously on the back step, blowing smoke into Fife. She regarded the growing junk heap that was the garden, shaking her heavy head. There was a dip in her thick, bleached hair, where she'd slept on it and hadn't bothered to brush it out.

"Do us all a favour, will you? Away and get a job, save some money, and get lost."

"Can I leave school at fifteen?" Helen was behind her, picking at some flaking paint on the sill by the kitchen door.

"Of course you bloody can. What do you think you're going to do, go to bloody university? Aye, that'd be right." Her foster mother flicked ash on the step. Some of it blew onto her slippers.

"What will I do for a job?"

"I don't know, do I? Get yourself down to the bakery, do a paper round, work in the shoe shop. There's plenty places. Use your brain. Just stop buzzing around me. You're always there."

Helen hovered near the doorway, wondering if she'd catch some morsel of kindness from this woman. Did she mean it? Or was she just in one of her moods again? The Scottish cold coming from outside made her shiver and she rubbed her hands together.

Her foster mother looked up at the sound. "What are you still standing there for? Did you not hear what I said?"

"Aye, I did."

"Are you stupid? You need to get out. You've outstayed your welcome with your bloody weirdness, and all that skulking around. No wonder your real mum didn't want you."

"What?" Helen wrapped her arms around her body.

"Have you lost your memory along with all of your other brain cells? I'm not your real mother, am I? But where's she? How did she get out of it? She just didn't want you, did she? Not for anything. I can't say I blame her, bloody strange one you are. Can I ask you

43

something, Helen? Who'd miss you if you didn't show up at school tomorrow?"

Helen was silent, rolling her finger across the grimy backsplash tiles above the sink.

"You see?" Her foster mother stubbed out her cigarette on the step, flicked the butt into the garden, and lit another one. She looked pleased with her conclusion. She pulled at the greying cardigan around her white shoulders and sucked in the smoke.

The laptop on Helen's bedside table was open, a screensaver of innocent blue sky drifting around as if tempting her to pick it up. She stared at it, willing it to do something to take the anger away. But still it meandered in a slow and irritating fashion. At least there were no fluffy clouds, the ultimate in false escapism. She'd turned it on that morning but lost interest in what the Internet had to offer rather quickly. She used to belong to an online forum, an exclusive club at NondescriptRambunctious.com, but it had disbanded a year ago due to a security risk. Something about a new member leaking some information; she didn't know the full details. She had been one of the most trusted and respected subscribers, having met Oliver, the owner of the forum, some twenty years ago when they did community service together at the Cat Rescue Centre in Edinburgh. It was her understanding that all members of the forum had some personal connection with him, which made the leak particularly disappointing. That said, it had happened and it must have been for a reason because Helen, and some select handpicked members, were now a part of Oliver's Circle at The Audacious. So in the end, it was a good thing. No online forum could ever be a full substitute for the real thing, in the flesh. She realized that now.

The email pinged. She had a new message.

It was probably just spam as usual, a message from Nigeria about her account number or a sales pitch about Viagra. These things made her boil; it was all she could do not to send a hate-filled reply, but knew that any engagement would be a mistake. She picked up the laptop and the dream-sequence screensaver disappeared.

Thursday 20th, 1 a.m., The Audacious.

It was from an anonymous email address, but she knew it was Oliver. He gave only the crucial details, in order to attract and inform all the members. None of them shared full names or contact information. It was too dangerous. He made sure everyone changed their email addresses monthly.

Thursday. Tomorrow.

She got out of bed, and took off the stiff woolen socks and the tracksuit bottoms that were bagging at the knees with overuse and under-washing. She sniffed her armpits. It really was time for a shower. Why couldn't she smell herself before? The simple pleasure that came with anticipation of The Audacious often brought with it great clarity on everything else.

She was stinking.

Her dirty clothes were strewn all over the bedroom floor, plates of half-eaten food scattered underneath the bed. She must get to the launderette, sort out what she would wear tomorrow, and make sure she was clean and presentable for the others. The white cotton shirt would do, with black trousers and perhaps a scarf. She threw some clothes in a pile on the floor, and made her way to the bathroom. She used to be such a meticulous clean freak, always scrubbing and tidying. As she'd got older, the obsessive gene had subsided somehow into this.

There was a ring of grime around the bath, hairs covering the rim of the plughole. She looked around, but couldn't remember buying any cleaning equipment recently, let alone using it. She showered off the base of the tub first, and got in when the water was nice and hot, steam masking some of the stains on the painted ceiling. There was a speckling of green mould at the bottom of the shower curtain, but that was a hopeless case. She would buy a new one soon; save the bother of scrubbing.

It was time to go. Her watch said twelve midnight and it could take over forty minutes to get to Soho, depending on the late buses. It was raining too hard to walk anywhere, and she didn't want to arrive sodden and hurried. It was best to remain calm, sedate, to get the most enjoyment from The Audacious. Helen closed the front door quietly and walked out into the night, towards the bus stop outside WH Smith. There were some lads hanging about, must have been in the kebab shop for after-closing-time food. They were singing and cheering. She stood inside the shelter, looked ahead, and ignored them.

"Hello, darlin', want a bite of my shish?" One of them held out a paper bag, chili sauce spilling out onto the pavement.

The others laughed. She zoned out the sounds and waited; they could carry on taunting her, but she didn't care and wouldn't listen. One of them stood directly in front of her and pulled a face. She could see some acne on the base of his neck, red and sore looking. Some shreds of lettuce had spilled, resting on his collar. She studied them, wondering how long it would take him to notice they were there.

"Weirdo," he said, and traipsed back to his friends.

She knew he wouldn't be back to try and scare her again; he was just a boy. Here it was, the night bus. She made her way to the middle section. Too near the back and there would be some trouble; too near the front and the driver would try to start a conversation, and she hated that. Helen turned and looked out the window. Two of the kebab lads got on after her and went straight to the back. There they go, she thought, bypassing me. It was a special gift she seemed to have: turning people off.

As the time dragged by, Helen prepared her mind for the viewing. She would get more out of it by being focussed, present. This required a huge effort of concentration, something that she had trained her mind to do over the years. It wasn't a natural state for her to be in, but if she knew she had to, she would do it. She didn't want to miss a thing.

Ten to one. She knocked on the middle of the three doors using the sequence they had been given. Helen looked behind her to double check that there was no one following her in the alley. She knocked again, a repeat of the same sequence. There was a short pause, a deadbolt was pulled across, and the door creaked open.

"Come in," said a male voice from the shadows.

Helen slipped inside and nodded at the doorman, who shut the door with a bang behind her. He sat down on a chair part way into the corridor and motioned to her to continue. He always wore a baseball cap, pulled down to cover his eyes. Tonight he was wearing a baggy skater top hiding any shape he might have, and a pair of those hideous distressed-look jeans, too tight. At least his leather jacket was nowhere to be seen.

It was bright: bare bulbs shining in intervals all the way down the ceiling of the corridor. She screwed up her eyes as she walked to the end, turned right as always, and stopped in front of the first door on the right. She took a deep breath and knocked on the door, this time with a deliberate single tap.

The door opened and she was, at last, going to join The Circle.

"You're one of the first," said Oliver. "There are a few more to join us, I believe, before we begin."

She nodded at him. He had always worn hats, even in the days when she would watch him on the web forum. Tonight he was wearing a grey felt fedora, which fit him well and somehow didn't seem at all pretentious on him. Helen was pleased to be one of the early ones, so she could take her place in one of the positions that she liked. She put her envelope containing the cash donation into the box on the floor, and then chose a chair directly facing the door. When anyone entered the room she would be able to watch their faces, all the reactions. There were four others already sat down, all gazing at the space in the middle of the circle, in expectation of what was to come. They were all men. With conscious effort not to look directly at anyone, she became aware of them through her peripheral vision. One was quite old, the brown suit man. The one opposite her was about her age, forty-ish, with greasy hair and ill-fitting black clothes. The third was in his thirties, pallid skin, someone who might typically work on a computer all day long. Oliver, the leader, was the fourth. He sat down and crossed his legs, casual, waiting for the others. He'd always been a nonchalant victimizer. Admirable.

She put her bag underneath the chair and zoned out. No one talked, used a phone, read or noted anything. They were not allowed to take any item out of their bag or use any electronic device for the duration of the viewing. Understandably, things had to remain firmly within The Circle. Their bags would be searched after the viewing. There were no windows, but everything was painted brilliant white, giving the feeling of airiness and light. There was a familiar smell of newly applied paint and she wondered how often they gave it a fresh coat, perhaps to cover up the stains, or to maintain the illusion of clinical cleanliness. The floor lights were set to low for the time being. They would be turned up eventually; she remembered last time, the sharpness of the shadows that were cast on the white walls. Spectacular.

There was a tap on the door. Here was number six, which meant they were half way there. It was the only other woman of the group. She came in and sat down as quickly as Helen had done. Her small bag was patent leather, which didn't seem to match her khaki and black military clothes, the cropped hair. Helen wondered who she was and if, given their feminine minority in the group, she was wondering about Helen. There were some things that women didn't do, and this was one of them.

SIX

The Lemon Wis Gubbed

He couldn't move his legs. Steve tried to sit up but his head was so heavy, it might as well have been stuffed full of haggis and neeps. It was probably better he kept still, on the ground. The grass was getting damp; the sun had disappeared along with the fix he'd taken before D appeared. Bad timing it was, to come down off the drugs just as he'd seeped into consciousness. Usually it was the other way around, coming up and sinking happily into the back of nowhere.

"Shite, fuck it, you bastard."

So even talking hurt. He wouldn't swear out loud again, just keep it inside. Dew from the grass was soaking one side of his face, or was that blood? Touching his fingertips to his cheek, he winced at the pain. A terrible ache seeped through his body, from his toes to the ends of his hair. He looked. His fingers were covered in thick, dark red. So there was blood, then. *Fuck.*

His phone should be in the inside pocket of his jacket. Was it still there? He rolled to one side, very slow, and felt for it. There. He reached in to get it, gingerly, and flipped it open. There was something to be said for old technology: robust and reliable. He couldn't phone Ed, seeing as he'd probably kick him some more for taking that last hit off him. No, Ed would just tell him he was an arse, which he was.

Jake was on speed dial. He managed to hold the phone to his ear and spoke as best he could. "Jake? It's me, Steve."

There was a pause. "Stevie-boy? Is that you?"

"Aye, I need some help, pal." His head throbbed with every syllable. *Jesus, this was bad.*

"You sound close to dead, Stevie. Where are you?"

"Links." It was all he could manage before the phone dropped from his frozen, bloody hand. Then everything went to black.

Ma was smoking in the kitchen, the smell drifting through to the living room just like always. It would have woken Steve up, if he'd been asleep in the first place. It had been a rough first night on the sofa after a marathon stint in Emergency. He was glad he'd given up smoking himself all those years ago, otherwise he'd be hacking up a lung just now and it wouldn't feel good, not with two cracked ribs. His ex-wife Sandra's endless nagging to give it up had been worth it in the end. She'd been good for something. "You're a stinking heap of shite," she'd said to him more than once. He could see now that she did have a point.

He shifted slightly on the sofa and tried to move a cushion that had trapped itself in one of the cracks. Bastard fucking plaster cast on his right leg made everything awkward.

"Ma? You up, then?"

Ma looked through the doorway and waved her cigarette. "You're awake, son. Do you want anything while I'm in here?"

"I'm dying for a pee, Ma."

"I'll get the bucket."

There was some clanging around and he could hear her sucking in a few times in rapid succession. Ma never liked to waste the first fag of the day, and she was obviously trying to finish it quick, before she came through.

"Here you go, son. You do your business and shout me when to come back." She put the bucket on the floor, roughly below his fly. "Then I'll make you a nice cup of tea."

"Thanks, Ma. Sorry I'm such an idiot." Steve held out his hands, black and yellow with the bruising. He'd put them in front of his face while D was kicking him, and it had saved his nose, right enough, but bruised hands were terrible painful.

"Away with ye, it's nothing. Let's just get you sorted and then we can talk about what the hell is going on."

Steve rolled over and pulled down his trackie bottoms, just enough to be able to relieve himself in the bucket. A few drips went on the sofa, to mingle in with the other stains and many years of alcohol spills. Wouldn't make any difference, he thought, not in the scheme of things.

"Right, I'm done, Ma." He rolled onto his back, trying to get into a position where as few places as possible hurt.

D had done him good this time. Steve wondered if that meant he still owed him money and realized miserably that it probably did. So now he was broken, crushed, as well as being in debt to the hardest dealer in West Edinburgh. Jesus, how did he do it?

Ma came back for the bucket. As she bent to pick it up, Steve caught a close-up of the plastic rollers in her hair, tight and alien looking. She slept in them every night, had always insisted that they weren't uncomfortable, but he couldn't figure out how that could be. They looked like spiked sausage rolls that had been glued onto her scalp. She took the bucket away, and he heard the slosh of his pee in the toilet down the hall, as she emptied it out. So it had come to this.

"Thanks, Ma. I'm glad you're here to look after me, or I don't know what I'd do." He had shouted unnecessarily, as she'd already appeared back in the room, with another cigarette between her lips.

"I'm your mother. Of course I'm here, ye numpty. When Jake dropped you off at my front door, with those ambulance men, I nearly died, so I did." She lit the cigarette, waved her hand in front of it.

"Sorry. I didn't want to worry you before. When I was in the hospital getting fixed up, they said I looked worse than I was. I asked Jake not to call you too early, didn't want you all feeredy."

"Well. You're here now." Ma looked at the bandage on his head, her face wrinkled and set into a lifetime of worry. "Are you going to tell me what happened? On your birthday as well, what a shame."

"I got beaten up, Ma, simple as that. Just one guy, it was. I can't even pretend I was mugged by a group of schemies." Steve sighed, felt a lump on the side of his face. "Do I look really bad?"

Ma looked away, pursing her lips. "Remember when your uncle Sam fell from the second floor of a tenement when he was washing windows?"

"Aye."

"You look worse than that."

They fell silent for a few moments, Steve taking the opportunity to study the cheap gold vase perched on top of Ma's coffee table. A bunch of fake tulips, pink and yellow, drooped around it. Were they plastic or felt?

"If you're going to make fake flowers, as least make them stand up a bit, eh?" He managed a smile.

"Right enough," Ma wheezed a laugh and went and stubbed out her cigarette in the Rothman's F1 ashtray on the sill. "So do you know the guy who did this?"

51

"Aye, I do. I was going to pay him back some money I owed him, but he got me before I had the chance to hand it over."

"Owed him for what, Stevie?"

"Pub money, that's all. I had the money to pay him back; it wasn't that much. He's a hard bastard. I think he was just looking for an excuse to gub me."

"Right." She looked at him, tapping her foot on the shag carpet. Her expression said she didn't believe him and he didn't blame her.

"Why am I such a disaster, Ma?"

She turned and padded back to the kitchen. "Be careful, Stevie, or you'll turn into your father. Then you'll never have a hope."

He'd been asleep for a while on his makeshift bed. Stiff and sore, Steve became aware of some folk in the hallway and tried to focus. The painkillers were wearing off again and he reached down to get some more, feeling for his glass of water and the white prescription pot.

Ma came through, all smiles. "There's a couple of nice pals here to see you."

Ma was always soft with Ed and Jake. She'd known them all their lives and sometimes claimed to have wiped their arses, usually when there was a room full of people to show off to. Steve winced, wondered if he smelled really bad, but couldn't bend his neck enough to sniff his armpits. The lads came in and Ma disappeared.

"Jesus fuck." Ed stood in the doorway, frozen.

"Looks like a dug's dinner, eh?" Jake had been with Steve all the time he was at the hospital, so he was more used to the sore sight of him.

"Did you bring me some grapes?" Steve grinned, but neither Ed nor Jake smiled back. "I suppose not," he said.

His pals hovered in the middle of the room, on the other side of the coffee table and the plastic flowers. Neither of them looked him in the eye.

"Anyone seen or heard from D since he did this?" Steve asked, but he didn't want to know, not really.

"I've no' seen him," said Jake. "But I wouldn't count on him disappearing or nothing. He always turns up when you're not expecting it, you know? He'll have figured out where you are, no doubt. You don't need a degree to know you'd be at your ma's place if you're not at your own."

"I've learned that from experience, pal. It's like there's a special radar that dealers use to hunt for the poor bastards that owe them. I could be anywhere and he'd find me." Steve shut his eyes, even more sorry for himself now. Ed and Jake couldn't seem to take the sight of him. He must look terrible.

Ed cleared this throat, his leg twitching now.

"What?" Steve had known Ed long enough. Something else was up.

"I saw him." Ed sat down on Ma's telly chair, the one with the patterned footstool in front of it. He sank into the fabric, and looked like an old man now, with that baldie head of his.

Jake sat on the floor. "You never fuckin' told me."

"Aye, well, it was only this afternoon, keep your melt on."

Steve felt a panic fluttering inside his chest, a cold sensation that contrasted with the rest of the dull, warm throbbing. "Well, where did you see him? Did he talk to you?"

"He was waiting for me when I finished my shift down the docks, stepped out from behind the office building in those steel-toed boots of his. He caught me unawares, so he did. I knew what he'd done. Jake had phoned me. I nearly shite myself, I don't mind saying." Ed looked behind his shoulder, as if D could show at any minute, come flying through the window like Batman.

Ma came into the room and they stopped talking. Her wiry hair was brushed out and she was patting the sides of it, as though pushing it closer to her scalp. Steve let out a frustrated sigh.

"I'm putting the kettle on," she said. "Would you boys like a nice cup of tea and a scone?" She beamed at them, like nothing in the world was wrong.

"That would be lovely, Diane." Jake gave her a smile, pushing the glasses up on his nose like he was a wee boy again, come 'round for his tea after school, like he did in the old days.

She stood for a moment, looking between Ed and Jake, making some awestruck murmuring noises, before turning back to the kitchen. "I'll be away then, leave you boys to it. It's lovely to see you all together, so it is. And thanks to wee Jake there, my Steve is safe back home."

"Tell me what he said to you, Ed," Steve whispered when Ma had gone.

"Word for word?"

"Aye, whatever. Just spit it out, will you?"

Jake chipped in. "Fuck's sake, Ed, will you just tell us?"

Ed leaned forward for dramatic effect. "He says, 'See your pal Stevie? You tell him he's a dead man if I don't get three hundred cash by Friday.'"

"Is that it?" Jake stretched out his legs underneath the coffee table and grinned. "Three hundred quid? We can do that easy between us, boys."

Steve stared at Ed, at his tensed-up body and tight fists. "What else did he say?"

Ed paused. "He says, 'And you tell him something else. He's mine now. When he's all fixed up, he's running for me, to pay off the rest of it.'"

"No. You're fuckin' joking. I can't work for him, I couldn't take it." Steve found he was half shouting now, which made his head pound. "No way. Not that. Anything but that."

"He means it, Stevie-boy. It might be your only way out of this mess." Ed leaned back in the telly chair, resigned.

Jake lay down on the floor and stared at the stucco ceiling. "Fuck."

"What if I can come up with all the money?" Steve was asking, but he knew it was a daft question.

"Can you come up with all the money?" Ed looked up.

"No. Not unless I win the lottery."

"Then you're fucked. I'm sorry, pal."

Steve was melting into the sofa, becoming one of the stains, a giant mess. "You got any gear on you, Ed?"

Ed growled. "You're done with all that, now. Finished, you hear what I'm saying? Don't ask me again."

Steve looked over at Jake. He was staring at his shoes, shaking his curly head. So it was like that, was it? They were looking out for him proper. He should feel grateful he had two solid pals, but a hit would feel so good just now.

"Fair enough, lads." He forced himself to stay calm about it, although he'd started to get the sweats, seeping into his blood, deep inside. A familiar sensation. He reached down for the painkillers. They would be better than nothing.

Ma's words repeated themselves in his head then, reminding him of what he could be. *Be careful, Stevie, or you'll turn into your father.*

"Yous two are good pals." He just about managed to say it before his eyes closed and his body lapsed into recovery mode again.

SEVEN
A Proper Home

The sun was out and the birds were chirping on the windowsill, but Lizzy didn't feel like this was a good morning. As she left the hostel, she nearly stepped on a homeless guy, who was lying in a sleeping bag on the front step. He'd probably missed his curfew. He was dead to the world. As she jumped over him, she could smell his unwashed body, rank alcoholic breath filling the air. This was London all over, the streets like home to the homeless.

She thought about Simon, like she did every time she saw young guys with lost souls on the street. They'd escaped Dalbegie together, and he used to be there for her no matter what. Until he got too caught up in the drugs. Immersed in the street scene, Simon stopped caring about anyone but himself, and it had taken her a long time to realize that included her. Now she had no one, not really. Ever since Nat disappeared a week ago, Lizzy had felt sick in the pit of her gut. Natalie was the only person she'd felt like getting close to since Simon, and it was getting more likely every day that her new friend was gone forever. Was it her? Did she attract bad things?

Mum never came back.

The police had been buzzing around the market once they'd accepted Nat as a "missing person," but they'd not found anything out. That was familiar to Lizzy too; the disappointment of a failed investigation, just like when her mum disappeared. They'd questioned Spinner, seeing as loads of people had pointed the finger at him, but he had two alibis for the night Nat went. At first, Lizzy had been scared they might wonder if she was a missing person herself, but they were too busy concentrating on Nat to care about her.

The bus was coming down the road and Lizzy broke into a run. It looked like it wasn't too full and it would be a shame to miss it. She'd promised Dave she wouldn't be too late, but she had to get down to Kidbrooke and back, which might take a while. Keith had asked her to go to Nat's parents' first thing. Apparently Nat had told them all about her. They wanted to meet her and hear anything she might know that would help them find Nat. As she ran, she accidentally brushed against some woman walking her dog, just a wee touch on her elbow.

"Watch what you're doing, you stupid cow," the woman scowled, yanking her lead to pull the dog close.

"Get a life," Lizzy shouted back as she hopped on the bus.

The driver grinned at her. "Picking a fight already, are you? A bit early for all that, isn't it?"

"Some people are just so miserable." She punched in and went to the back. Some start to the day. The tears had already been waiting behind her eyes and now she fought to keep them where they were, looking out the window at the shop fronts and busy people whizzing by, trying to focus on something—a yellow "Yaaz Bazaar" awning or a road sweeper. Anything.

A tear escaped, just the one, and dripped onto her hand. She didn't look down, in case any more came, not wanting to get all puffy-eyed. She wiped her jacket sleeve underneath her eyes and some black eyeliner smudged on the cotton. The magazines all said not to put eyeliner underneath, only on top, but she liked the fiercer look it gave her. Now she'd just look like a panda, a sad one as well. Nat's mum and dad wouldn't notice, anyway—no one did.

Lizzy rang the bell of number 84 Swan Road. The door opened almost immediately. It was Natalie's mum, bedraggled, with dark rings around her eyes. She looked like she hadn't slept in days, which was probably because she hadn't, Lizzy realized. Her leggings were baggy at the knees, and her jumper looked like it might be inside out, thick seams down the sleeves.

"Here she is. You must be Lizzy. Thanks for coming all the way down here, darlin'. I'm Karen." She waved her hand to follow her inside.

Lizzy went with her through to the living room. The house smelled of burnt toast and tea bags and laundry. The shelf above the telly was covered with photo frames, all different shapes and sizes, black-and-white and colour prints, kids and oldies and families together.

This was a proper home.

"You sit down on the sofa and I'll put the kettle on." She shouted upstairs. "Darren, she's here."

There was a thump and heavy footsteps coming down. Lizzy slotted her hands under her thighs and slumped back. She hoped Nat's dad wouldn't get angry, or try to blame her.

He filled the doorframe when he appeared, his hair ruffled up so it stuck up on end. "Thanks for coming over, Lizzy. Nat told me you'd been a good mate to her. We wanted to meet you, just in case there's anything else you've got for us." He sat down on an armchair and crossed his legs.

"The thing is, I don't know anything about where she went. I'm really sorry. She didn't say anything to me that day about it." Lizzy looked back at the kitchen, hoping Karen would come back soon.

Darren leaned forward. "It's just that, you know, if there was something you didn't want to tell the police, you can tell us. Anything that might help. Me and Karen, we won't get angry or nothing. We just want our baby girl back."

"I'm sorry. I want her back too. If she'd planned something, she would have told me. I'd know. But she didn't, did she?" Lizzy didn't like to spell out what she thought, that Nat could have been abducted. "There's a guy called Spinner who sniffs around the girls in the market. I saw him talking to her that day. But that's all I know."

Karen reappeared with a tray full of teacups and biscuits, and set it down on the table in front of them. "Yes, we've heard about this Spinner. The police have questioned him. He sounds well dodgy."

"He is. I don't know if he's got anything to do with it, but I don't trust him." Lizzy took a tea and a biscuit from Karen. "Thank you."

There was a grandfather clock in the corner of the room, and it was ticking quietly, filling up the gaps. Karen looked lost in her own thoughts, staring into her tea. Nat's dad slurped at his and murmured a few words about what a scumbag Spinner sounded. Nat was still their baby girl, then. She liked to be a bit of a rebel, work where she wanted to work, and have a row with her parents, but at home she had all this. Lizzy looked around the room, at the framed school photo of Nat in a blue uniform, at the crystal animals in the glass cabinet next to the fireplace, parts of their lives, stories to be told and treasured. She felt a pang of jealousy, but brushed it away. Nat might be hurt, anything. This was no time for thinking about her own miseries. "Don't worry," she said. "Nat'll be back soon and then we'll know who to go after."

"You all right there, darlin'?" Dave looked up as she arrived at the stall.

"Yeah, course I am."

"How was it with Nat's mum and dad? Didn't give you any grief, did they?"

"Nah, they were nice. They were hoping I had something else to tell them. I wish I did, Dave."

"Chuck on a pinny then, and give us a hand, will you? I've got Granny Smiths coming out of my bleedin' earholes over here."

Lizzy put an apron on and mucked in. She'd known Dave for so long that they felt comfortable in silence, no need to talk if they didn't feel like it. They shifted crates, put out the fruit and vegetables, working quickly and in sync like an old married couple.

When they'd finished, Dave reached up, stretching out his back. "She'll be back, Lizzy, don't you worry."

"How do you know?"

"I don't really, do I, but I'm sure she'll turn up. Kids always do."

Lizzy frowned and started to turn some of the apples. Dave was just trying to make her feel better, but there wasn't any point saying anything if you didn't really know. He was just getting her hopes up. But then she'd said the same thing to Nat's parents, which was a stupid thing to do.

"Dave, you know when I started working on the stall, that day when I just showed up and you gave me a day's work? Did you not see me before that, sitting over there on the pavement?"

"There's so many weirdies around here, I never pay much attention to be honest, darlin'. When you showed up, you said I'd promised you some work for that day, jabbering on about some letter I'd written and slipped in your pocket. It weren't me. I was busy, though, wasn't I, needed the help, and you had a pretty little face. So there we were."

"So what are you saying? I'm a pretty weirdo?"

He puffed out his cheeks. "Yeah, I s'pose so. We never did work out who'd put the note in your pocket, did we? It came out of nowhere. It wasn't you, and it wasn't me. But it don't matter now. You're here, and we're okay, ain't we?"

"No, it doesn't really matter. But I'd still like to know who dumped me on that pavement and wrote the note. I think about it sometimes, and it freaks me out."

A young guy came over, all black denim and horn-rimmed glasses. He nodded at Lizzy and went to pick up one of the apples.

"Don't touch," she snapped.

He jumped, pulled back his hand. "Jesus, you gave me a fright," he said.

Dave grinned. "Don't mind her, she hasn't had her dog biscuits yet this morning."

She hadn't meant to sound like that. Lizzy tried to smile and grabbed a bag for the man's fruit. "Sorry about that."

When he'd gone, she looked over at Dave to apologize, but behind him a familiar figure was coming out of the shadows and made her forget all about feeling sorry for herself. She gasped. "Natalie?"

It was her; it was Nat, still dressed in the same clothes she was wearing on the day she disappeared. They were dirtier and crumpled now, and she looked thinner, or just different.

"It's you, darlin'!" Keith ran to Natalie, put his hands gently on her shoulders, and bent over to study her face.

Nat seemed confused, disorientated. She looked back into his eyes for a moment, then fell forward into his arms. Lizzy went closer, heard her friend's sobs, mixed in with Keith's low voice trying to calm her down.

"Let's sit you down over here," he said, motioning to Lizzy to unfold one of the traders' picnic chairs used for tea breaks.

Lizzy pulled out two chairs and sat on one of them, putting her arm around the back of the other one. Natalie sat down and leaned in to her. Lizzy could see lots of streaks on her face, where tears had washed tiny rivers of clean through the dirt and grime. Her friend's hair was greasy and hung in strands around her face.

"Where have you been? What happened, Nat?"

Keith stood in front of them, hands on his thighs. "I'm going to call your mum, my love, let her know you're here." He was shouting, as if Natalie couldn't hear though all the upset. He pulled his phone out of his jeans pocket and dialed, walking a few paces away to make the call.

Nat looked at the ground. "I don't know where I was. I must have been somewhere."

"What do you mean?" Lizzy squeezed her hand.

"I can't remember anything."

"Where did you come from just now? Did someone drop you off around here?"

Nat pressed her fingers into the sides of her temples and screwed up her face. "I was in a car. Something was covering my eyes, so I couldn't see. Next minute I was in the street, looking at the market. It was weird."

"It wasn't Spinner, was it? I've not seen him around for a few days." Lizzy looked up, and glanced around at the growing number of people. She'd been looking out for Spinner since she saw him on the day Nat disappeared, hoping she'd be able to question him again. She thought she'd catch him out, watch his expressions. She imagined a shadow of recognition when she mentioned Natalie, or some glimmer of satisfaction in his evil eyes that the police would have missed when they questioned him. But she hadn't had another chance.

"I just don't know, Lizzy. I'm so tired. Will you take me home?"

"Of course."

"Mum and Dad. They're going to kill me."

Lizzy squeezed Nat's hand. "They're not, Nat. They've been so worried about you. This ain't your fault." She waved her fingers at Dave, who was watching them while serving a customer.

He thrust a bag of fruit at a woman and came over in three huge strides. "What's going on?"

"Do you mind if I take Nat home? We can't let her go by herself."

"Course you can. Is Keith still trying to get hold of her mum? Where've you been, Nat? We've all been having a heart attack around here. Good to see you back, girl."

"She can't remember anything. I'll wait 'til Keith is off the phone and then I'll go. Cheers, Dave." Lizzy grabbed her bag and her jacket, throwing the apron on top of a crate. "There's a bit of change in there."

"You're a good girl, Lizzy. I'll see you when I see you. As long as it takes, kid." Dave hopped back to the stall.

Dave would have to stay for her shift, but this was important. Lizzy was pretty sure he wouldn't mind even if she was gone for the rest of the day. She watched Keith slide his phone in his back pocket and pause for a moment before coming back.

"Just spoke to your mum, Nat. She's over the moon you're back." He looked at the ground. "It's been a tough week for her."

"I'm going to take her home. Dave says it's all right," Lizzy said.

"I said I'd take her back, but there's the stall I suppose. That would be great, Lizzy. Goes without saying, but be careful. Don't talk to no one."

Lizzy rubbed her friend's arm. "Let's go, Nat, come on."

Keith held out some cash. "Here's the bus money. Thanks, love."

Lizzy took it. "I'll look after her, don't worry about nothing." She grabbed Natalie's hand and pulled her gently away. "Let's get you to your mum's. I know the way now."

Nat coughed, her chest wheezing. "They never wanted me to work here."

"I know, but that don't matter now. You're back and that's all they'll care about. Promise."

"Nat! You're here. My Natalie." Karen's voice was hoarse, desperate. She pulled her daughter in, and wrapped her arms around her.

There were a few moments of silence as the two of them buried their heads into each other. Lizzy kept back until someone acknowledged her, turning her head to one side so it didn't seem like she was watching. There was an empty pop can underneath the hedge that separated Natalie's house with the neighbour. It was half covered in dirt and leaves, forgotten.

Karen looked up at last and smiled at Lizzy. "Come in, darlin'. I'll get you a drink and something to eat. You both look like you could do with a good feed."

Lizzy felt anxious, like she was in the way. "She hasn't said much. Says she can't remember anything."

Karen led them into the living room and they sat down on the sofa. Natalie leaned into Lizzy and closed her eyes. Karen fussed with the plastic coasters on the coffee table in front of them, brushing away some imaginary dust. She didn't take her eyes off her daughter.

Lizzy felt like she should take charge. "Should we get her to bed, do you think? Have you called the police, to let them know she's back?"

Karen straightened. "Yes, I should call and let them know she's here. I don't want them 'round here, though, not yet. She needs a rest, get herself a bit sorted out."

Lizzy didn't want to say out loud what she was thinking. What could have happened to Natalie. But she had to say something. "They'll want to take a look at her properly, as soon as they can. There might be evidence."

"I wish Darren was home." Natalie's mum looked out the window, as if he might appear, as if Lizzy hadn't said what she'd said. "I couldn't get him at work; he hadn't been there long. I left a message. Hopefully he'll get it soon." Her eyes filled with tears. "He must be down the warehouse."

Lizzy pulled Natalie up and helped her walk to the hallway. "I'll get her upstairs so she can lie down for a bit. Where's her room?"

"I'll go up first, show you where it is. I've changed all the sheets all ready for her. I knew she was coming back, even though the police were all doom and gloom. And here she is, completely fine. You were right, Lizzy. We just had to wait a bit longer."

Lizzy helped her friend up the stairs. Natalie seemed so light, frail, like her bones were empty. She wasn't "completely fine"; Lizzy was sure of that. They followed Karen into the bedroom, which was white and pink and airy. There was a white wardrobe and matching chest of drawers, and pink curtains with tiny white flowers. Natalie lay down on the bed, curled up her legs and fell asleep straightaway. Her mum stroked her hair away from her face and put a blanket on top of her.

"There we are. My baby girl back in her room, just like I always knew."

The two of them watched her for a moment. Lizzy didn't want to leave until she knew the police had been called, that Natalie would get a proper check-up. If they were to find out who took her, what they did, she would need professional examination. Even she knew that.

"My Keith told me she just appeared by the stall. Do you know anything, darlin'?" Karen was wringing her hands around and around, her sweatshirt sleeves stretched and baggy.

"No. Nothing. She was just walking towards us, come out of nowhere. We think she must have been dropped off by someone, but we didn't see who it was. She's got some money, a wad of cash, stuffed in her pocket. It doesn't make sense." She tried to keep her voice gentle. "Shall we go downstairs and try Darren again?" Perhaps Nat's dad would help move things along.

Karen looked grateful. "Yes, let's have another go, shall we? And I'll make you a nice bacon sarnie. You hungry, darlin'?"

"Yeah. I'm always hungry, to be honest."

"Look at you, like a skeleton." She trudged down the stairs, her slippers a little too big, the backs of them flapping against her heels.

In the kitchen, Karen put the gas stove on, and soon bacon was sizzling in a pan. There were three stools at a bar on one side of the kitchen and Lizzy sat up on one, watching as Karen made up two rolls with bacon, sliced tomato, and ketchup. She slid a large glass of orange juice over as well and Lizzy gulped at it, realizing she hadn't had a drink since the tea she'd had that morning. Karen ate her roll standing up, facing Lizzy.

"Thank you. This is brilliant." Lizzy spoke with her mouth full, but covered it up with her hand.

"You enjoy it, my love. It's been quiet around here while Nat's been gone. She's got no brothers or sisters, as you know. Thanks for bringing her home to her old mum. The things you girls get up to, I don't know."

"Someone took her. I don't think she got up to anything."

"That's not what I meant. It's just that I'm pleased she's back. I don't want to think about where she was just yet. Okay, darlin'?"

"Yeah, I know. But we need to call the police before she has a bath."

Karen didn't answer. She licked her finger and pushed it into some crumbs on the plate in front of her. Lizzy studied her face and could see the understanding there, along with a lot of worry. She thought about the money in Nat's pocket. It was obvious what young girls usually got paid for. Natalie's mum knew what she had to do, but needed to enjoy this moment. Her daughter had come back, safe, alive. What had happened to her they could worry about in a few minutes, when they'd finished the bacon rolls.

"Good, ain't they?"

"The best." Lizzy put the last piece in her mouth and chewed it with her eyes closed.

The front door burst open and Nat's dad rushed through to the kitchen. "Where is she?"

Karen smiled. "Your daughter's upstairs asleep on her bed. She's all right, Darren."

"Thank Christ for that. I'll go see her." He ran upstairs, heavy boots pounding on the carpet.

Karen looked at Lizzy. "Here we go," she said. "Darren will sort this out, make the calls."

"Shall I go back?"

"No, stay for a bit. Maybe you can help the police, tell them where she appeared from and what she was doing, that kind of thing. I'll make you up another roll, if you like."

They went through to the living room while Nat's dad came down and called the police. He sounded like a kind man, Lizzy thought, the way dads should be. Not like hers, not at all interested and violent when he chose to be. He was scary when he was drunk, which was often, if she remembered right. Hers was in Yorkshire somewhere, a place she'd never been, because he'd never invited her. Not that he knew how to get hold of her since she'd left Scotland. She used to see him once a year, at Christmas, when he made the trip up to Dalbegie. She didn't miss him, the stress of him. He'd never hurt her physically, but had beaten up her mum plenty of times when they lived together. Good riddance to him.

She listened to Nat's dad on the phone, the worried parent, and wondered what it would be like to have two people care about you that much.

"Karen and Darren," she said, before she realized she was saying it out loud.

"I know, funny isn't it," said Karen. "When you rhyme with each other, you know you're a proper team."

"I suppose so," Lizzy said. "I can't remember anyone I know rhyming with their other half."

"I bet you'll rhyme with someone one day, darlin'. Or as good as."

Maybe she would, although it would be a first in her family.

Darren came bouncing into the room, clapped his hands together and went to the window. "Right, the police are on their way. She'll have to go down the station, get examined. I tell you, that's the last time she's working on that bloody stall. I'll have your Keith, for not watching her proper."

"It ain't my brother's fault and you know it." Karen crossed her arms and nodded over at Lizzy. "She was getting that bus home every day by herself, and we were okay with it, Darren."

Darren sighed. "I know. I should never have let her take that bloody job in the first place, all that way up town. No place for a young girl." He turned to Lizzy. "You don't look much older. What do your parents make of it all?"

"Not much."

"There we go. It ain't right."

Lizzy nodded. "Glad she's back safe."

"So are we, love. You're a good friend." Karen patted her hand.

They waited for the police to come, to take Nat and find out what they needed to know. Lizzy felt a bit sick at the thought of all the prodding and probing and wished she hadn't had that second bacon roll. She hoped Nat's dad would eventually change his mind and let her come back to work. She'd really miss her otherwise. Nat hadn't disappeared for good; she was here, in the flesh. But was her spirit still there? As the police car drew up, lights flashing, Lizzy closed her eyes and wished for her friend to be whole again. There was nothing to do but wait and see. She might as well get back to the market, and help Dave with packing up. There was no point going back to the bedsit early, and it wasn't warm enough to sit out in the park. And even if it was, she could never relax properly, always looking over her shoulder, with that shuddery feeling that someone, somewhere, was looking for her.

EIGHT

Oliver the Overseer

I've been watching you for so long, my dear Lizzy. I feel that you belong to me. I hope that doesn't offend you. Anyone or anything that might affect your progress in this life is an imposter, unwanted, and superfluous to our needs. You are not a puppet; I do not control you, but I do have the power of influence, as your unseen guardian.

I found an excellent vantage point some months ago, quite by accident, when I discovered an open door to a derelict bedsit, flea-ridden and damp. It's better than it sounds, simply because the place directly overlooks the market. It must belong to someone, perhaps the owner of the other ten or twelve ratholes in the building, but so far it has remained empty, and the lock I added to the door means that it stays free from homeless chancers. With bleach, disinfectant, and insect powder, I scrubbed the place with a wire brush until it couldn't possibly hold any germs, and made it mine. I use it just for daytime viewing, an activity with which I'm long familiar.

I used to watch your mother too, from my cottage opposite the newsagents in Dalbegie. The Scottish Highlands, so fresh and clean. I should have appreciated the purity of the air more than I did, but of course I was focussed on other things. London is stale, as stagnant as a tropical pond, but you know all this. I've seen the grubbiness under your fingernails at the end of each day, spotless again each morning. You look after yourself, despite the relentless filth of it all. Your mother was much the same; my Lauren. I enjoyed the neat way she dressed, the delicate earrings she thoughtfully chose and changed each day. The details were the most interesting to me, the finer points that I gleaned from the eyes of my high-grade Nikon Sport Optics. I've never felt the need to upgrade them; their clarity is superb. I also liked the way she said my name, with the enunciation on the "O" in her beautiful singsong Scottish accent. I wonder what she'd think of her daughter trying so hard to lose her Highland tones. What would you call me, now? "Olivah" like the orphan boy in the film, spoken like Nancy Sykes. Poor Lizzy; you do slip up sometimes, and your accent is still there for the trained ear. My fondness for you is like that of distant uncle; it's hard to believe there was a time when I considered your death so eagerly, following that of your mother.

The desire still burns, but the flame fluctuates from low to blazing. And so I hold back.

Finding you wasn't difficult, even though I came to London some time after your disappearance. My tardiness was partly because I had some loose ends to tie up in Dalbegie, and partly because I didn't want to rouse suspicion if my departure had coincided with yours and Simon's – and of course the despicable Roy's. I have a small but effective network in the city, and street youth are predictable in their choices of location. When I first spied you, however, sitting on some steps near Trafalgar Square, it was still a shock. You were dirty and thin, a lost soul with a vacant look that only someone high on drugs can have. You were with Simon, who had clearly sunk even further, his waxy skin a mass of sores. I detested him even more than I had before, this boy who was pulling you down with him into some irretrievable place.

You wouldn't remember, but I picked you up that day, took your hand, and guided you to the streets of Soho. I felt, even then, that you were in some way a part of me and I needed to show you what to do next. I'd seen young people working the market; it was a lifeline to many, offering cash in hand for an honest day's work. Some people survive on the streets, and some don't, and you are a survivor. In you, I saw a tough exterior with the soul of a gentle fawn, and too much intelligence to waste on sitting on steps with idiots like Simon.

I'd seen a stall at the end of the market, run by a hard-working man, one of the only ones without an assistant, and I left you on the curb nearby, to work off whatever it was you'd consumed. In your coat pocket I left twenty pounds and a note.

Fruit stall, Berwick St. Market
Start Tuesday, 7 a.m.
Cash in hand

It was a simple plan that could easily have gone wrong, but when I returned to my lookout the next morning, there you were, talking to the man at the stall, brandishing the note as if it were his. You looked alert, an endearing aura of hope about your bright face. I should imagine it would be hard to resist an offer of help so early in the morning, a long day ahead of setting up, selling, standing on tired feet. To my delight, he eventually nodded, held out his hands, and you immediately began emptying cartons of fruit. He liked you. Of course he did. You're young, eager, attractive, and strong. I felt proud of you, for grasping at a chance and making it happen. You were given money at the end of that day, and you used it well. The rest of your emergence into the real world was all your own doing and I was satisfied you'd come good.

As you've matured and grown stronger, so too has my protectiveness of you. Roy, you would be pleased to know, is not someone you ever need worry about. I saw to that personally. I sense your nervous tension, that constant darting look, and I can't blame you for worrying that he'll come after you. If only I could tell you that I removed his revolting body from this world on the night you left Dalbegie three years ago, it would make your life a calmer one.

I've seen Spinner trying to talk to you, and I delight in your revulsion at his presence. Admittedly he is odious. He is, however, a useful pawn in my underground business. He seeks, recruits, and sometimes even sits on the door there. He loves the market, with all those impressionable, desperate people. The way he dresses, the tight jeans and that leather jacket, disgusts me, the clinging fabrics a breeding ground for bacteria. I could swear that I can smell his body odour from up here. But he is the one who sniffs out the victims, and brings them to me like a dog, and so I endure his physical repulsiveness for now.

I instructed Spinner not to touch you. You cannot be a part of The Audacious. He doesn't know the reason: that I cannot have anyone else hurt you but me. He doesn't need to know; he will do as I tell him and knows not to ask questions. I have a modicum of regret that we viewed Natalie at The Audacious. She is, after all, part of your new world and offers no threat. She wouldn't have been my choice, but Spinner brought her that day for defiant reasons of his own. If not you, then your closest friend. But of course we went ahead; why wouldn't we? As it happened, she was an extremely popular subject, and was one of the lucky ones, a survivor in our final game of risk.

If you get abducted, Lizzy, if you are killed, it will be with me. Your fate is not in the hands of The Circle's game of chance; it is mine to play with. I have the ultimate power, because I will choose when you leave this world, and how you will do so.

NINE
Helen in Tandem

Helen had been in bed for almost a week. She only knew this because the midday news was telling her that it was Friday, not because she'd been keeping any sort of tally. She had collapsed into oblivion last weekend, and the days had uneventfully merged into each other. At first, she basked in the glory of the viewing at The Audacious. Then, as the days passed, her skin began to itch again, her mind shutting down with the lack of stimulus. Most of the time, she was unaware of the clock or the sun or the moon. The curtains remained drawn, and she ate only when her stomach told her she had to. The bed sheets smelled of her unwashed hair, she realized, but it wasn't an unpleasant thing, this cocoon of herself.

The television came into focus. A newsreader with a stiff, blonde bob and a fake smile was telling London about another incident on the tube. More pointless deaths; just another day. Helen shifted slightly, just enough to be able to make a gun with her fingers and shoot at the screen. Her right leg was still aching for no apparent reason, despite the painkillers, but there was nothing to get up for, to stretch it out. The ache was inside, in her bones, and she wondered if something more sinister was wrong.

The next viewing at The Audacious was this Monday night, after another long wait. The Circle often gathered on a Monday. The beginning of the week meant there were fewer people around to witness anyone going into the building, and less trouble generally. On Friday and Saturday nights the police were always patrolling, looking for something to kick off.

She had three more nights to get through.

Helen got out of bed, another twinge of pain shooting down her shin. She would go outside for a walk, feed the ducks maybe, before diving back into hibernation for the rest of the weekend. Perhaps exercise would relieve this relentless ache. She put on her coat over the leggings and T-shirt that she'd been wearing for several days. No point in changing into clean clothes before she'd showered. The world would have to make do with her just the way she was.

As she left the flat, a wave of excitement drifted out with her. The positive thing about her dreary existence was that time disappeared without much of a bother, and before she knew it, the next viewing would be looming. Helen would spend the next round of hours in a trance, not quite in real life but aware that something good was coming.

She emptied out the plastic bag of broken-up bread into the pond, and scrunched it up in her pocket. The ducks pecked and flapped, happy with what they were given and how they were given it. No need to make a show of the delivery.

Reflections in the water were shimmering in the sunlight. There was no one else around, and she felt calm in her solitude. Lifting her face to a touch of warmth from the sky, she closed her eyes and listened to the delicate splashes and squawking coming from the pond.

She sat. There was no one. It was so quiet.

Then there was a voice behind her. "You all right, missus?"

Helen sat up straight, felt some saliva on one side of her face, her fingers cold on her skin. Time had passed again without her realizing.

"I thought you was dead for a minute!" A man walked around to face her.

She didn't answer, wiping her face with her coat sleeve in case there were any other signs of her temporary disappearance. The man looked harmless enough, a middle-aged construction worker in orange overalls, probably on his way home from work. She tried to smile, but wasn't sure if it had looked like a grimace.

"You look terrible, darlin'. Were you asleep? You need to get yourself home and warmed up a bit." He looked at his watch, as if he was late.

"Yes. I will do." She rubbed at her right leg, as it had stiffened up again.

"Want a hand getting up?" He came closer.

"No." She had shouted a bit. It wasn't intentional, but she didn't like strangers in close proximity, even if they were trying to help her. It had just come out that way.

"Keep your hair on, I was just trying to help," he said as he went on his way, shaking his head.

Helen could hear his thoughts. They sprang out of his head and found their way over to her. "*She's not all there, the poor woman,*" and "*You can't help some people.*" She turned and hobbled in the opposite direction, towards the bus stop, with a sudden urge to go somewhere, any place away from here. She'd go to Dina's Diner, have her usual brunch in Soho. She hoped that Dina herself would be there this time, not just her long-suffering daughter. It was sad, to look forward to seeing a café owner, but Dina was one of the few people who spoke to her.

She was there. "Egg, chips and beans!" Dina was calling out the orders and throwing plates on the bar for her daughter to take to the tables. She shouted at a customer by the window. "Is it scrambled or fried eggs you want with the full English, darlin'?"

Helen sat down at a table near the counter, her usual spot taken up by a group of men who looked like they probably worked on the market, dirty fingernails and tired faces. Missy nodded at her as she took two plates overflowing with baked beans and put them down in front of a pair of grubby workmen. "There you go, my loves, tuck into that and see what happens."

Dina called out again. "Missy, there's no ketchup on table one. And Helen's table here needs wiping." She waved at Helen before turning back to the frying pans.

"Bleeding slave driver, she is," Missy murmured as she wiped the table over with a damp cloth.

This was how it went when Dina was there. Helen enjoyed their banter; it was entertaining once in a while. She took off her coat and hung it on the back of the wooden chair, not bothering to look at the menu scribbled on the whiteboard above.

"Your usual, is it?" Dina called, brandishing a spatula.

"Please." Helen managed a smile and forced out another few words. "It's hard to change from it." Did that sound awkward? Probably.

"Of course it's hard to change your order. It's made by the best cook in the world," said Dina. "Sunny side up, here I come."

The bacon was sizzling, the smell of it making Helen's stomach ache. When was her last proper meal? She studied her own finger-nails and realized they were just as filthy as the workmen's. Hands under the table now, she looked around the café, trying to find distraction from her dull hunger pangs. There was someone she recognized, sitting behind the workmen's table, alone. Perhaps she'd seen him around the market, or even in Dina's before. He wore ripped jeans and too much gold jewellery for a man. Rough. He was looking around the room too, his narrow eyes surveying the place. He was probably looking for someone to take advantage of, she thought. He looked like the type who was out for what he could get, always on the sponge for opportunity. She had known his type before, many times over. But there was something else in the way he was slumped in the chair, this curve of his thighs.

Her interest in him was lost as Missy announced the arrival of her food. "Double egg and bacon. Get it in you."

Helen picked up the knife and fork and cut into one of the yolks, watched the dark yellow of it run onto the buttered toast. There were some things that you could rely on in life and one of them was Dina's perfectly cooked eggs. She looked up just in time to catch Dina watching her. She held up her knife, egg running down it, and smiled.

The smile had come naturally. There was a thing.

A chair scraped across the floor. The man with the gold chains had got up and was leaving some change on the table. Helen watched as he slid towards the door, past a young girl sitting on one of the high stools at the window. He turned to grin at her and she gave him the finger. His grin didn't waver; it was as if it was stuck on his face like the Joker's.

Helen thought of all the ways The Circle could make that fake smile disappear. And all the ways it could dampen the girl's spirit too, for that matter. She was too shiny for her own good.

Back home, Helen showered and threw some clothes into a laundry bag. The meal and fresh air had given her some momentum. She would get her washing done that night, leaving the weekend to keep to herself. She wouldn't need to eat until Saturday, not after that breakfast, so she had already cleaned up the kitchen knowing that it would stay spotless for the rest of the day. She hated washing up, then dirtying the plates again; there didn't seem to be any point to it. But it had been surprisingly satisfying, wiping the surfaces, leaving cutlery to drain and making things smell of tangerine Fairy Liquid.

As she prepared to leave the house, there was a ding from her laptop. An email had come in. She hurried to the computer.

Monday 12th, 2 a.m., The Audacious

So now she had a time as well as a date. It was even later than usual. She stared at the screen. The anonymous message was all she would be getting, but it was enough to make her heart beat fast enough for her to feel it, to imagine blood pumping around her body instead of floating around like stagnant water. She grabbed the bag and left with renewed energy.

Friday nights were fairly quiet down the launderette, as most people had other things to do, especially working folk whose sole purpose seemed to be to get as drunk as possible at the end of the week. When Helen arrived, she was pleased to see only three other people there, and it looked like two of them were finishing up, folding and packing.

She found her usual place in the far corner, where there was a seat facing the back wall, and emptied the whole bag of clothes straight into the machine. Once the coins and the powder were in and it began to whir, she sat down, empty bag at her feet, and stared into the water and soap suds. This was one place where her ability to shed time was a benefit. No sooner did she sit down and daydream, the washing was done.

The last two viewings at The Audacious had been intense—something gloriously new with each of them. First, the man who'd been picked for The Circle was a homeless drunk, and older than they'd ever had previously. Some of the subjects were "taken," but others, like this one, came of their own accord with the promise of payment in return for being "watched". Despite his poor situation in life, he fought back furiously when he realized what was involved. But it didn't put a stop to things, not at that late stage, when time and effort had been invested.

"Stop this now, just fucking stop," he had shouted, arms flailing, before he was finally handcuffed and injected again. He must have developed a high tolerance to drugs after years of abuse, and he seemed too "aware," a risk.

As an extra precaution, they hooded him, but it kept slipping, the elastic not positioned quite right, and Helen would occasionally see a wild eye, bloodshot and angry, before it was covered up again.

The other woman in the circle spoke out. "Think of the money you're making."

"I don't want your fucking money. I can't take it," he said through gritted teeth as he kicked at the shackles.

His spirit was surprising…and interesting. When Oliver gave the man the gun at the end of the session, she half imagined him pointing it away, shooting one of them into oblivion. But he was so crazed and confused by that point that he did what Oliver told him, just like they always did. They'd finally beat him down for the final spin, the crescendo of the performance. Oliver inserted a bullet into the canister, and run his hand across it so that it revolved, clicking into place. The man would have a one in six chance of shooting himself dead. He cowered on the floor, sweating profusely, while Oliver calmly gave him the instructions. One chance. The man had whimpered, and did it quick. There was a loud bang, then a muffled gurgle as a river of blood poured out one side of his head, thick and dark, a surprising quantity. *Unlucky for some.*

The other exceptional viewing of late was the girl.

Helen had felt like something special was about to happen, had hoped for a submissive in The Circle that night; she enjoyed that kind the most. It was as if they were enjoying the procedures, taking them willingly, lucky to be a part of it, not like the previous man who'd made such a fuss. Once, a young prostitute had apparently found her way back to that alley, days after her release, and knocked on the door. The doorman had been expecting someone and opened it despite the erratic knock, surprised to see her there instead. She had told him she had a vague recollection of leaving the place with a good sum of money. Could she come back again? He told her the rules; no one was allowed to come twice, and if she showed her face there again, she would be sorry. Helen heard he'd given the woman a scar on her cheek with his flick-knife, so she wouldn't forget. They'd increased the dose of the memory inhibitor after that.

That night, Helen had been early, deciding to get off one stop too soon and walk the rest of the way. She'd stepped off the bus onto the pavement in front of a clothes shop, dark now, and covered with a metal gate. The route was familiar. She kept to the main roads, only a few taxis and the occasional truck keeping her company. She kept a mace spray and a knife in her coat pocket and held onto them, in case of trouble, would use either one without thinking about it. But it wouldn't happen; it seldom did to a drab person like herself, invisible to most folk on the street.

When she reached the alley, she paused for a moment at the corner, looking and breathing in. The air was thick, full of desperation and hunger. It was beautiful, the tension. She knew it was going to be a good night.

She knocked, the special code, and was let inside. It was the same man on the door, hooded, silent, cap down over his face. Without looking up, he gestured towards the other end of the corridor. As if he needed to tell her where to go. She walked slowly along that last brief passage that led to ecstasy.

In the room, over half the members of The Circle were already present, including the other woman. Helen took a seat facing her so that she could surreptitiously study her. She was wearing army greens this time; proper camouflage. The trousers were tight with pink socks underneath, a glint of feminine. Her bag was a canvas satchel, bulging under her chair. Was that a hair clip on one side of her head? Helen couldn't quite see it from that angle.

Oliver stood by the door. He was wearing a black wool hat, knitted to incorporate a short peak at the front. At some angles it looked like his hair. Helen wondered if he was balding underneath now. There was a red scratch down the side of his face, starting from his scalp. It wasn't bleeding, but it looked raw and tender. She remembered his penchant for scalding showers, scrubbing perceived germs from his being.

A few minutes later, the viewing began. The timing was always strict and no stragglers were allowed in. Not that anyone was ever late.

A girl walked in, her legs bare and shaking. "Not doing this," she was saying. She seemed rather young. Her accent was working class, like all the voices in Dina's café.

"Give her a little extra," said the other woman.

The man from the front door appeared with a syringe and put it into the girl's arm in one experienced movement.

"What you doing?" The girl swayed a little, then went quiet.

"We're going to do just what we want," said Oliver. "And you're going to see if you can take it." Then he addressed the rest of the group. "Are we all sure about this? She's young."

Everyone nodded. Helen's skin tingled.

The girl couldn't have known that all that pain she would endure that night would be gone, erased. There would be no significant marks on her skin after a few days in the recovery room. If she was one of the lucky ones, if she chose a blank at the end, she'd leave with good money. They often left cash in the surviving victims' pockets, to discover once they were kicked back out into the street. It was mainly to let them think they'd done a sexual act for the money, something they didn't mind forgetting and wouldn't want to talk about.

The girl slumped, arms down at her sides as if they had become heavy. Helen nodded her approval. Now they could begin. She'd never been the one to start things, but she felt her dry mouth opening and the words came out.

"Spin her."

The washing machine had stopped and the light was flashing. Helen started, alert now, a rush of adrenaline giving life to her body. She opened the washer door and surveyed the tightly wound clothes, damp and wrinkled. That girl. She'd given quite the show, a viewing to remember, and it had made Helen realize that she had a preference, a type of person she liked to see at the viewings. It was girls, too young to get angry or violent, but old enough to know what was happening to them. The golden age. There was also a sweetness and vulnerability with a girl, even with the more streetwise of them. Tough, but only on the outside.

TEN

Steve's Visiting Hour

He could walk to the toilet and back to the sofa, and to the kitchen to make a cup of tea. That was about it so far. The thought of all the tenement stairs made Steve shudder, even though they were his only way of getting out. It would be a while before he'd be able to go up and down them, even with a stick.

He needed a drink.

Steve pulled himself up using the arm of the chair, where he'd been sitting for two hours watching shite on the telly. It was all driving him mad bored. His walking stick was propped up against the chair, and he held onto it as he went through to the kitchen. He grabbed the white plastic kettle that Ma had owned for twenty years or more. It took ages to boil, so he only quarter-filled it under the tap. It made a hissing noise like it was going to explode, but it would no doubt last another twenty years, despite its brown stains and lime-scaled insides.

Ma had gone out to get the messages, and it was nice to have the place to himself for a bit. Bless her, she looked after his sorry self so well, but she was also full of blether when he didn't want to hear it. What he should be doing with his life, which women he should be spending it with, and whether he had enough put by for the future were all Ma's favourite subjects. They were things that he didn't want to think about just now. There was only one predicament on his mind, and that was how he was going to get D off his back.

Ed and Jake had delivered the three hundred, no problem, and he owed them at least half of it. Good pals, they were; the best. But D wouldn't forget about the rest of the cash in a million years, and so Steve owed him big, in time spent as his runner.

The only thing was, he couldn't run yet.

He made himself a tea, plenty of milk and sugar, and took a packet of biscuits out of the cupboard. They were the plain, Rich Tea kind, no chocolate. Ma liked them, god only knew why. There was some clanking around outside on the stair. She was back already. Maybe she'd bought more interesting biscuits to dunk.

"Hello, darlin', it's me," Ma shouted from the door as she turned her key in the lock.

Steve put the Rich Teas back in the cupboard. "I just made a cup of tea. Are you wanting one?"

"That would be lovely. Get an extra cup, though, I've got one of your wee friends with me."

The door slammed.

"Right, okay. Is that you, Ed?" Steve took two cups out the cupboard and set them down next to his.

There was no answer. Ma appeared with two shopping bags, bulging with packets and boxes and store-brand tins. Steve could see the blue-and-white striped labels through the plastic. She put them up on the counter and rubbed her forearms, then lowered her voice. "He was sitting at the bottom of the stair, says he's a pal of yours. He said his name, but I didn't quite catch it."

Steve felt the blood drain from his face and into the soles of his feet. He nodded at Ma and went through to the living room.

"All right, there, Stevie-boy?" D was sitting on Ma's armchair, clutching the end of the two arms like he was trying to crush them, his big dirty shoes up on her footstool. His hair was in its usual tangled clump, his face unshaven.

Steve leaned on the walking stick in a more exaggerated way than he needed to. He thought he could see a leaf trapped in all that hair. And what the fuck was he wearing? Looked like a sleeping bag cut up to make a jacket. "D. This is a surprise."

"You're nearly better, then, walking around." D made a sweeping gesture around the room.

"I've been sleeping on the sofa, haven't been able to get down the stair yet."

"Won't be long though, will it, Stevie-boy? A couple of days? Three?" D's hands tightened on the armchair ends as his eyes narrowed.

"The doctor says it'll be another three weeks."

"The doctor says?"

"Aye."

Steve switched off the telly, then changed his mind and turned it on again. It might drown out some of what D was going to say, for Ma's sake. He limped over to the sofa and sat down, while D watched quietly. He put the walking stick beside him and held onto it.

"Here you go, boys, you forgot your tea." Ma came through with two mugs and set them down on the table. "And I've some chocolate biscuits. I'll just get them."

"Thanks very much," said D.

"Ach away, any pal of Steve's is welcome in my house any day," she said as she disappeared again.

Steve wanted to roll his eyes, but didn't dare.

D picked up his tea and slurped at it. The mug said "Best Mum in the World" on it, with a picture of a Labrador puppy. Steve looked at his, but didn't feel much like drinking it now. Ma came back with the biscuits. She grabbed one for herself and disappeared back to the kitchen. She wouldn't want to be in the way, but she didn't know the half of it, Steve thought.

"If I find out you're putting any of this on, I'll fair murder you." D spoke through a biscuit that he'd crammed into his mouth.

"You broke my leg in two places, cracked a couple of ribs."

"Well, you fuckin' deserved it."

They sat in silence, save for D's slurping and some numpty on the telly presenting a reality show. Steve could hear Ma crashing around with the pots and pans, whistling to herself in a way that said "I'm not listening to you, I'm just minding my own." He wondered what she'd heard. He waited for D's next move, what he'd say, and guessed at how long he'd give him to get stronger. A couple of extra days maybe, at most.

Eventually, D stood. "You've got a week, then you're mine."

"Right." Well, that wasn't as bad as he thought. He was half expecting to be thrown down the stair, maybe break the other leg. Steve stood up to face him. The coffee table, the mugs of tea, the plate of biscuits and those plastic flowers, all stood between them. It all seemed strangely ordinary in the stark light of day. D seemed like a caricature of himself away from the sinister atmosphere of a dim pub or a damp, cobbled street.

D made his way to the door, walking slowly, like he was mulling something over in his mind. He turned to face Steve again, looked him up and down. He scratched his head and the leaf drifted to the floor.

Steve waited.

"Don't forget. A week today. I'll be back here to get you for the first job." He took two paces towards Steve.

"I'll do my best, D."

D stared for a moment, then in one move, he jumped forward, knocked the stick out of Steve's hand and grabbed his wrist. He pulled his hand back so far it felt like it was going to snap off. Steve grabbed the back of the sofa to stop himself from falling over and the pain seared through his arm. He yelled, couldn't help it. "Jesus, D, stop!"

D put his face right up to Steve's. "Just so you won't forget. See you soon, Stevie-boy. Make sure you're fit for anything." He went for the door, and was out of the flat just as Ma appeared from the kitchen.

"Is everything okay in here?" She came behind the sofa to where Steve was bent over.

"He's not exactly one of my pals, Ma." He rubbed his wrist, feeling for any more broken bones. It was probably just strained. He felt for his stick and sat down.

Ma came and sat down next to him and put her hand on his. "Who was he, then? What did he just do to you? I've a good mind to go after him, the wee scally."

"He was the one that did all this. I'm sorry he came 'round here. I don't want to get you involved in all my crap, I really don't. I'll need to move out in the next few days, get back to my own place as soon as I can, while I think about what I'm going to do."

"You can't live by yourself just now. Look at the state of you."

"I got myself into this mess, Ma, and now I've got to get myself out of it."

"Will I phone Ed, get him 'round? He'll know what to do."

"Not yet. Let's have a wee drink, shall we? Is it dinner time yet?" Steve swallowed, his throat so dry it felt like sandpaper. He wanted her to leave him alone, just for a few minutes, while he gathered his thoughts.

"Aye, it's nearly five-thirty, right enough. I've got us a pie and some oven chips. I'll make some peas with it. We'll have a drink. You'll be okay, son." She got up and managed to light a cigarette before she got through to the kitchen.

Steve heard the click of the old-fashioned gas lighter as Ma put the oven on. She shouted over the noise of the telly. "Your ma's dinner will make you feel better, you'll see."

Steve slumped back. He'd need more than that.

There was HP Sauce encrusted on the plates on the floor, a few pie crumbs scattered on the carpet. Steve's leg was propped up with pillows and Ma was sat on her chair in front of the telly. Where D had sat. They'd eaten off their laps while they watched *Pop Idol*, occasionally shouting abuse, mouths full, knives pointed at the judges.

"That was delicious." Steve belched and wiped his mouth with the back of his hand.

"Do you want another can of beer, son?" Ma got up with her glass. She was drinking whisky and lemonade with ice, which was her favourite drink next to tea. She'd already had three strong ones.

"Aye, why not? I feel like getting blootered, if you must know."

"Would you like a wee whisky with it?"

"Have you got any of that Red Label left? I'll take a nip of that."

Ma pointed a finger to the ceiling. "I'll see what I've got. Your uncle Hamish left a couple of half litres behind the last time he was over from Fife."

Steve switched the telly off, which was getting more tedious by the day. He was getting too much of it, with nothing else to do except sit and stare. He'd never understood the fascination for ordinary people doing everyday things, and calling them reality shows. There was nothing real about them. What was the point of it? Give him a cracking actress in a thriller movie any day. He'd get Ma to rent some films for him tomorrow.

"Here you go, son." Ma brought him a can plus a tall glass of whisky, setting both down on the floor in front of him.

"Thanks," he said. "You're too good to me."

He took a gulp of the Red Label, felt the burn down his throat. He must be getting soft; he was a bit dizzy with the beers already. He wondered if it was because he hadn't drunk anything for a while, what with being in hospital. Or maybe because it was mixing with the cocktail of painkillers he'd been taking to take the edge off things. He looked over at Ma. She was sipping her drink, staring at the blank telly. Her mouth was downturned, her eyes a bit glazed.

"What's the matter with you? Has the drink got you, Ma?" He cracked open his can and took a big gulp of it, the fizz feeling good after the burn of the nip. "Try not to worry yourself."

She paused. "What are we going to do about all of this?"

Ah, here was the question he'd been thinking about, and that he'd reached a decision about twenty minutes ago. Everything was clear now, despite the booze.

"I'm getting myself away, Ma. I can't stay here, or D will throw me over the banisters as soon as look at me. I can't go home because he'll find me and have my guts. I need to go somewhere else, where he can't seek me out. But that leaves you, and I don't want him to hurt you either. So you'll have to come with me."

"What are you talking about, son? Go where? We'll just call the police if he comes here again. He can't be making threats and hurting you just for some silly bit of money owing to him. We'll get Ed 'round, he'll know what to do."

"Ed's terrified of him. Jake is too. We all are. He could kill me."

"I'm calling the police, so I am. I'll do it now." Ma got up, wobbling slightly, spilling her drink on the carpet. She put it down carefully, her hand shaking. "That last drink must have gone to my head."

"We can't call the cops, not when this is about drugs and money."

"Drugs?"

"I'm sorry, Ma. I'm not perfect."

She sat down again, grabbed the drink and put a cigarette between her lips. As she spoke, the cigarette wobbled up and down. "He wasn't perfect either, your dad, but if he was alive, he'd know what to do. He'd kill that man with his bare hands, so he would. He'd skin him. So you're just going, then? Running away? Will you go to Glasgow? How long will you be away?"

"You'll need to come with me, so you're not left alone. We'll have to go in the next few days, before he comes back. He says I've got a week before I've to do his dirty work."

Ma lit her cigarette and took a deep drag. "I'm going nowhere; you're bloody joking. You get going if you have to. I'm staying where I am. Why should I leave my home for a hairy tyke like that? I'll just tell him you've gone away, disappeared one night. I'll put on the waterworks for him. Dirty work; what's all that about, anyway. You boys and your drugs. What drugs are they anyway?"

"It doesn't matter, Ma. Drugs is drugs and they get you into all kinds of trouble. I'll need to go further than Glasgow, I reckon. I don't know how long I'll be away."

"What will you do for money? With no job, as well. They've kept it open for you down the docks, but that's no good if you're not sticking around here, is it? Where will you stay?"

"I'll figure something out."

She sniffed, dabbed at her eyes with a screwed-up tissue. "Never have settled down, have you? Always looking for the next thing. Not even a woman can get you to sit still. And now you're off, wandering around Scotland with nowhere to live."

Steve drained the whisky, gulped at the can. He needed some fresh air, hobbled over to the sash window and opened it up, breathing deep. "I don't really know where I'm going. But I know I'll sort myself."

Ma went quiet. Steve stuck his head right out the window, smelled the hops of Edinburgh and the fresh sea air whistling through his face. He heard a sniff, then another.

"Are you crying again?"

"No." Ma crashed her glass onto the table. It was nearly empty now.

"You're greetin' there, so you are. Don't you be shedding tears for me; I'm going to get a grip of myself, I promise. D will never find me and I'll come back when I've got all the cash together. I'll get it to him with a wee bonus and that'll be the end of it."

She was crying openly now, not bothering with the tissue. "You're lost because of what I did."

Steve sat down on the table in front of her, tried to reach her hand. "You've done nothing but look after me. This is all happening because I'm an eejit with no sense. I'm not lost, Ma, I'm just a loser."

Ma blew her nose. "You were so tiny when you were born, the second one out. We couldn't afford both of you. Times were so hard. Your dad didn't have a job and I was in my early twenties, didn't know any better. He was so forceful, always telling me what to do, and I didn't question him enough."

"What are you talking about? The second one out?" An image came to him, of Ma with tears running down her face on every one of his birthdays. It had always been like that, her waving away the crying, claiming she was just being soft. But it was more than that. She was missing someone. *Jesus fuck.*

"You were twins, Stevie. It was the hardest thing I've ever had to do: choose between you. I'd always wanted a baby girl, and there she was, all pink and precious."

He shivered. "But you kept me instead. I'm glad you did, Ma, but why?" He imagined two babies on his Ma's lap, one tiny and pink, the other wrinkled and blue.

"Then there was you, my wee boy, the weakest one. How would you survive without me? Boys, men, you're all the same. You can't do anything for yourselves."

I'm a twin. I've got a sister. Steve shook his head, the alcohol combined with the fresh air taking a hit on his brain cells. "What happened to her?"

"I don't know. They took her into care. I didn't even give her a name, couldn't do it because I knew I'd think of it forever. Your dad did it. He signed the papers and handed her over while I was still in the hospital. I hated myself. And I hated him for years, I don't mind saying."

"Christ." He sat and stared, eyes blurry, blood tingling. "And this is why you greet every year on my birthday? Because it's not just my birthday, is it? Some woman somewhere just turned forty as well." *My pink, precious sister.*

Ma looked up at him, hope filling her face. "Will you find her, for me, Stevie? Bring back my baby girl. That's what you could do to get away from here, and it would be something useful."

"She could be anywhere, Ma." He thought of a shorter version of himself sitting under a palm tree in Africa, wearing a pink dress.

"There's ways these days; I saw it on the telly. We have rights now, rights we didn't have back in the day. Find her, before it's too late. Please, Stevie, you can do it." Ma grabbed her glass and drained the last of it, as if she'd reached a conclusion.

Steve went and lay down. His leg was killing him. He could do it, right enough; unearth his sister. It was a purpose. He hadn't really had one of those before. If he found her, it might complete the picture, somehow, make sense of his life. He'd do it alone, get Ed and Jake to keep an eye on Ma, just in case. It wasn't practical to take her anyway. He could sleep on the street if need be, but she couldn't. Not at her age, the way she was.

"Aye. I'll do it, Ma. I'll go looking for her."

A twin sister might be what he'd been missing in his life all along.

Ma wiped her face and smiled. "You're a good boy, Stevie. I know you'll find her, so you will."

He smiled at her and nodded. So he was the weakest one at birth. Well, that figured. He'd show Ma he was good for something, that he could be strong now. Enough of this neediness. This was his chance to prove he could be relied on, even make her happy. *That would be a fuckin' first.*

"I can't believe it, Ma. Why did you no' tell me before?"

"It's nothing to be proud of," she said. "Until now I didn't think you'd even care."

ELEVEN
Lizzy Sees a Ghost

It had been two years since Lizzy had seen Simon, when she had finally stepped away from him that wet Sunday morning. It had taken months for her to make the decision. They'd been through so much together. He was like a good but bad habit, and he'd been hard to shake. He was also the only link to her past.

"Lizzy? S'that you?"

And now here he was. The shocking mess in front of her, gibbering and dribbling, was the ex-boyfriend she'd let go in the wilds of London. She'd just finished putting everything out on the stall and Dave had gone off in his van. Keith and Natalie were busy with their stuff. She was on her own.

"Aye, it's me. I work here, Simon. You don't look so good." She felt cold at the sight of him.

He came closer and she could smell him. It was that homeless person stink again. His hair had grown out and it was wild and matted, nearly down to his shoulders. There were spots around his mouth, black circles under his eyes.

"I don't feel so good," he muttered.

"I've got to work, but I'll get a lunch break. If you go away and come back later, we could get some chips. You can tell me what's going on. Okay?"

He nodded, but didn't move.

She'd have to be hard with him. "I can't talk right now, Simon. You've got to go. Come back for twelve."

"When's twelve?"

"About four hours' time."

"Fuck."

Lizzy watched as he stumbled off towards Wardour Street, almost falling over when he dropped off the curb and into the road. He wasn't carrying a bag, she noticed, so he couldn't have much in the way of belongings. By the looks of things he was still sleeping rough, so probably no stash anywhere. His coat was too big for him, pockets bulging, and she imagined how emaciated his body was underneath it all. She swore under her breath. Just when things were getting better, with Natalie back, this bloody well happened. It was going to be difficult not to help him, but she would not be sucked back into his world.

It was hard to believe how close they had once been. She'd let him; she'd done it with him. She only had the nerve when they were high or drunk, but still. She'd turned fourteen, and had felt ten years older. The first time they did it behind a cardboard box in an alley. Afterwards she'd felt disgusting. After that, Simon took any chance he could, but she'd never felt good about it, like it was something they shouldn't be doing, and in all the wrong places. But there was a soft spot in her for Simon. It was a curse.

She must have been staring into space, because there was a customer standing there and she hadn't noticed. He was clearing his throat.

"Sorry, I was miles away," she said. "What can I get for you?"

While she was picking out his apples and bananas, she glanced over at Nat. Her friend was smiling at her uncle Keith and holding out a large bag for him to put veggies in. Looked like she was having a good day today. Some days she didn't turn up at all, sometimes because she couldn't face getting out of bed, and other times because Karen or Darren couldn't come with her to drop her off and pick her up at the end, which was a condition of her working there. Neither of them was happy about her being on the stall at all after what had happened, but Nat insisted, wanting to do anything her parents were against. Still, she skived off quite a bit. Keith had told Dave that if she wasn't his niece, he'd have done away with her for someone more reliable by now, but Lizzy knew he didn't really mean it.

The police had found nothing, no evidence of sexual activity, or so they called it. Lizzy had been relieved; although why Nat had been given cash was still a mystery to them all. She had no internal damage, just some light marks on her skin here and there. And she still couldn't remember a thing.

Nat was coming over now. Lizzy finished up and gave the man his change.

"Millionth customer of the day, eh, Lizzy?" Natalie leaned on the post next to the stall and sighed.

"Yep, and he didn't even try and squeeze the mangos. Did you see the other guy that was just here?"

"The homeless guy with the long hair?"

"Yeah, him. You'll never guess who that was."

"Who?" Natalie stood straight, hands on her hips. "Not one of Spinner's lot?"

"No, worse, sort of. The boy I left Scotland with, Simon, the one who got too into the drugs? It was him. He looked really bad."

"You're joking. I thought he was an old man from behind, all skinny and bent over."

"No, he's only seventeen. I said he could come back at lunch, so we could talk. I don't know why I said that. I should have told him where to go, but he looked so desperate."

"Do you want me to come with you?" Natalie looked worried.

"Nah, it's okay, I can deal with Simon."

Keith was motioning for Nat to return to the stall. She shrugged and waved her fingers at Lizzy. "See ya later, then. Good luck and be careful."

She'd need a bit of luck. The best thing would be if Simon never showed up, that he got lost in drugs again and forgot he ever saw her. That look on his face when he did see her though, it was so full of love and history. She knew he'd be back.

Simon was hunched over, cradling his skinny legs. They were sitting on the steps at the edge of Trafalgar Square, one of their old favourite places, watching the pigeons peck seeds from the palms of tourists and then adding to the piles of droppings all around them. The sun had been out all morning and Lizzy had stripped down to her T-shirt. It was pretty warm and so it was worrying that Simon was shivering. He'd been quiet since he'd come back to the stall at lunchtime, head down, watching his feet all the way to where Lizzy had decided they would sit. Dave hadn't been happy about her going off with him, but she convinced him she'd be okay. She was used to all this. She'd got Maccy D's on the way, two-for-one Quarter Pounders, just like the old days.

At first she tried to keep things light, talk about all kinds of stuff, while they ate. She pointed at the people feeding the pigeons. "I don't know why you'd want to stand in the middle of all that shit, with those things flapping around you. Like rats with wings."

Simon looked up briefly. "You used to say shite, not shit."

"Well, it's the same thing." So she had his attention now. He was listening, seemed more present than earlier that morning. She wondered if he'd had a hit. "Where are you staying now, Simon? Rough?"

"Sometimes rough. Well, most of the time. You sound a bit London now, you know?"

A stray pigeon waddled towards them, pecking near to Simon's burger wrapper in front of his feet. He kicked at it and it flapped away. One of its legs was grossly deformed, like it had been bitten in half.

Lizzy shrugged. "I am a bit London. It's been three years now. What do you do for cash? Not still running, are you?" She didn't dare look him in the eye.

"A bit."

"Jesus, Simon, is it going to end? You'll die on the street. Look at you." Lizzy bent to pull up one of the legs of his jeans, revealing a ghost-white stalk of a leg. It was filthy.

He groaned. "I want to stop, but I go around in a big circle. I need the money, I do the drop, I spend some of it on a hit because I'm so cold I can't stand it. Sometimes just speed, sometimes brown mixed with crack or whatever. I don't even know what it is half the time. There's no sleep on the street, not real sleep, because there's too much bad shite going on around, you know? The next day I've no money again. I don't know how to stop. When I saw you working the market, I was on my way to meet a guy to pick up. I've picked up, dropped, and got the money and had one hit, just speed. The rest of the cash is in my pocket; I haven't spent it yet. But by about dark o'clock tonight I'll want to spend it on a hit so bad, it'll be impossible not to." He pulled at his hair, and examined his fingernails, black and greasy.

"I thought you'd had a snifter since this morning. You were dribbling down your chin earlier; it was disgusting. Now you're eating and talking for Scotland. You could spend the rest on a place to sleep for the night instead. Get a hot shower."

"Am I stinking? I can't smell myself, but I bet I am."

Lizzy slurped at her drink, getting the last of it as the ice melted around the straw. "You do, Simon. You stink really bad."

He leaned back on his elbows and threw the last piece of his burger bun at the birds, and they pounced on it, clucking and pecking each other out of the way. "Thanks for the Maccy D's. Have you got any fags?"

"No, I can't afford to smoke no more." Lizzy looked at her own fingers, with none of the yellow stains on them like she had when she first moved down to London.

"Me neither, but I scab them off folk when I can, you know? Not that I was scabbing off you or nothing. You know what I mean, eh, Lizzy."

"Aye, I think so."

"Remember we used to nick voddy and fags from the offy?"

"We were good at that." She smiled at him for the first time. They did get up to some funny stuff in Dalbegie. All that seemed like a long time ago. She paused, not sure whether to ask. "What did you do with the rest of your half? Looks like it's all gone now."

When they left Scotland, they'd made off with a hefty package. They were supposed to drop it off for Roy, Simon's mum's skanky boyfriend. He'd threatened them at the time with more beatings if they missed his contact at Edinburgh Waverley, and they had missed the drop because the train was so badly delayed. Scared of going back to face Roy, they'd opened the package and discovered it was full of cash, enough to set them up somewhere else. They set off on the London sleeper train, full of dreams, but in the end they'd only traded that dark world for another one. She'd been terrified of seeing Roy again ever since they'd left.

"All gone. What about yours?" Simon was asking quietly, a glint of hope in his face.

"There's not much left. I've put the last of it in the bank for emergencies, like when I've nowhere to stay or nothing to eat. I used to keep it stashed in my pockets, but I was always worried I'd be mugged. But I'm not doing too bad on the market and I've got a place to stay, a room of my own, in a building I was taken to by the shelter folk. It's nothing special, but it's mine, for now anyway. And it got me a fixed address."

Simon nodded. She knew he wouldn't ask her for money, or even a place to stay. He wouldn't take from her. It'd be humiliating for him.

He sat up. "I've something to tell you. So I met this guy I used to know at school—Darryl. I was queuing up one time at the night shelter and he was a couple of folk in front of me. He turned 'round and I recognized him; he looked the same. Took him a couple of minutes to know it was me, though."

"I think I remember him. Did he have a gold earring, walk funny?"

"Aye, that's him. He told me a couple of things about folk back home."

"Who?" Lizzy felt nauseated. What if he knew any of her family? Or worse, Simon's family? Or Roy. What were they all thinking, saying, about their disappearance? She'd never been in contact with her auntie Maureen or anyone else, not even her best friend Molly. Too scared. She put her drink inside the brown paper bag along with the scraps left from lunch, a few chips and some half-squeezed ketchup sachets. Suddenly the taste of the burger was sour in her mouth. Pickles mixed with onions gave a gross aftertaste.

Simon looked into her eyes as she searched his for information. "None of your lot, don't worry. Have you never tried to get in touch?"

She shook her head, the relief making her eyes smart. "Never."

"Me neither. So this Darryl, he used to live down the road from me. I'd walk with him sometimes on the way to school."

"So what did he say then?"

"He asked me about you, and about Roy. Said the last he'd heard, all three of us had disappeared together, down to Edinburgh."

Lizzy went cold, rubbed at her arms. "Why would they think that? We left Roy behind, off his melt, after he'd kicked you half to death back in Dalbegie."

"Because that night he went out and never came back again. When we didn't either, everyone just assumed we were all in it together. Some guy that worked at the station remembered you from the ticket queue."

"Jesus. So what did happen to Roy, then?"

"That's what I don't know."

Simon didn't go far after he walked back to the stall with Lizzy. He sat, slumped on the side of the road, only a few yards away. As Lizzy worked the afternoon shift, she kept watch as he deteriorated to a trembling mess once more. She knew where it was all going, had seen it too many times before. He was scratching at his arms and rocking slightly. Once a shopkeeper came out onto the pavement to ask him to move. He must have been affecting trade. The street sweeper worked around him, but acted like Simon wasn't even there. The working folk sidestepped, rushed past him, occasionally throwing some loose change at his feet.

Nat kept looking, and as soon as it was time for a break, she came over. She was wearing a black T-shirt with a white peace symbol on it that Lizzy had bought for her in the flea market to celebrate her coming back. It was Nat's favourite now, and Lizzy hadn't seen her friend in the Hello Kitty one in the past few weeks. She'd grown out of it, a different, darker soul since her disappearance.

"Why's he still here? Not waiting for you to finish, is he?"

Lizzy couldn't help but feel happy that her friend was looking out for her, even though she didn't need her to. She could handle Simon and had always been able to look after herself. "I think he might be. I don't think he knows how to get himself clean again. I'm the only person he can rely on in this place."

"You left him, though. Don't he get the message?" Natalie tutted.

"I did, but he saw me here, didn't he? Something made him find me, so it was meant to be."

"He smells like a rat's arse."

"I know." Lizzy laughed. "Don't you worry, I'm just going to send him on his way."

"Lizzy?"

"Yep?"

"I got a weird flashback last night. I woke up with it, and it was well freaky."

Lizzy handed a customer some change and smoothed down her apron. "What's that about? Is your memory coming back?"

"I think so. I don't know. It seemed real." Nat swallowed. "You coming back with us for tea? Mum's picking me up, as usual, although I don't know why they insist on coming here. For god's sake, I'm fine. Anyway, she said she's doing pizza and popcorn and she got a film to watch. I'm to ask you. Sorry if that sounds lame."

"Yeah, brilliant. It's not lame at all. You're lucky, you know."

"For what?" Nat screwed up her face.

"For having a mum and a dad. For them caring about you."

Nat scratched her head. "I suppose."

"Look, I'll only be a few minutes with him over there. Wait for me at the end, okay? Hey, Spinner wasn't in the dream last night, was he?"

"Nah, he wasn't. Apparently he's been questioned twice now, and they've got nothing on him. He's not been around much, anyway. I'll see you later then." Natalie went back to Keith's stall, looking back every so often, as if making sure Lizzy wasn't going to disappear.

At four o'clock Dave came back with the van and Lizzy helped him pack up. By then, Simon was noisily retching into the gutter, spitting and moaning. Dave saw him and pulled a face. "How long has that bloke been there? Someone needs to move him. It's not the one you went off with at lunch is it? Christ, it is."

"It is him. Sorry, Dave."

"That's disgusting. It'll put people off coming to the market. I might go and move him myself."

"Don't." Lizzy held up two apples that had bruises on them. "Can I have these, Dave?"

"Yeah, course you can, darlin'."

She put them in the big side pockets in her combat trousers, felt them heavy on each leg. "I know him pretty well. He's the guy I came to London with, the one I tried to get rid of. I'll sort him when we're finished here."

Dave rubbed his hands together. "You're joking. Him? Let me get rid of him for you. It'd be a pleasure."

"That's what Nat said. Yeah, it's him, after a lot of drugs and not a lot else. I can handle him, Dave. He won't be back, I promise."

"Well, if he's here tomorrow, I'll be having a word." Dave put his hands on his hips and watched Simon spit on the pavement, narrowly missing a woman's shoe. He spoke under his breath. "I'll let you off for now, but watch yourself, sunshine."

Lizzy helped put everything in the van, and Dave gave her some notes for the day's work. He was good with that, paying at the end of every shift, the cash arrangement suiting both of them. She nodded thanks and pocketed the money, signaling to Nat that she'd be five minutes.

Simon had put his head on his knees, quiet now, trembling for his next hit. She sat down next to him on the dry side of the pavement.

"Simon?" She put her hand on his back. His jacket felt stiff and waxy with grime.

He moaned and heaved a little.

"I'm going to give you my wages for today. But you can't come back. You get somewhere to sleep the night, get a shower. Sort yourself out. I can't do that for you."

"I know." He said it softly, resigned. "Lizzy. I'm sorry for what happened. What I did."

She took the notes out of her pocket, rolled up and ready to go, and put them in his hand. His skin was cold and damp. She closed his fingers around it and felt them stiffen.

"It's forgotten, Simon. Look at me."

He lifted his head, whining with the pain, the heaviness of it. His eyes were watering, unfocussed, but managed to meet hers.

"Get yourself out of this mess. Promise me."

His mouth moved and he made a noise, but he couldn't speak. He wrenched his eyes away and pushed his hands on his thighs to stand up. Lizzy watched as he staggered away, clutching the money, and disappeared around the corner. She hoped her words had registered with him, that he just might not go for the next hit. But something told her he was on his way.

Simon had been a painful reminder of her past, of what she had escaped 'from and what was lurking for her out there. If Roy had disappeared from Dalbegie at the same time as them, where was he now? That was three years ago, which seemed like plenty of time to work out they weren't in Edinburgh, or even Glasgow. Was he here, in London, lurking in corners with the likes of Spinner? She often had that panicky feeling that someone was watching her, and it had been intense today. She was pleased that Nat had asked her back to her place. Her family and home had been a sanctuary recently. She kidded herself that she was going back there for Nat, to help her though her difficult recovery time, but it was for herself as well. She loved to be in the warmth of someone's kitchen, eat a hot meal from a plate with a flowery pattern around the rim. They would all sit together, her and Nat, and Nat's mum and dad, Karen and Darren. They'd have plates on their laps, watching telly and laughing and ribbing each other. That was why people lived, wasn't it? To be happy.

Poor Simon didn't have any of that. He'd never had a real family, even when he lived with his mum. She was a drunk, a waste of space. You only had to look at her boyfriends to know she was a skank. Still, he wasn't her problem now. She turned to see Natalie anxiously waiting, biting her nails. Her proper friend. She needed to move on and not look back.

TWELVE

Oliver Steps In

Good for you, Lizzy. That dreadful Simon from Dalbegie, whose family I despised, arrived back on the scene and made you waver. But in the end you sent him on his way. I knew he was somewhere in central London, begging and scraping, but still. How dare he find you. I watched as you passed the odious boy some money, probably all of the cash you'd earned that day, and turned away. An act of kindness, yet not entirely selfless, as you must have known it was the one thing that would get rid of him. For the time being, anyway.

I was not going to sit back and have him undo all that you'd achieved for yourself, to pull you back down with him again. You're hardly at the top of the social ladder, but you've got a home of sorts, and you earn your money through honest work. I decided I would have to intervene. Otherwise he would be back, time and time again, sniffing around and taking advantage of you.

Yes, Lizzy; I followed him.

It was hardly difficult to be furtive, because he moved so very slowly, with hardly any senses about him. He staggered through Soho, stopping in doorways, holding onto railings, and even pitching into lampposts as though their sole purpose was to guide him. I had to pretend to look in shop windows as I went, while I waited for a chance to take him aside. It was soon rush hour, and the streets were growing crowded with working people rushing in all directions to get home. He was alone, yet never without an audience.

But I am a patient man now. My days of rushing into things are gone. I waited in the shadows until my opportunity came, much quicker than I expected. Simon eventually blundered down to Leicester Square underground station, becoming one of the crowd. It's a fact that when there are more people, there are fewer eyes on the target.

He got through the barriers with a dirty ticket he found discarded on the floor, disturbing the flow by bending to grab it amidst the surging crowd. When he stood to study it, wobbling slightly, a few people tutted in that impatient commuter way, as though their life was dependent upon reaching the platform within the next minute. God forbid they have to wait sixty seconds more than necessary to get on a train. I purchased my own ticket during the holdup, plenty of time, then followed him down the escalator to the northbound platform. He began asking people for spare change, mumbling almost incomprehensibly. It seemed he had reached a desperate stage in the drug cycle, even though he had your wages in his pocket. Perhaps he had even forgotten the roll of notes was there, although that seems unlikely. Or perhaps he'd decided to go clean. Unlikelier still. He held out his hand, eyes watering, and people either ignored him or stepped away from his repulsive presence. No one gave him any money.

The train was due to arrive. Simon staggered to the far end, nearing the edge of the platform, and I made my way towards him. He was talking to himself, some angry words I couldn't make out from where I was standing with my back to the wall. The throng moved in sections, regulars taking their places where the doors would fall open when the train stopped, everyone focussed on their own space, judging where to be. I knew exactly where I had to be. I edged forwards until I was within reach of Simon. I could smell his skin, dirty and pungent. He was sweating now, muttering, "I need some change to get home, I need to get home," to no one in particular. Well, there was no home for that boy. I felt the wind from the tunnel on my face and the crowd tightened.

The train was coming.

It was all about the timing. I turned my body, and pushed, fast. It was more of a nudge, really; it didn't take much force to send Simon on his way. He was down in a second, the train almost upon him when he hit the tracks. A few people gasped when they saw his flailing body, but most didn't see him go, and no one witnessed my own small movement. I read about it in the *Standard* tonight. Apparently the tube driver was aware of a flash of colour, but there was nothing he could do to avoid the accident.

Most were irritated at the delay it caused them.

It was satisfying to be able to walk away without having to deal with the aftermath: a body and its leavings to dispose of. Cleaning up can be exciting in its own way, but it's mostly a chore. This was an easy, clean procedure and now I have one less irritation. When the excitement of the "accident" was over, and I had stepped back on the escalator out of the abyss, I wondered how many people died underground each year. Occasionally, one of the free newspapers would report a jumper, or a collapse, but surely out of the millions of people who frequented these tunnels every year, there must be more than a handful of casualties. Hidden statistics mask the brutality of the world. Simon is one of many, an insignificant number, and you shouldn't feel bad that he has joined a growing list. That is, if you ever find out.

Simon had no hope of survival in London, what with his background. He's better off dead. His deadbeat mother was a drunk, becoming a whore to drugs when she met that Roy, and she looked away when he began to take advantage of her own son, and of you as well, which I witnessed frequently in the days when I was following your progress in Dalbegie. I confess I rapidly became rather fond of watching your life unravel in the wake of your mother's death. Her slow, fascinating departure from life, by my hands, is something you may never know. It came as a surprise to me that I would feel a kind of protectiveness towards you, as if you had become my responsibility.

When I took Roy three years ago, at the same time you and Simon were on your way to London, I simply removed one of the world's monsters. No doubt Simon's mother replaced him with another, similar creature in no time. What chance did her son have alone in the world? He'd never had the guidance of a parent, so how could he guide himself? You tried to help him, but even you couldn't change what was inherent in his character: self-destruction. And so you've lost a threat in your life, someone who was once a friend but had become the enemy. I did it all for you, Lizzy.

Am I a friend or an enemy? You could never imagine how deeply

I care about your well being, dissonant with my deep desire to make you my victim. You are beautifully ignorant that you are in my hands. By all means, maintain your low profile, and continue looking over your shoulder. It's endearing that you're keeping an eye out for the wrong person. Because there is only one real threat left, and that is me.

THIRTEEN

The Other Woman

The email had been short and to the point. It was from the other woman in The Circle, and she wanted to meet. Helen had read it several times, as if a hidden message might appear, giving an underlying reason. But there was none. Helen had been curious about her since The Circle began. Perhaps this woman had a passing interest in her too. Her latest email address began "LuLoo@" and Helen noted that all her addresses to date had started with "L." Was she a Lucy, a Leila, perhaps something paradoxically feminine like a Lily?

Last time at The Audacious, when Helen had spoken up for the first time and ordered the spin, Lucy or Lily gave her an admiring look. There were few women in the world who relished evil with as much enthusiasm as men. When you meet a like-minded woman, Helen thought, it might be interesting just to compare notes. They could meet in Soho, which was likely to be common ground, given they both travelled there for every viewing. The next one hadn't been announced yet, and Helen hadn't made the journey for over two weeks.

She sent a short reply. *What about Thursday 1 p.m. Soho?*

She stared at her inbox for a few moments. Nothing came back. It had been many years since she'd had any form of friendship. Helen removed her slippers and peeled off her leggings, which were covered with milk spills, Marmite stains, and drips from the teapot. They were filthy, she realized now. She put them in the laundry bag and took a long shower. It was time to get the place in shape once more, get presentable, now that she had something to look forward to.

When she finished in the bathroom, Helen checked her email, a small towel still twisted on her head, strands of escaped hair wet on her chest. There was no reply yet. She got dressed and began to pick up dirty clothes, plates, and empty tins from the floor as she moved around the room. She used her left hand more than her right, as for some reason that wrist was aching. Rubbing it didn't seem to make a difference. She'd take an aspirin and it would probably go away. Her leg felt better, though.

She looked around the small space. Housing benefit didn't offer much for a single woman with no dependents, and yet she didn't care about the state or the size of her home. She had never bothered about material things, only the psychological. How people could be mentally affected and scarred had fascinated her from a young age. There was a time, in her awkward teenage years, when school bullying reached new heights. She'd been picked on over the years, many times over, but because she showed no reaction, the bullies had tired of her. They turned to one of her classmates, taunted her daily, and Helen found that she enjoyed observing those incidences from afar. The sequence of events, the causes and effects, were compelling to her even then.

"You're a freak, a monster from Planet Zorb, so you are. Where'd you come from?" Cassie pointed at the girl with the birthmark.

"Did the gypsies leave you on the doorstep? I would have done." Cassie's friend, Sass, joined in.

The girls were in the classroom, waiting for the teacher. Helen sat at the back of the room, as usual, watching with the others.

The girl with the birthmark was standing with her back against the blackboard, her head rubbing out some calculus notes from the previous class. She fidgeted with the hem of her dress and looked with longing at the classroom door. Helen studied the mark on her face. From a distance it looked very dark, a deep aubergine purple covering one side of her cheek, nose, and chin. The girl would have to deal with stares and snide comments for the rest of her life.

Cassie poked the girl in the chest. "Look at me. I'm talking to you, you wee shite."

"You deaf as well as pig ugly?" Sass brought her fist up close to the girl's scared face.

One of the other students got up, as if about to step in, but she was beaten to it by the teacher, who burst into the room with her arms full of books. Cassie and her sidekick pulled faces and sat down at their desks. The girl with the birthmark was frozen at the blackboard, shaking. She looked guilty, as if it was she who had done something wrong.

"What is going on here?" The teacher dropped the books onto her desk with a bang. Dust flew up and Helen could nearly smell the mustiness of them. Everyone fell silent, waiting to see what would happen next.

"Why are you standing up here?" the teacher asked the girl, her voice gentle now.

The girl shrugged as her eyes filled with tears.

The teacher turned to Cassie and Sass. "Can you two enlighten me? You were up here a second ago."

"Don't know, Miss," Cassie said, chewing imaginary gum.

"Beats me, Miss," Sass smirked.

The teacher stared at them before turning back to the front of the classroom. "You may sit down," she said to the girl. "Were these two bothering you?"

The girl barely nodded, but that was all that was needed. Teachers in Fife didn't hold back on punishments. Cassie and Sass were getting it, thought Helen. The girl was as good as dead.

After school, Helen walked a different route than usual so she could watch the next act of the afternoon's incident. Something would happen; it was inevitable. Among the crowd of skipping, laughing girls, she was focussed on one. The girl with the birthmark was walking slowly, head bent, her canvas satchel dragging on the ground. She left the school and turned onto the side street that led to the main road. Helen kept a distance behind the sorry figure. There were bushes lining the street and she wondered which one was hiding Cassie and Sass. The girl quickened as if it would make a difference.

Finally, Cassie jumped out from behind a parked car, with Sass close behind.

The girl stopped and tightened her grip on the satchel. Helen paused and tucked herself behind a lamp post. Cassie and Sass grabbed her and dragged her towards the playing fields. She didn't struggle, as far as Helen could see. Perhaps she was pulling back, but she was so weak the resistance wasn't visible. Helen followed, far enough behind that they wouldn't notice, but near enough that she could see.

They got to the fields and pushed the girl to the ground. They kicked her and pulled her hair.

Helen discovered that she liked to watch the pain. She felt invigorated, as if she'd taken a drug that had hit her bloodstream and sent pulses of happiness through her body. The drug was highly addictive.

Helen was on the bus once more, on her way to meet "LuLoo@". They'd agreed to meet in a bar on Old Compton Street at one o'clock. She was unfamiliar with the place, but knew roughly where it was, on the same side as The Stock Pot, a restaurant she sometimes went to for a cheap, filling lunch. She got off at Leicester Square and walked. It was bright, and the air had that smell of warmth and light perfume. With summer on its way, everyone was dressed for going out. Even the working-lunch types were sprayed, brushed and made over for the afternoon. Two girls walked in front of her, arm in arm, wearing matching Burberry bandanas and leather handbags. They were on their way somewhere, thought Helen, to meet men probably. It was all beyond her. She hadn't felt inclined to be close to a man for as long as she could remember.

The Stock Pot was busy, a queue already forming outside. Helen walked past it, looking up at the signs for the right bar. It was four minutes past, which was the perfect time to arrive. Not too early and not late.

There were a few empty seats outside, and music playing inside, but not too loud. She stood by the door for a moment, scanning the tables. A woman at the bar waved. It was her.

"Afternoon," the woman said and offered her hand.

Helen took her hand briefly and sat down on the stool next to her. She hung her bag on the hook underneath the bar and loosened her scarf. "What are you drinking?"

"I'm having a blueberry vodka and soda. What'll you have?"

She frowned. "Same, I think."

The woman behind the bar came over and smiled, adjusting a bra strap.

"She'll have one of these, when you get a minute, please Cindy." The woman held up her drink. She turned to Helen. "I'm Lou."

"Helen." She didn't think it necessary to change her name. What was the point? They were both a part of the same underground corruption and neither would want to be found out. "This your regular, then?"

"Yeah, sort of. I come here once a fortnight or so. Don't really go out that much."

"Me neither." Helen didn't like to admit that she didn't go out at all. She felt self-conscious about what she was wearing. She'd thought the grey trousers and sneakers would make her blend in, but they served to make her feel very ordinary compared with the other women in the bar. Lou's dress sense seemed strange and contradictory to Helen when in The Circle, but here it fit. Combat trousers mixed with a floral top; cropped hair contrasted with pink lipstick. It made sense now, her style. Helen had never been good at dressing herself.

"So what do you do, Helen?"

There was a pause as the bartender put the blue drink in front of her. Helen nodded thanks and took out her purse.

"No, this one's on me." Lou pushed a ten-pound note across the bar and smiled.

"Thanks." Helen took a gulp of the drink. What was she doing here? She shouldn't be here. Two women sat near them at the bar. They were young, with tattoos and fresh faces.

"So." Lou swiveled around to face her. "What do you do when you're not watching people get hurt?"

Lou's knee was touching hers and she didn't like it. She shifted slightly to one side. "I'm not working at the moment. I used to be a nurse, but it didn't work out."

"A nurse? That's a good one." Lou chuckled, scanning the room as if she wanted to let someone in on the joke.

"What about you?" Helen didn't want to talk about nursing, or even mention the Cat Rescue. Best deflect with questions, she thought.

"I work for the post office."

"Oh."

"I'm a postman. They have to say postal worker to not be sexist, but I'm essentially a postman. Got the uniform and everything. And the bike."

"Early mornings, then."

"You bet, I'm up at dawn but then I'm finished by lunchtime and the rest of the day is my own. If you're not working, we could hang out in the afternoons sometimes if you like."

"Yes. We could." Helen couldn't think of what to say next.

Lou picked up her drink and took a long swig. She held two fingers up and caught the bartender's eye. The bartender nodded and grabbed two glasses from behind her. Helen drained hers, for courage, and to seem normal. She sensed the conversation was awkward, but wasn't sure how to put it right.

Two more drinks came and Helen passed over a twenty. "These are good drinks," she said, and took a sip.

Lou looked relieved and held up her glass. They chinked them together.

"Can I ask you something?" Lou lowered her voice and leaned towards her a little.

"Okay." Helen didn't think there was any chance anyone could overhear them, what with the music and the endless chatter of women. Were there any men in the bar? Helen couldn't see one.

"When you watch at The Audacious. Do you get turned on?"

Helen took off her scarf and put it on the hook with her bag. It was too hot in there. "No. I feel very happy, like I've taken an amazing pill. But not turned on. I suppose you do, then."

Lou was looking into Helen's eyes intently, the blue of them flashing. "Yes, I do. Very much."

"Right." Helen sipped at the drink, the ice banging into her teeth. "Why is that, do you think?"

"I don't know, Helen. I like the power, being in control. I want the person in the middle of The Circle to beg for mercy, and for us to give it to them in the end. After they've been on the journey with us. I feel turned on right now, just thinking about it."

Helen looked at her with pity. For her, neither the viewings online nor the recent ones in the flesh had been sexual. She had sensations, feelings of elation, but that was different. If everything was about sex, then this woman, Lou, missed out on all the more subtle, more ethereal emotions. They talked for a while more, a short, broken conversation, as they downed their second drinks. Helen felt the alcohol go to her head. She hadn't seen any change from the twenty, so they must make them strong and worth the money, she thought. Lou's eyes were slightly glazed.

"Let's go." Lou put her hand on Helen's thigh.

Helen shifted away again. "You hungry?"

"Something like that." She raised her eyebrows. "I don't live far from here. We could go back to my place."

The way Lou was looking at her gave Helen a familiar feeling, one that she'd experienced before. She grabbed her scarf and bag, and stood up. "I'm going to the loo. Then I'll just get off."

Lou replied, but Helen didn't wait to listen. When she reached the Ladies, she glanced back at the bar. Lou was watching her, those laser eyes meeting hers, boring through her. She looked away, opened the door. Inside, she chose the furthest stall. There was some noise coming from one of the others, two-people noise, feminine sighing and low voices.

When she came back to the bar, Lou was gone, their stools already taken up by two girls, leaning in towards each other and laughing easily. One of them was holding up a lighter for the other. What was it like to be that comfortable with another person, to touch and talk and not care about anything? She would never find out.

Helen walked back out into the afternoon. Relief washed through her as she made her way to The Stock Pot, where she should have gone in the first place. She could eat alone before heading home, the way it should be. There was something to be said for one's own company. The Circle, The Audacious, they were groups of anonymity. It had been a bad idea to think she could collaborate on a more personal level with one of the members, except for Oliver of course, who she'd partnered with once before. Other people, even family, were unpredictable. Life was simple the way she had it.

There was still a queue at The Stock Pot and she was so hungry her stomach hurt. Dina's wasn't far and she'd get food that much quicker. Helen walked along the crowded streets as fast as her short legs could manage, until she could nearly smell the bacon fat, just the way she liked it.

But as she turned the corner, she caught the shape of a figure in a doorway, stepping forward to look into the street. It was a tall man, wearing a trilby hat. Was that Oliver? She paused and waited until he turned his head a little. Yes, it was definitely him. What was he doing? Forgetting about the bacon, Helen slid across to the brick siding of the next building. He was watching someone in the market, she was sure of it. He was leaning forward again, staring in the direction of a stall at the far end, the one with the girl in black, working alone. She was busy serving customers, chatting and passing over bags of produce. Then Oliver turned, opened the door behind him and disappeared into the building. Helen looked up. It looked like there were flats or bedsits above the shops, all with dirty windows and broken blinds. He couldn't live there, surely; he was too much of a clean freak. She waited a few moments, then passed Dina's and made her way through the market. As she got to the far end, she saw that the girl in black couldn't be much older than sixteen, similar to the one they'd had at The Audacious recently. Perhaps this one would be next on the list.

The girl looked up; she must have felt Helen staring. Their eyes met. She was the one who flicked the finger at the pimp in Dina's that day. Tall and blonde. Compelling. Should she buy some fruit? Talk to her? Helen wasn't sure what to do. In the end, she simply turned and walked back to Dina's, her heart filled with excitement. Oliver had been making some good choices of late. That girl might be another one. There was something about her, a little spark of wisdom beyond her years that was appealing. A young, defiant personality was interesting in The Circle, their reactions unpredictable, the results all the more vibrant.

FOURTEEN

Steve's Revelation

He could get about with just the one stick, had practiced getting down the stair with Ma beside him. He held onto the banister and she clung to his shirtsleeve. Steve's ribs still hurt, but he could move without his lungs feeling like they were being punctured now, and he'd got used to the plaster on his leg. It would come off soon anyway; he could get it removed when he was in Glasgow, no problem.

Ma was making mince and tatties for his tea, which had been his favourite since he was a bairn. It had to be with peas on the side, and HP Sauce and ketchup squirted all over it. She had been fussing around him all day, packing wee things in his rucksack, making it heavier by the minute. Over all the simmering and clarting about in the kitchen, she carried on shouting out orders.

"Don't forget to send me some postcards from wherever you end up."

"I'm no' going to Tenerife, Ma." He smiled to himself, switching the telly over to the national news.

"Aye, I know that, you besom. Send them from anywhere. I don't care if they've got the Queen of England on them, as long as I know you're all right."

"I'll put 'wish you were here' on them. I'll see if I can find some of the ones with the cheeky nurses on."

"You will, as well, knowing you. This is ready, will I dish it up?"

He could hear Ma tutting away in there, even though she'd have found his comment about the dirty postcards quite funny. Steve listened to the rest of the news story before he got up to get his tea. A young homeless guy had thrown himself on the tracks at Leicester Square tube and brought the Northern Line to a standstill. Poor bastard; things must have got rough to have done that, to have gone down the hard way. *Ripped to shreds by a fuckin' train.* He'd never let that happen to himself. As soon as he found his sister, made some money, he'd be back to Edinburgh to live the clean life and look after his ma.

"Give us that delicious tea, then, will you." He went through and grabbed the HP bottle.

"Don't put too much of that stuff on. You won't be able to taste it," Ma grumbled.

They sat on chairs with their trays on their laps, as Steve was sick of the sight of the sofa. Ma had taken the rollers out of her hair that afternoon and had been fussing with a brush for what seemed like hours. It was like she was dressing up to see him off, give him a lasting memory of how she looked when she wasn't all trussed up with plastic space-alien pins in her head.

They ate without talking, Steve occasionally making a moaning sound that meant he was enjoying the meal, Ma chewing noisily and sucking on her false teeth. The news was still on low in the background. When they'd scraped their plates and put them on the floor in front of them, it was time to discuss what was about to happen.

Steve picked his teeth. "You look through the spyhole before you answer the door, no matter what day it is or what time."

"Yes, I will. And I'm to call Jake right away if it's that D."

"Right. Everyone's been briefed. He'll come over with Ed right away. They'll not let D hurt you. Although there's a risk he'll do a

110

wobbler and have a go at them when he finds out I've done a runner. They're good pals, so they are, to step in."

"Well, it's not their fault, is it? Or mine. D can see that."

"No, but D is mental."

"True enough." Ma considered this. "Should I go to my sister's place in North Berwick for a wee holiday?"

Steve looked at her face, flushed and anxious and trying not to show it. Look at her. She was his ma and he loved her to pieces. What was he thinking? Call Jake, call Ed, they'd be useless against D. What good was all of that going to do? He'd have the door smashed down before she'd even finished dialing the number. He could threaten her, do anything. He was unpredictable. Jesus. *What was he thinking?*

"Aye, that would be a good idea, I think, Ma. Can you get down there the day after tomorrow, get away before D is supposed to be coming back?"

"I would think so. I've not very much to pack up, have I?"

He leaned forward, head hung low. "I'm so sorry to put you through all of this. I'll make it up to you a hundred times over, I promise."

"Just find my baby girl, Stevie." Ma clenched her hands together and shut her eyes like she was praying, even though she'd never said a word to the boss up there in her life.

Steve knew he had to go, that he had to find his sister. It could be his chance to make everything right after a lifetime of wrong.

"I'm getting off right now. You take care." He stood up. "Get to your sister's. Pack tonight, right? You promise?"

"I will do. I promise, son."

He got up and kissed her cheek. It was wet.

The train pulled out of Edinburgh Waverley and Steve felt inside his jacket pocket. Jake's younger sister had a way with the Internet and she'd been looking up all sorts of things for him the last few days. Eventually she'd found out about his twin on the ScotlandsPeople website. She'd given Steve a piece of paper with the details of the place in Glasgow that had put her into care all those years ago. Now the search had begun.

He studied the notes. Helen. So that was her name. Stephen and Helen, born in Edinburgh in 1962. He'd not told Ma, didn't want to get her hopes up by giving her a name. She'd be thinking about it all the time he was away, and who knew how long he'd be. He put his cane next to him on the empty seat and shifted his legs so the broken one stuck out into the aisle. It was a short journey to Glasgow, not too much time to be jolted around. Only a couple more days and he could have the cast taken off, then he'd be more mobile. His ribs felt good, and the bruising on his face had gone completely so didn't look quite as scary. It wouldn't be long before he'd be able to find building work and make some cash. Ma, Ed, and Jake had all subbed him before he left, but it wouldn't last long. He'd made a solemn promise to all of them that he'd pay them back twice over, and hoped he'd be able to keep his word.

He looked out the window at the houses by the side of the tracks, wee fences and plastic slides and washing lines with sheets and towels flapping in the wind. Helen could have grown up in any one of them, with some family that wasn't her own. Maybe they'd loved her, brought her up right, but they weren't real family, were they? His dad must have thought of her name, when he signed her away. What kind of a man would do that, sign his daughter away to strangers? He'd never been close to him and now he felt even more removed, if that was possible with a dead man.

He tried to remember his dad's face, but could only think of his voice, hoarse from smoking roll-ups, always angry or exasperated. One of the last times they'd spent together was when they went to the building site down at Portobello. They'd got the bus over, so Steve would know what to do and where to go when he started the job. He was sixteen, had just left school, and was excited to be a working man earning his own money.

His dad had spoken to the windowpane. "I done a job near here once, fuckin' hard work it was. Tiring getting the bus at the end of the day, covered in cement and all kinds of shite."

"When was that, Dad?"

"Good few years ago, now. Got paid good money, better than what you're getting."

"It's only my first job."

"Aye, and you'd better do what you're told on site. Don't be getting any funny ideas. This isn't school, this is real life you're in the now, and it's no' a fuckin' picnic."

"I know."

"You don't know the half of it yet, son."

He'd been right about that one. He hadn't known the half of it, and look at the mess he was in. If his dad was around now, he'd have broken his other leg, right enough, he'd be so angry. He was never one for holding back. Like the time him and Ed were caught stealing from the corner shop. Dad had sent Ed home with a clip around the ear and then beaten the life out of Steve with a leather belt. He still had a scar on the back of his leg where the belt had cut into his skin. Best not think about that.

A woman with a toddler was coming up the aisle, trying to find two seats together. He moved his leg over so she could get past him, and she pretended not to see the seats next to him, moving up the carriage. Perhaps he did look bad after all, or maybe he was born rotten, and everyone knew it just by looking at him. He wondered if Helen was his better half, the good one, and when they came together they'd somehow cancel each other out and he'd become normal, a whole person.

As the train powered its way through to Glasgow, Steve made a decision. He'd had enough of all this, normal people not wanting to sit near him, drug dealers after him, leaving his own ma behind. He'd not had a hit for some time, and he'd been thinking about getting a wrap 'round the back of Queen Street Station when he arrived. But he mustn't do that now; it would set him back all the way. He needed to stay focussed on the job, get somewhere to stay, find Helen. He'd need to get building work when the cast was off as well.

He decided to stay clean, and it was the hardest decision he'd made in his whole life. How sad was that? Forty years of nothing to show.

"Got a room for a couple of nights, pal?"

Steve could only afford to stay in Dennistoun and it wasn't too special. There was a sign outside the grey stone building that read "room" and that was it. Not "room for rent," or "spacious suite," or anything like that. Just "room."

The guy at the door of the hostel looked him up and down. "You from Edinburgh?"

"Aye, sorry an' that." Steve held out his hand in apology and hoped he'd get some sympathy because of his leg.

The guy sucked hard on a roll-up and nodded. "Two nights, then you're away." He threw the stub on the ground near Steve's feet and glowered at him. "Fifteen quid a night."

"Cool." Steve handed him some notes and stepped inside after him. The hall smelled of damp, sweaty feet, and weed. He'd be keeping his clothes on, including his socks, to keep the bed bugs out. The Royal Infirmary wasn't far, so he could get himself there in the morning to get the cast off early. Bloody thing.

"In there, lock the door behind you." The guy pushed on a door with the number 13 on it. Then he left without another word, lighting up a fag as he stomped down the corridor.

Steve crept into the dark, feeling along the dewy wall for a light switch. There didn't seem to be one. There was a small bedside table with a lamp and he groped up the shaft of it and felt a metal pull chain. Yellow light seeped into the room, showing bare walls, a filthy sink, and a single bed covered with a thin orange quilt. It crackled static when he ran his hand over it. He locked the door and sat down on the bed, dumping his rucksack on a threadbare pink rug. It wasn't the Hilton but it was somewhere to stay.

There was a knock on the door, a deep voice booming on the other side. "Okay, there, pal? You looking for some white or maybe a wee toke?"

Steve sighed, would have killed for something. "No thanks, pal," he shouted. He didn't open the door, in case he got weak and stuck whatever the guy had in a vein.

"Suit yersel."

The footsteps faded and Steve lay back on the quilt. He'd managed to say no. Now the first time was over with. The bed sagged in the middle and the pillow was so thin he could feel the lumps in the middle of it. Things were going to get better; he could feel it, now that he'd decided to pull himself together. He wasn't crying; his eyes were watering with the smell and the damp and everything. Two tears escaped and ran in opposite directions to each ear. He left them, felt the trail of them on his face, a warm reminder of things. Then he slept.

FIFTEEN
Nat's Dream

Lizzy and Nat were on the bed in Nat's room, flicking through some of her mum's weekly magazines and occasionally giggling at some celebrity. They were trying to take their minds off things, escape the traumas that had got a hold of them both.

"No way." Lizzy held up one of the magazines. "Look at this shot of Brad Pitt. He looks well dodgy with that beard."

"Gross. He's old, anyway." Nat waved him away and moved her attention back to the glossy pages in front of her. She shifted onto her stomach and kicked her slippers onto the floor.

Lizzy gazed out the window. "Simon used to look so cool when he shaved his beard and his head the same length. He had a tattoo on his neck, which you wouldn't have seen with all that hair he'd grown. He didn't seem bothered by it, even though it hung there, all greasy around his face."

"I don't think he really knew what was going on." Nat looked up.

Lizzy felt the tears welling. "Why didn't I just take him back to the bedsit with me? He was asking for help. I was his only real friend, for god's sake."

"It ain't your fault he was a druggie. It wasn't Simon's fault either, really, was it? He took your money, at the end of the day, and went off to buy more drugs. It's obvious what happened. But it don't mean anything. He couldn't help himself, could he?"

"I gave him my day's wages, just to get rid of him. I asked him to get somewhere to stay the night, but I knew he'd go and get another fix. What if I hadn't given him anything? If I'd taken him back with me, he might have slept on it and I could have talked to him properly in the morning." She was crying now. Her tears ran down her face and dripped onto the magazine cover. "I just feel so bad for him. He had a crap life."

Natalie sat up and gave her a hug. "He'd been like that for a long time. And that was nothing to do with you. You could have taken him back to your place and he could've robbed you."

Lizzy managed a smile. "I don't have anything to rob."

"True. But he could have got violent, hit you or worse. It's not like he would've come down off the drugs and been all normal."

Simon had only hit her once. It was on the day she left him. It was because he was so angry, at everything, himself, with her, with life. She'd had enough of the highs and the lows, told him she was off to make something of herself, alone. She'd done her first shift with Dave, and had regular work if she wanted it. Simon growled and hit her hard right on her cheekbone. All it did was seal it for her. She had to go, had seen men hit women before, and knew once it started it didn't stop.

Dad used to hit Mum.

But that was then. Simon went too far that day and it was a mistake, and a long time ago. Lizzy couldn't bear to think what had happened after the last time she saw him, clutching the few crumpled notes she'd given him, staggering away from the market. There was about two hours from that moment to when he jumped under the train at Leicester Square. His picture was on the front of the *Metro*, and Keith said it was all over the local news on telly. They said he was "a homeless man." He wasn't really a man, though, more of a boy who'd never been shown the right way. After what they'd been through in Scotland together, and especially when they escaped to London, she should have showed him more sympathy, a bit of loyalty. Everyone deserved another chance, especially Simon, who had seen her though the worst time, when her mum disappeared.

"We'll never know, will we, because I didn't give him the chance. I sent him off, and now he's dead, Nat."

"I know." Nat went quiet.

Lizzy could see her friend's eyes were static, that she was staring at the page but not reading anything. She wiped her face with her sleeve and looked at the pink alarm clock on the bedside table. "I should get going. It's nearly six."

Natalie jumped. "Stay for tea. Mum's doing spag bog, she said to ask you. Stay the night as well. Please. We'll go top to toe, or you can stay on the blow-up on the floor."

"Nah. I don't want your mum to think I'm scabbing off you."

"She don't. Please, Lizzy, stay. I don't like sleeping by myself no more."

"What?"

"I'm getting the dreams, the flashbacks, even more, and it's horrible. I wake up screaming sometimes."

"Do you think they're real memories, of what happened?"

"I can't think where they would have come from if they weren't. I could never make them up myself."

Nat's mum put down a basket of garlic bread wrapped in silver foil on the table. The smell of it nearly brought Lizzy to tears again. She hadn't realized she was so hungry. What would she be having for tea back at the bedsit? Toast, probably. Sliced ham, maybe, if it was on special.

"Thanks for having me stay for tea again, Karen," she said.

"Don't be daft, she loves it." Nat's dad grabbed the bread and ripped off the end. "Don't you, love? She ain't happy unless she's feeding an army."

"Too right, Darren," shouted Karen from the kitchen, "especially if they was in uniform." She laughed at that, a loud and infectious laugh.

Nat winked at her. "See, I told you."

Karen came bustling back, carrying two plates of bolognaise. "Anyway, it's nice for Nat to have someone her own age around. She don't want to sit around with us two boring old farts, do you Nat?"

"Not really."

"Cheeky." Darren pulled at his daughter's ponytail.

"You staying the night, are you Lizzy? Stay over." Karen stood at the doorway, waiting for an answer, wringing her hands. "We'll get the blow-up out for you. I've got a horror film we can all watch. We can stay up late and eat ice cream. What do you think?"

Lizzy looked at Nat. "Yeah, that would be good."

She saw Karen give Nat a smile as if to say, "there you are, you'll be all right now." So they needed her and she needed them. That was a good way to be. She twisted her fork in the spaghetti and ate the first mouthful. Homemade, steaming hot, and sprinkled with parmesan; the way pasta should be. It warmed her insides instantly, tasted even better than it looked. Was it the way Mum used to make it? She couldn't quite remember.

It was past midnight and Lizzy was lying awake on the air mattress beside Natalie, who was breathing deeply. It was more comfy than the bed at her place; there were none of the lumps or that squeaky headboard. It wasn't exactly quiet, as there were still sirens and barking and all of the outside noises that she usually got. It was the inside noises that were different. Instead of shouting and doors banging and people running up the stairs, there was the distant hum of the fridge, snoring coming from Karen and Darren's room, the odd creak in the house. These were nicer, more comforting sounds to have at night.

Being in Nat's house with a proper family made Lizzy think of her own blood. She'd been twelve when her mum disappeared and no one had ever found anything of her, not one clue as to what happened. Of course, her dad in Yorkshire had been a suspect. He had a history of violence towards her mum, but they'd been divorced for years and it didn't make sense that he'd suddenly come after her. The police had found nothing on him and he had plenty of alibis back in Yorkshire. Lizzy had never really suspected him in her heart. He was hard, but not evil, and she had always looked forward to seeing him every Christmas, like a loyal and stupid puppy. Not any more. He never wanted her around the rest of the year, did he? She could see that clearly now. He could go to hell, and might have done by now, for all she knew.

She remembered the night about a week after the disappearance when she felt the spirit of her mum go. She was staying at Auntie Maureen's, in baby Noah's room, while he slept with his parents. Everyone had been talking about what they thought happened to Mum: she'd been abducted by some guy in the Chinese; she'd been lured back to Dad and was too embarrassed to admit it; she'd run off with some guy from the social club. Everything was made up, because no one actually knew where she was. That night, Lizzy had been in a kind of half-sleep, thinking about the time they were all in Portobello eating ice cream with Granny Mac. One minute they were all laughing and closeness, the next, her mum was touching her face in the dream before drifting away. She'd woken up cold and crying. She knew her mum had died, that she was never coming back. With Granny Mac already dead, her dad away with his new life, and no brothers or sisters, Auntie Maureen and Uncle Brian became her closest family. The thing was, they had the boys, and didn't have much time for her. She'd been on her own. She still was.

I wish this was our house, and that was you in the next room, snoring. Not with Dad, but with someone else that made you happy. I know Dad wasn't exactly good at that. Or maybe just on your own, because it seems like men have always made problems for us. Yeah, you're by yourself, taking up the whole bed. Earlier we had our tea on our laps and watched Britain's Next Top Model, *just like always. Afterwards I lay back on the sofa with my feet on your lap. You held my toes with one hand and drank a cup of tea with the other. We laughed at all the girls who took bad photographs, and at the catwalk teacher, who had legs like a giraffe.*

We're back in Scotland, in Dalbegie, and you've got work in the morning at the newsagents. Jessica will be skiving off all the jobs again, and you'll have to lug all the papers inside and sort them out yourself. It's Saturday tomorrow, so no school. I'll make you some toast and tea before you go to work, look after you. Someone has to.

I miss you every day, Mum. It's something that's never going to fade away, not ever. If I could have you back, I'd never let you go. I've no photos of you, because I left everything behind, I had to. But I could never forget your face. If you are up there, looking down, you'll be able to watch my face growing old, getting wrinkles. But yours will never change for me. I remember you had that broken jewellery box. When you opened the lid there was a ballerina inside that didn't turn around any more when the music came on. When I was younger I didn't see the point of hanging onto it when it didn't even work. You told me that Granny Mac had given it to you, so it was sentimental. I didn't understand what that meant at the time. If I had it now, I'd treasure it forever.

I know what sentimental means. It means never letting go of a memory.

It was almost two in the morning. Lizzy could see the glow-in-the-dark hands of Nat's clock on her bedside table. She must have fallen asleep after all, though earlier it had felt like she never would. Nat had woken her up; she was making funny noises and fidgeting around. She'd pushed her pillow off the bed and onto Lizzy's head.

"Stop. No. Stop it," Nat was mumbling.

From the dimness of the streetlight outside, Lizzy could make out the shape of Nat's body on top of the bed. She'd thrown off the covers and was leaning up on one elbow.

"Natalie?" Lizzy whispered, not sure if her friend was awake or dreaming.

She didn't answer. Still asleep, she started to kick her legs a little. It was like she was having one of those nightmares, when you're trying to scream but the sound won't come out, or you're trying to run but your legs won't move. There was a low groan coming from inside her and she made small, sharp movements.

Lizzy thought about waking her, but wondered if that would freak her out. "It's okay, Nat, you're just dreaming," she whispered.

Natalie started to scream. It was high pitched at first, like it was trying to get out, then it grew louder and deeper. It was a terrified scream. Lizzy jumped up and put the bedside light on, put her hand on Nat's shoulder to try and calm her down. Nat moved away from her touch, like it had hurt her, and opened her eyes. She was looking at something behind Lizzy, perhaps whatever was in the dream.

"Let me go. Please, let me go," she cried, hands together, her face streaked with tears and sweat.

"It's me, Lizzy. It's just me. You're dreaming, Nat," Lizzy kept repeating.

The bedroom door opened and Karen came in. "You're all right, Nat, it's another one of your dreams, babe." She sat on the other side of the bed and waited.

Gradually, Natalie calmed down. Her eyes began to focus, and she lay down on her back, breathing heavily. "Sorry."

"You've nothing to be sorry about, darlin', you can't help it." Her mum pulled up the duvet and smoothed it over her daughter's body. "It's not real. Just a dream."

Natalie looked at Lizzy and her eyes filled with tears.

Karen got up and studied them both for a moment. "Tell Lizzy what it was about, Nat. Try and remember."

Lizzy grabbed her hand. "Tell me. It might be important, Nat."

Nat waited until her mum left the room. "It was so real. I'll tell you, but it's really horrible."

"Have you had the same dream before?"

"Yeah. But I can't bring myself to tell Mum about it. She couldn't handle it."

"I want to know. It might give us a clue about what happened, and who took you."

Natalie rubbed her eyes and pushed the pillows up against the wall. She sat up, and she told.

A cloth held over her face; that's the first thing. After that, she's in an alleyway. It's still light so Natalie can see it clearly. There are dumpsters, rubbish spilling out all over the ground. The place stinks of something terrible, like dead bodies or sewage. She wants to cover her nose with her sleeve, as the stench is making her gag, but she can't because her hands are tied together. She doesn't panic because of the cotton wool in her head, the drowsiness. There are low and high windows all the way along the buildings. The roads are busy on either side; she sees a double-decker go past at the far end. There are three rusty doors in front of them, covered with graffiti. The middle one says "CUNTS" in big letters, as though it's meant for the people inside. Nat wouldn't forget that; it was one of the forbidden words at home, school, every-where. They go down the steps to that door and enter.

How had she got here? The journey is vague, fuzzy, but it couldn't have been long. She's still in London by the looks of that bus, the buildings. Who brought her here? She tries to catch a glimpse of the man behind her, steering her. He is wearing a black balaclava, a cap on top of it, pulled low over his face. He doesn't smell of anything. He doesn't say anything.

A long walk down a white corridor. A drink and a tablet. Every-thing starts to sink deeper in the cotton wool.

Now she's in a large, white room, standing in the middle of a group of people. They are sitting on chairs, forming a circle around her. They are faceless, nondescript, except for one man who is tall and wearing a black knitted hat with a peak. He's the one who let them in the room, and now he is sitting with the rest of them. Someone is behind her, up close. Perhaps it's the man in the balaclava again. There are chains fixed to the floor and the ceiling. There's a table near the wall, with a machine and wires coming out of it.

There is pain and the people are just watching it happen.

Sometimes there is too much pain and the world goes black.

She spins around, catching the pain, which comes from all angles, from everywhere. It doesn't stop, even though she begs it to. She thinks it will never end, but then the worst of it comes. Finally, she must hold a gun to her head, and fire.

She doesn't die, but wets herself.

She wants to die, but doesn't.

Lizzy lay thinking for a while after Nat had sunk back into sleep. The dream her friend had described seemed too full of small details and weirdness not to be part of what she'd seen in real life. Something really bad had kicked off in that place she'd described. Stuff she couldn't even imagine. Lizzy would find out where it was, who had done these things to her friend. Spinner was definitely part of it, she was sure. Next time she saw him she'd follow him. He might be dangerous, but it would be worth it, to find out what he was up to, maybe stop him from doing it to someone else. The police didn't seem to be having any luck; maybe she'd do better.

She plumped up her pillow and turned onto her side. She'd need to get some sleep if she was going to stay alert at work tomorrow, and keep watch for Spinner. The next time she saw him, she'd go for it. It was all down to her, now.

SIXTEEN

Oliver's Game

I came with you this evening, Lizzy. You and your friend left the market together, as you've been doing quite regularly of late. I was curious to know where you were going, and if you were meeting anyone. I hoped not. At first, Natalie's parents would accompany her to and from the market, and I can't say I blamed them, but recently they have entrusted you with the job, as if a teenager could fend off the same kind of bad company they could themselves. A foolish move.

Any fears that I had of you girls drifting, venturing into relationships that would jeopardize my control, were put to rest. It seems that you've been accepted into the fold of your friend's family home at number 84 Swan Road in South East London, and that is where you both ventured. The area is rough around the edges, certainly, but not one of the worst. From what I can see they are what you might call "salt of the earth," and I'm sure they will look after your best interests. I know you'll be appreciative, as you've already shown your loyalty and protectiveness towards Natalie, or "Nat" as you insist on calling her.

Natalie's mother came to the front door to welcome you. I overheard Natalie say "all right, Mum," as she jostled past, leaving you to smile politely and wait to be invited in. You're conscious of being in the way, I see, but I suspect they think you're delightful. The mother, who was wearing pink slippers and a rather garish apron, threw her arms around you and pulled you inside. She would be attractive were it not for her obvious hair colouring and drawn-on make up. You, on the other hand, had made an effort with your hair. It was tied back in a neat ponytail, light wisps of blonde touching the sides of your face. Your make-up is too severe, with those thick rims of black around your eyes, presumably to hide your pain and protect yourself. I can see a trace of the twelve-year-old you, the little girl you once were. You are at once angelic and street savvy, and I've admired the dichotomy of you for a long time.

I hid and observed, just for a while. The curtains downstairs were drawn and the lights were on, even though it wasn't yet completely dark. I made my way to the side of the house, hidden from street view by the laurels, and listened at the window. I couldn't make out the details of your conversation, just laughing, chatter and the sounds of the television. There was a man's voice, deep and distinct, but not threatening. I assume it was the father. Satisfied that you were safe, I left, navigating the dirty streets, past men in baggy football shirts, their bellies slung over faded jeans, some of them walking their dogs and leaving excrement in the gutter. I suffered all the way to the tube station, but it was worth it, to know where you were, and that you were still mine.

I had a viewing late tonight, one of my finest at The Audacious. It was the icing on top of a good day's observations. As I already mentioned, your friend Natalie was one of the lucky ones in my game of chance. She walked away, alive and oblivious, young enough to recover quickly from her physical traumas. Tonight's recipient, however, wasn't quite so fortunate. Let me explain.

Russian Roulette; I wonder if you've heard of it? You might not, being so young. Apparently, Graham Greene played it a few times as a young man, this terrible but compelling game of chance. There was one of our greatest writers, bullied and profoundly depressed, holding a gun to his own head. But we can all play; we don't have to be someone special. Simply put a bullet in a revolver, leaving five empty chambers in the barrel. Then spin the barrel, point the gun to your head, and fire. You might die; you might not. When I think of it, I picture Christopher Walken or Robert De Niro in *The Deer Hunter*, their sweaty headbands, fire and killing. It's one of my favourite films. I'm interested in statistics, because they always present a pattern, whether you think they will or not. Statistically speaking, if you use the same gun and don't spin the chamber, someone will die by the sixth pull of the trigger. But of course, these odds change if, each time you play, the chamber is spun. Each time we give our player the gun, they have a one in six chance of getting the bullet. It never changes. And yet, at The Audacious, we witness more than our fair share of deaths.

I know, because I keep a log.

In the past two years, we've had twenty-two viewings. You would think the number of deaths would equal around a sixth of this, so therefore no more than four. But we've had eight bullets enter eight numbskulls: a beautiful result. I write down the details of each gathering, including the kind of person we watched within The Circle, their age, sex, disposition, and where we found them. Then I jot down some notes about their reactions during the viewing, and of course, whether they caught a bullet at the end. Bang.

Whether they live or die, they all have something in common: they've done it to themselves.

You might wonder at the audacity of it all, the risk of The Audacious itself. In the early days of the Internet, the good old nineties, my double password-protected website was secure, but in the digital age things move quickly, and the world becomes too sophisticated for security to be guaranteed. I've turned it all on its head, Lizzy. We, as a collective, have moved on from online intrigue to live, stark reality. In our desensitized society, we have come to expect darkness on the Internet, and there are many on the case to uncover evil—or simply to enjoy it. Nothing is sacred any more, or different. If we really want to hide, it is now more difficult to be found in the flesh than it is online. Unbelievable, isn't it? Here we are, brazenly set up in the heart of Soho, our meetings monthly at minimum, without a breach of security in sight. A simple knock on the right door, in the right alley, will get you in. Tap, tap, tap.

But my dear Lizzy. You need not worry your pretty head about any of this. You'll never have to suffer through the game, in front of my avid witnesses, even though they are respected members of The Circle. You're too good for it. I'll have to think of another, perhaps more figurative, way of playing roulette with you. A special game. Let's wait.

SEVENTEEN
Helen Feels It Coming

It had been a terrible day from the beginning. She'd had one of her headaches when she first woke up, could hardly open her eyes for the pain. They came once a month, predictably regular, but still the pain was a shock. She kept a big bottle of Anadin in the bedside drawer for these mornings and, as she'd fumbled around for it, she'd knocked over the glass of water sitting on top of the table. The contents of the glass had somehow expanded into a pondful that soaked half the floor, the contents of the drawer, and seeped up the side of the duvet.

Helen didn't leave the flat until midday, once two lots of pills had worked on her head. There was hardly any food left in the fridge and she needed to get to Tesco Express at least, for the essentials. Grocery shops were vile places, full of people overspending, sucked in by two-for-one deals and cheap out-of-date products. At least the Express was straightforward. You went there for the few things you'd run out of, and the queue moved quickly.

Today, it was full of people jostling, trying to grab their sandwiches, bags of crisps, their low-fat yogurts, as quickly as possible. She'd timed it all wrong, hadn't thought about the lunch hour. People worked for a living, unlike Helen who could lie in bed all morning with a headache. Usually she didn't care, but today they made her feel inadequate and removed from society. There she was, standing with her empty basket, wearing her white trainers and grey coat, not quite hiding her polyester pyjamas underneath. Everyone else wore suits and leather shoes; fifteen denier tights sheathing slim calves.

"Excuse me, can I get to the salads, there?" A young woman in a smart black suit and high heels was trying to get past her, looking at the contents of the aisle rather than at Helen as she spoke.

Now they were really annoying her. Helen didn't budge. "In a rush."

The woman looked at her. "What?"

"You're all in a rush."

"Oh, for fuck's sake." The woman reached past her, grabbed a prawn salad and darted towards the queue.

Helen could feel the red rising from the bottom of her neck. She could leave and come back in a couple of hours, but she wanted bread, butter and jam, and to go home and not have to come out again. She went to the bread section, grabbed her usual loaf and contemplated the English muffins.

"I want to go park. Want to go." A toddler was whining further down the aisle, pulling at his mother's jacket.

Helen turned and watched as the mother wrenched the corner of her jacket pocket out of her son's grimy hand while simultaneously grabbing a packet of mini croissants. "Stop it, Nigel, we'll go in a minute."

The boy started to cry. "Want to go swings. You hurt my hand."

"I didn't hurt your hand, for goodness sake. Let's just get Mummy's sandwich and then we'll go. Do you want a bag of cheezies?" She grabbed his other hand and pulled him towards where Helen was standing.

The boy carried on whining, like a continuous siren, the high-pitched noise piercing Helen's head and triggering the headache again. She had never understood why mothers referred to themselves in the third person. "Mummy's going to do this" and "Mummy will be cross at that." It made her dig her fingernails into her palms and she did this now, as they came closer. She was in the way, of course, and the mother had to skirt around her, dragging the boy behind. His face was red and wet, trails of viscous green oozing from his nose.

Helen trod on the boy's foot. It wasn't an accident exactly, but she was confused by the noise and her anger about the mother, and the boy whining. She pushed down with her foot for just a moment but it meant he stopped in his tracks and pulled back. The mother assumed he was simply resisting and pulled his arms harder, muttering and swearing under her breath. He stopped whining and wailed even louder than before.

Helen turned back to the English muffins and took a packet down from the shelf. She felt a bit better.

Back at home, after two rounds of toast, Helen had started to feel panicky again, and lay down on the bed. There had been no word from The Circle for over two weeks, and she needed something to focus on, so the world didn't drift. She even contemplated emailing Lou to see if she'd heard anything, but resisted. The very thought of that woman, so intense in the Soho bar, urged Helen not to contact her directly again. Something would come through soon, with a date to fix on, a viewing to look forward to.

Everything was closing in now. The walls had shifted, the ceiling had dropped, and now the floor was rising up. Helen could feel tension in the air, all around her, swirling, making tiny vibrations and a low hum. She was lying on the bed, on top of the duvet, arms by her sides. In her heart, she knew the room wasn't really shrinking, but didn't know how to make it stop inside her head. She should just ride it out, maybe, go along with it. Like a bad trip.

She thought of the boy from earlier, whose foot she'd stepped on, not too hard but enough. It had felt good, the physical contact, and balanced, like she was giving something that she had received herself as a child, like a reversed redemption. If she dealt the bad, some of the things that had been given to her would somehow leave her psyche. As the stain on the ceiling grew closer, the past welled up and she took deep breaths and tried not to think of it. Some of it she knew would never leave her memories, but would lodge deeper into her soul with every recollection.

She was fifteen and old enough to leave school, but not legal or even mature enough to live on her own. Fife had been a lonely place, especially coming from the anonymity of Glasgow. She stood out because of the way she was, and that hadn't been a good thing.

"Happy Birthday, Helen. Fifteen at long bloody last." Her foster mother placed a single cupcake on the kitchen table in front of her. It had white fondant icing on it, and a tiny silver ball in the middle. It was one of the ones from a Sainsbury's box of six. There was no candle.

Helen looked down at it. She smelled the icing.

"What are you sniffing at it for? You're no' a dog." Her foster mother lit up a cigarette and sat down opposite, her mouth puckering. "You know what this means, don't you?"

Helen looked up and shook her head. She picked off the silver ball from the cake and popped it into her mouth. It tasted like sugar.

"It means you're leaving school. And it means you're leaving us. You're going to London, to a new foster home, 'til you're eighteen. Then you'll be an adult, ready to face the world." She smiled crooked, as if she thought it was the last thing that Helen would be able to do.

"Why?"

"Because I can't have you here any more. It's no' fair on the rest of us. And because it'll do you good to go somewhere else, get in with another family. You might even change if they're lucky."

Helen peeled the paper from the base of the cupcake and took a large bite. It was slightly stale, but she ate it regardless. She didn't know how to respond to the news. It had been presented to her as an inevitable part of her life, of growing up, and not as a choice. She didn't have any concept of what London was, the size of it, how many lived there. Just that it was a big city in England, where all the telly programmes were filmed and where Margaret Thatcher lived. Everyone hated Margaret Thatcher. She looked up at her foster mother, but she had gone, a trail of smoke drifting through to the living room, where the rest of the family were watching some comedy show and laughing.

A week later she was on the train to King's Cross. She was put on the bus in Fife and waved off from there, had to find the right platform and train at Waverley by herself. Her bag was wedged between her body and the side of the train. It contained everything she owned, so she mustn't let it out of her sight. She didn't have much, and so the bag wasn't that big. Stuffed inside were all the clothes that she hadn't grown out of, a spare pair of shoes, a stuffed bear that she'd had for as long as she could remember, and her toothbrush and comb. Toys and books had to stay behind, too heavy to carry, and apparently promised to the Salvation Army. She realized that she had nothing to read or do for the five-hour journey.

An elderly man sat down opposite and put his own bag in the hold above the seats. He nodded at her and she stared, unsure whether to nod back or to say something. They spent the rest of the trip in silence, the man reading and napping and Helen looking out of the window at disappearing Scotland. At first she wondered when England started, if there was a border of some kind, but there was no such thing and the time disappeared into nothing until the train slowed into King's Cross St. Pancras.

This was London, where she would become an adult. Then she would be set free.

Her name was written in blue crayon on a piece of paper, held up by a thin teenage boy with bleached hair and black roots, wearing tight jeans that flared at the bottom. He was standing with a couple in their early thirties or so. Helen moved towards them but they didn't notice her until she was almost touching the paper sign.

"Oh, hello, dear. You Helen, then?" The woman bent over slightly, putting her hands on her thighs, as if talking to a small child.

"Yes."

The man grabbed her bag from her and slung it over his shoulder. "You made it, then. This all you got?" He was at least six-foot-two and the bag looked tiny perched up there.

"Well, she came down on her own, didn't you, me dear? Don't s'pose you could carry much more." The woman was still bending over.

People were hurrying past them, trundling hand luggage, pulling children, shouting at each other. The four of them, Helen and this family, stood still. They were all looking at her expectantly; for what, she didn't know.

"Well," said the woman. "I'm Kelly. I'm going to be your foster mum. This is Mick, he's going to be your foster dad. And this here string bean is Kevin. He'll be your foster brother, I s'pose. Ain't that right, Kev?"

Kev nodded and screwed up the sign. He looked disappointed. Kelly took his arm then Helen's arm on the other side of her, and walked them towards the exit. Helen noticed when Mick widened his eyes at his wife.

"It's all going to be all right," Kelly was saying.

Things are never all right, thought Helen.

The ceiling stopped moving and settled into a place that was neither close nor far away, the grey stain on the stucco blurred and misplaced. She herself was a stain, both marked and anonymous, a dark spot tarnishing everything she touched. Helen had come from somewhere unspecified, and her only sense of place was when she surfaced somewhere, unwanted and unsightly, and put her mark on life. Was this it, where she was ending up? She had decided long ago that to be alone was best for her, for everyone, but now she couldn't see where it was all going. It was like she was spending her life waiting.

As she came out of half-sleep, Helen wondered: what exactly was she waiting for? She thought of Oliver and his bold ventures, his secret vantage points, the constant proactive recruitment of both victims and members. She had been passive by comparison, some kind of background watcher, and now this didn't seem enough to fulfill her desires. She should be out there, searching, looking more actively for projects and people that would satisfy. She liked the girl at the market, the one who Oliver seemed to be watching so intently. If that girl didn't turn up at The Audacious next time, then perhaps Helen would go after her as a solo venture. She had a soulful innocence about her that would be fun to break.

No more. There was no sense in waiting for something to materialize, when she could make it happen herself. Helen sat up and rubbed her eyes. She would make herself come alive, or she would wither and die.

EIGHTEEN

The Prodigal Sister

Steve stepped out into the bright lights of London, which around the train station were covered in a layer of black grime. From Dennistoun to King's Cross; things were on the up, he thought, rolling his eyes. The guy who worked on the platform had told him there was a bed and breakfast nearby that wasn't too expensive and not too full of druggies. It didn't sound glamorous exactly, but it would do for a couple of nights until he found work. He was strong enough now, could walk without a limp, and he was ready for labour.

He'd been to London once before, and now remembered the scale of it, that overwhelming feeling flooding back, that he was completely out of reach of the ocean, of the end of the city. Seven million people crammed in, and not even a seaside, with its fresh air and horizon to calm things down. No wonder everyone was in a bad mood.

"Standard!" The newspaper seller on the corner was scowling as he shouted.

"Spare some change?" a homeless man muttered, shaking a plastic cup with a few pennies in it.

Someone bumped into him, hurrying towards the steps up to the station. A pigeon with one leg pecked at his foot. Steve shivered as he made his way to the bed and breakfast, telling himself that tomorrow things were going to get better.

The office in Glasgow had told him about Helen's first foster family. They said "first" because they said it was never guaranteed the family had worked out, although they had no record of any further changes in her situation.

Later that day, he had found this family, if you could call it that.

The foster mother was still living at the address he was given, on a run-down road by the train tracks in Fife. May Faddyan looked older than his ma, cracked and worn about the face, deep lines around her mouth from sucking on cigarettes. She answered the door with a lit one hanging off her bottom lip, squinting through a wisp of smoke.

"What do you want?" she growled, half-closing the door on him.

Steve stepped back a bit so she wouldn't be intimidated. "Are you May?"

"Aye."

"I'm looking for Helen."

"Helen who?"

"Helen that you were foster mother to, from forty-odd years ago. Do you know where she is, now?"

"You from Social Services?" She shut the door another few inches.

"Naw. I'm her brother. Her real brother. I'm just trying to find her, that's all. Can I come in for a wee minute? I'm harmless, I promise."

She stepped inside and motioned for him to follow. The place stank of stale smoke. They walked into the kitchen and she put the kettle on, threw her stub in the sink and lit another cigarette. "Sit down and I'll have a think."

"I appreciate it. I only just found out I've got a sister and I'd like to meet her, you know? So would her ma."

"You think you do, son." May leaned back on a kitchen cupboard and blew smoke into the air between them. She seemed to know exactly who he was talking about. "Aye, you think you do, the now."

"So you know where she is?"

"I know where she went. After. My husband was still alive, and my eldest boy was in secondary school. The wee 'un had disappeared. Helen had been watching him after school while I went to the shops. I came back and neither of them was home. When Helen came back she was alone, said he'd run away at the park and she couldn't find him. Well. I never believed her."

Steve watched as she took a long drag on the cigarette, her hand shaking. He frowned. "What do you think happened, then? How old was Helen at that point, anyway? She must have only been a kid herself."

"I don't know what happened, because the wee 'un was never found. This sister of yours. She wasn't right in the head. She was acting funny when she came home that day, like she'd done something bad. I think she'd done a terrible thing, so I do. I had her in my house until she was fifteen or so, and I couldn't have kept her for a minute longer."

Steve was trying to take it all in, couldn't imagine what a young girl would have done. It was a bit ridiculous. "So where did she go? To another foster family?"

"We wanted rid of her, quick. She had to go. We were all in mourning over the loss. She was questioned but she was a minor, they had nothing on her. There was a family looking for a teenage girl in London, so that's where she went."

"Jesus."

"It split us up, the rest of the family. I always thought it was her, that Helen, who killed him. She was jealous of my wee boy, getting all the attention. Not everyone believed she could do it, but I did, I don't mind saying. A mother knows."

"Can I have a glass of water, please, May?" Steve was parched, and the smoke was catching his throat. The cigarettes must have been even stronger than the ones his ma smoked. His leg, fresh out of the cast, was aching after the long walk from the bus stop and he stretched it out under the table.

May took a chipped glass out of the cupboard and held it under the tap. "I don't know where she went, exactly. But there'll be some office for fostering in London that'll have a record of her. I just hope the next family didn't get the same grief that we did, god help them."

"She was just a kid." Steve took the glass from her and downed it. The water was warm and tasted faintly of chalk.

"She wasn't just any old kid. She was Helen. Just before she went, it was her birthday. I got her a big cake, candles, the lot. She just sat and stared at it; it was dead weird. There wasn't anything we could do for her, in the end."

"I think I'll be off, then. Thank you for your time, May." Steve stood up and made for the front door, anxious to get out of there before this woman told him any more of her made-up shite. It was obvious she couldn't cope with keeping her house clean, let alone bring other folk's kids up right. No wonder Helen had felt weird being there. She should have been at home with him and Dad and Ma. It wasn't right. May was old, mind, and he didn't want to be rude to her, show her some respect, but if he hung around any longer he wouldn't be able to keep it shut.

As he opened the door, she called out. "I hope you find what you're looking for."

He didn't answer. He hoped the London people Helen had ended up with were better than this. They couldn't be much worse, right enough. Stepping over a rusty frying pan, he shuffled through the litter, leaves, and weeds to the garden gate. He wanted to believe that the place had deteriorated since Helen had lived there, but a nagging feeling told him it had always been like that.

The main foreman on the building site seemed like a reasonable guy, said he had work coming out his ears. The city was putting up a high-rise apartment block in Peckham and it wasn't happening fast enough. Steve had experience, and didn't mention his leg. He could hide the injury well enough now.

The foreman regarded him, head tilted, his clipboard under one arm while he scratched his arse with the other. "We got a couple of other Jocks on site."

"You have, eh," said Steve. "Glasgow or Edinburgh, or someplace else?"

"Dunno, mate, you all sound the same to me. Makes a change from the Polacks though, dunnit. They're fuckin' everywhere, they are. Good workers, mind."

Steve nodded, not sure what to say.

"You want to work for cash for a couple of weeks, so's I can try you out?"

"Aye, sounds good to me."

"Then you can start tomorrow. We got boots and hats you can borrow down the office there. You can get them now, say Dave sent you. If you don't show up tomorrow, I'll send the heavies to get 'em back. That's a joke. I trust you, thousands wouldn't."

And there was his first job in London. The money was good and there was no sea wind here to blast through your skull and freeze your nuts off like there was back home. *Fuckin' magic.* Steve got his boots and his hat and took them back to the bed and breakfast, where he had a celebratory lie down on the nylon until the noise of the traffic outside lulled him into a nap. Life was good for once.

That evening, he counted out his money and worked out he could afford to get a burger and fries and maybe a bottle of cider to bring back afterwards. There was a battered telly in the corner of the room and if he bent the ancient aerial right back, he could just about make out the picture. He'd watch some crap, drink the cider, and hopefully get a good sleep before his first day at work.

Outside it was buzzing, with people everywhere. He'd never seen so many people in one street ever; it was mad. They were all colours as well: black, all shades of brown, not just the peely-wally white that you got on the cold stone streets of Leith. There was a Maccy D's on the corner, and they were doing a two-for-one deal. That would do. And forget the cider, he needed a clear head in the morning. This was the new Steve, all right. *Some kind of fuckin' temple.* He'd work like a dog, make money, find his sister. He felt nervous about her, about the life she'd had. Had she been loved at all as a kid? It didn't seem that way from that witch in Fife.

It wasn't his fault. How could it be? He didn't even know she existed until recently, but he felt responsible. He'd been the chosen one to stay at home, and there was his twin somewhere else in the world, sent to this city by a family who'd accused her of something she didn't do. That was terrible. He'd make it up to her, somehow. And hopefully she would find it in her heart to forgive Ma.

Steve got to the site ten minutes early. He was to drive one of the big Cats to dig out the far corner of the pit. He'd never used one before, but he wasn't going to admit that.

The foreman nodded at one of the other construction men. "Jock Number One will show you what to do, mate. Just keep digging it out until lunch. I'll ring the buzzer. It'll be cash in hand at the end of the day." He disappeared and left them to it.

The other man held out his hand. "Where you from? My name's Billy, no' Jock Number One obviously. He's a bit of a numpty that guy, but he's all right, you know?"

Steve took his hand. "Hello there, Billy. I'm Steve. I'm from Edinburgh and I'm pretty sure you're Glasgow. But it's better than being English, eh pal?"

"Aye, you're no' wrong, there." Billy grinned. "You used one of these Cats before?"

"Naw."

"Then I'll show you what to do, it's dead easy."

Once Billy had showed him the levers, Steve gave it a go and it was much harder than he thought it would be. Billy was a good guy, stuck around to help for a bit, even though he had a job to do himself. Turned out he lived in a house share in Dulwich, not too far, and one of the guys was moving out. Billy offered it to him. It was a lad's pit apparently, but it was cheap and Steve calculated it was less likely that he'd get robbed or shot than in the B&B. He accepted the offer of the room and would move in that weekend. *Brilliant.*

Now all he had to do was find that sister of his.

The adoption office he needed was open on a Saturday, so he went down there after paying up at the B&B. They found Helen's details fairly quickly—he couldn't believe it—and gave him the family name and address that had fostered her from 1977. They were in South East London, a place called New Cross. They said it was on the train line from Charing Cross and so it'd be easy to get to. *Maybe it was a bit too easy*, he thought.

He never did like calling ahead. Steve went straight to the tube and bought a ticket to Charing Cross, then got an overland train. He found it wasn't exactly a step up from the previous place in Fife, as he found himself on a platform covered in graffiti. There were crushed cans, butt ends, and even a couple of needles on the floor. He sighed, looked at the bit of paper scrunched up in his jacket pocket. Kelly and Mick Hartnett. He'd found the address in his *London A-Z* earlier, and he worked out it was probably about a twenty-minute walk. He wished he still had his stick; the leg was playing up a bit after his first week at work. It was okay though. Every time he got a twinge, he thought of D's pitted face, and it made him even more determined to get on with it.

Number 36 didn't have much character, a small terraced house with no flowers or plants outside it, just a plain wire fence and moss-ridden grass. The pathway had weeds growing in all the cracks, although the place was swept and clean. Superficial clean, maybe, Steve thought. He knocked on the door and stepped back a few paces, learning from his last visit that he might seem a bit intimidating to older folk. He heard someone shouting inside. "I'm on the bog, Mick, can you get it?"

The door crashed open and a large man looked at Steve with suspicion. He was wearing grey sweatpants, his belly hanging over the top of them. He scratched it, and it wobbled. "What you selling?"

Steve showed his empty palms. "Nothing." He pulled out the piece of paper, and studied it, although he could easily remember the names. "Sorry to bother you. I'm looking for Kelly and Mick Hartnett. I've come a long way."

"Yeah. I'm Mick. Who are you?" He widened out his stance, folded his arms across his chest.

"Steve Stinson. From Edinburgh." He stepped forward and held out his hand. "I'm looking for a girl you fostered some years ago. Her name's Helen. She's my sister and I'm trying to track her down."

Mick's arms seemed to unfold and slump involuntarily. He shook Steve's hand and stared at him for a moment. "You better come in, mate."

He went through to the living room, calling out to his wife. "Kell, we got someone here wants to find Helen." He motioned for Steve to sit down on one of the armchairs.

Steve sunk into the chair. "Thanks very much. I think I will sit myself down. I broke my leg recently and it's killing me just now."

Mick stood by the doorway and called out again. "You nearly done there, Kell? We got company, darlin'."

His wife appeared, wiping her wet hands on the back of her jeans. "All right, all right, I'm coming, for god's sake," she hissed. Then louder, "Who've we got here, then? Something about Helen? What's she done, then?"

Steve stood up. "She's done nothing. I'm just trying to find her, because I found out recently that she's my twin sister. She was taken away when we were born. I'm down in London to find her. My ma wants her back." It sounded a bit daft, he realized. That his ma had never even told him until now. What did that say about his own family? He sat down again, put his hands on the white covers of the chair's armrests. They were scratchy.

"I'll put the kettle on," said Kelly, and disappeared into the kitchen.

"The thing is, Steve. Steve, is it?" Mick was staring.

Steve nodded.

"The thing is, Steve, we haven't seen Helen since she left us when she was eighteen. We had her for three years and they was hard years." Mick sat down at last, on the armchair opposite. He also put his hands on the armrests.

"Do you know where she went when she left yous two? Was she working or did she go off to college?"

"She was working, all right, she'd had god knows how many jobs. You name it, she'd done it. Worked in a shoe shop, the bakery, selling advertising space in a directory, cleaning down at the school. She couldn't seem to stick at anything for more than five minutes, or else she'd be fired for not doing the job right. I hate to tell you this, but she was a bit strange, not quite the full shilling. We couldn't seem to get through to her, could we, Kell?"

Kelly had come in with a tray of tea and biscuits. She put it down on the glass-topped coffee table and started fussing with coasters and cups and saucers. "No one could get through to Helen. She'd been sent to us because the family in Scotland couldn't deal with her no more. We'd had some experience with difficult teenagers, had a young lad with us at the time, and we thought we could take on one more, easy. She weren't easy, though, was she Mick?"

"No, she weren't." Mick scratched at the stubble on his chin.

Kelly passed around the plate of biscuits. They were digestives, but not the chocolate ones. Steve took two anyway.

She continued. "The young lad we had when she arrived, Kev, he disappeared about a year later. Just like that, no warning, nothing. One minute he was here, the next he was gone. No one ever found him. Far as we knew, he'd gone off to school in the morning, with his lunch. He was no angel, bunked off sometimes, but still, off he went. Helen said she was going to walk with him partway then get the bus to work, so off she went as well. At the end of the day, she came back and he didn't. End of story."

"No trace of him at all?" Steve tried to eat the biscuits without getting crumbs everywhere.

"Not a dicky. Well, we felt responsible, didn't we, Mick? It was awful, social services interviewing us, questioning Helen. Turns out a little boy disappeared in her last family, the one in Scotland. They never found him neither. I'm sorry if this upsets you, but I always wondered if Helen had something to do with it. They never got anything on her. But still."

Steve found he was sweating, with the hot tea and the information that he hadn't expected. "Did she turn up for work that day? The day the other kid disappeared."

"She did. The police checked. She was there, but poor Kev never showed up for school."

"Probably wasn't her doing, then, eh?" Steve wiped his brow with his sleeve.

Mick and Kelly looked at each other and didn't answer.

"So. Do you know where she is now? How will I find her? Does she keep in touch?"

Kelly answered. "Soon as she turned eighteen, she was off. She didn't seem ready to be out there on her own, but she wanted to be independent and so that was that. If I'm honest, we encouraged her to go, didn't we Mick? We didn't really know what to do with her. She didn't seem to have the same emotions as the rest of us. Well. She didn't seem to have them at all."

Mick shook his head. "Like I said, not all there, mate, I'm afraid. She told us her new address, a council bedsit, but that was twenty-odd years ago. We tried to see her a few times. Whatever had happened, we'd looked after her for nearly three years, wanted to see how she was getting on. But she wanted none of it. So we gave up eventually. You still got that address, Kell?"

"It'll be in my address book by the phone. I've had that old thing forever. I'll go and get it, then at least it's something."

"Thanks, much appreciated." Steve hoped she'd hurry up because they were starting to give him the willies about his own sister. She was just a kid even then. All teenagers want to be away from their parents, where he was from. *Jesus. She can't be that bad, for fuck's sake.*

While they were waiting for Kelly to get her address book, the two men went quiet, awkward with each other now. Steve began to whistle tunelessly, which annoyed him when other people did it. He was annoying himself now. He stood up when she came back, anxious to go, and stuffed the piece of paper she held out into his pocket without looking at it.

"Well. I hope you find her, I really do. You might be just what she needs." Kelly wiped her hands on her jeans again, even though they weren't wet.

Mick stood up, hands on hips. "Yeah. Good luck, mate."

"Well," Steve said, "thanks for all this. Whoever it is I find, she'll still be my sister, now, won't she?"

"Yeah. I s'pose so," said Mick. "You don't look nothing like each other, though, mate. I'll tell you that much."

He left the two of them, looking at each other with secret-code faces. He was getting closer to his twin, to Helen, but he found that the nearer he got, his feelings of dread got stronger. They weren't anything to do with excitement or anticipation at seeing her, but definitely dread. What the hell was he going to find? Well, he was going to soldier on, of course he was, and deal with whatever came along. He could do this. He'd make Ma proud of him at last.

As Steve reached the end of the road, a black cloud came into view, heavy and ominous, and his leg throbbed like it was angry. Then a crow swooped down from the sky onto a nearby fence and stared at him. He stopped in the street. Was someone trying to tell him something? The crow turned around and squirted out some runny shite onto the bonnet of a Ford Cortina. He laughed. *A sign from god, eh? Get to fuck, that was a load of shite. Pull yourself together, man. She's your sister. How bad could she be?*

NINETEEN

Lizzy Follows Spinner

Lizzy and Nat were sitting on a bench in Soho Square. Lizzy had taken off her Doc Martins and rolled up her socks inside them. "I think I'll need new flip-flops soon. It's getting too hot for these boots and they're all I've got." She waved her bare feet around.

"You can get them cheap in Portobello Market, I've seen them all colours for two quid." Natalie wiped her eyes with a tissue and screwed it up into the palm of her hand. "We should go down there Saturday."

"That'll do me for the whole summer. I might get black ones."

"You get black everything, you do. I'm going for silver or purple."

They'd got chips and Cokes for lunch. Keith and Dave had treated them both; it was like they couldn't give them enough at the moment. Nat's uncle Keith felt terrible about what had happened to her, and Dave felt protective over Lizzy as it was, let alone now her friend had been abducted. They were both more vulnerable than ever in the eyes of everyone else, but the two of them didn't want to be thought of as kids. They could look after themselves.

Lizzy screwed up her chip wrapper and tossed it on the ground beside her boots. She'd put it in the bin when they left the square. "I'll paint my toenails black and all. I've always done them black, since I was thirteen."

"Goth." Nat poked her friend in the thigh.

"Chav." Lizzy grinned. "You've cheered up a bit. It's good to have a good cry sometimes, though."

"Yeah, sorry. I've stopped now." Nat poked her tissue down her sleeve.

"That social worker yesterday. What was she wearing?"

Nat giggled. "I don't know. I think it was pyjamas. She kept asking me questions about sex and that, if anyone had touched me down below, if they'd tried to have it off with me, or if there was anyone in the nude in my flashbacks. She was obsessed with it, seemed like."

"They didn't though, did they?" Lizzy shivered.

Nat shook her head. "Not as far as I can remember. You think I'd know wouldn't you? If someone had sex with me. It just didn't seem like it was about that. It was about pain. All over my body pain, not just in one place. Like an electric shock."

Lizzy had persuaded Nat to tell the police about her dreams, or flashbacks. Two officers had come to see her at home, then had taken her down the station. Later in the week they sent her to see a social worker. There was no shortage of ears, but no one seemed sure of how to help, to move forward. They all agreed that Natalie had suffered a severe trauma and that the details and the memories were slowly coming to the surface. The social worker had said they were "manifesting in night terrors." The details in the dreams could have been real facts about the place that Nat was taken to, but unfortunately they didn't include the people responsible for taking her there. The D.I. on call described their task as "looking for a needle in a city full of needles." Lizzy thought this was pretty pathetic. She'd seen it all before, people in high places not being able to help. They'd never found a trace of her mum, so how could she expect anything more for Nat?

Lizzy lay back on the grass and watched the clouds go by. "When I was in the waiting room at the counsellor's office, the woman behind reception kept staring at me. I'd look up at her, and she'd look down again. Then she'd stare again. It was getting really annoying. Maybe she thought I was going to nick the *People's Friend*. Silly cow. So what else did they ask you?"

"They mainly wanted to know what I could remember. I had to say everything over and over again. Then all the questions about touching and that. It was exhausting." Nat looked at her watch, pink and little-girlish. "Shall we go back? It's half past."

"Yeah, I s'pose." Lizzy hadn't got much sleep in the bedsit the night before and was flagging. She grabbed all the rubbish and took it to the bin in her bare feet. The grass felt good, not too dry and scratchy yet. The beginning of summer was the best time of year, the smell of warmth in the air before it got sticky and heavy. It seemed like the start of bigger and better things, although she didn't know what just yet. Maybe it would be something good for a change.

They'd been back on the stalls a while when Lizzy saw Spinner. She'd been watching the plummeting sun, hoping Keith and Dave would be back with the vans soon, and that Nat's mum might ask her back for tea when she came to pick up Nat. Karen's dinners were so good compared to a cold slice of pizza in the bedsit, sitting with headphones on, trying to forget about all the noise, the trouble, the endless shouting. When she was alone, she'd think about Simon and about her mum and then she'd start crying. The loss of Simon was like breaking another link to home. His death, in a way, meant another step away from Mum, more memories fading.

"Not long, eh Nat!" she shouted over.

Natalie gave her the thumbs up, since she was taking money from a customer and couldn't shout back.

Moments later, Lizzy noticed a familiar swagger coming towards her, those tight jeans. It was Spinner, had to be. She flushed as she realized this could be her chance to follow him. If he didn't have something to do with Nat's disappearance, she'd be amazed. He kept his head down, didn't stop at the stall and try to charm folk like he usually did. Busy texting, he went inside the café, almost bumping into a woman coming out. She scowled at him, but he was concentrating on his phone and didn't notice.

Dave arrived, reversing the van right up to the stall so they could pack up. "All right Lizzy, darlin', good afternoon was it?"

"Yeah, not bad. My apron's pretty heavy. I'm totally knackered now. Didn't get much sleep last night."

"You get going. I'll pack up, no problem." Dave held out his hand for the apron and gave Lizzy her money for the day. "Get some rest. You done well today."

"Cheers, Dave." Lizzy turned to pick up her cardigan and her bag. As she did, she saw Spinner leaving the café with a sausage roll in one hand, his phone still in the other. "I'm going to run," she said.

Fuck it. I'm going to follow him.

"See ya tomorrow, Nat! Got to go," she shouted at her friend, and waved. Natalie frowned and held up her hand, probably wondering where she was going, what she was doing. They didn't do much without each other these days.

She'd explain in the morning. There was no time to stop and she should do this alone. Nat wasn't ready to be following creeps around the city, and if it led her to a place she recognized from her dreams, she might lose it. Spinner was marching, in his funny, lopsided way, down Broadwick Street, and Lizzy was right behind him.

Left and right, through an alley, down a street, and walking fast. Lizzy kept her distance but never took her eyes off the swagger. Spinner made calls and texted continually, so she didn't think he'd notice anyone following him, but still, she wouldn't take any chances. He stopped to talk to someone standing in a disused doorway and something passed between them, but she couldn't see what. She thought of the plastic wraps that Roy used to dish out back home. The most attention Spinner gave anyone was when he looked up from his phone briefly and nodded at a man serving customers behind the counter of a chip shop. She noticed that the man nodded back, but didn't smile.

Eventually they came to a narrow alleyway, all shadowy, the sun behind the buildings. Spinner turned into the alley and hurried partway down. Lizzy watched from behind the wall at the entrance, as he went down three small steps, barely visible from where she was standing, and knocked on a door. After a few moments, he disappeared inside the building. It must have been a basement, as there were shop fronts on the main street in front of her. There was an independent electrical store, a tiny bakery, and a travel agent. They all seemed empty. She hesitated and then turned into the alley.

It stank. Lizzy held her too-long sleeve over her nose. There were a couple of dumpsters opposite the door that Spinner had gone through, and the smell must have been coming from them. Either they hadn't been emptied for a while or there was something really bad in them. She heaved, her eyes watering. What if he came out and saw her there?

She'd have to be quick. She jogged further in, and found there were actually three doors in a row. There was litter and discarded needles and crushed beer cans on and around the steps leading down to them. They were covered in graffiti, dirty and old. On the middle one, in big letters, was the word "CUNTS."

Adrenaline coursed through her. Lizzy felt her heart, the blood rush. This was where Natalie had been taken. This was the place in her nightmares. The smell, the doors, that word. *Fuck. This was the place she'd described.*

The door handle was rattling. Someone was going to come out.

She jumped. There was no time to get to the end of the alley, so she had to hide behind one of the dumpsters. There was just enough room to slip between the cold metal and the brick wall. Her eyes were streaming now; the stench like rotten fish mixed with human shite.

The door clanged shut and some heavy feet took their time to climb the three steps up to the alley. Whoever it was paused. Lizzy held her breath, and buried her nose in her sleeve, worried they would be able to sense her somehow. She checked her feet weren't showing. The person wasn't moving, very still, and only a few feet away. Was it Spinner? Had he seen her following? Maybe he was playing games with her.

She heard some faint beeping and realized the person was texting. That must be why they'd stopped. But Spinner texted, called, everything, while he was on the move. Either he knew she was there, or it was someone else.

She listened, trying not to breathe too loudly, until she couldn't stand it any longer. What was going on? She had to look.

Shifting sideways, slowly, gradually, she peered around the side of the dumpster. It was a man, standing with his back to her, and texting on his phone just like she thought. He was tall, slim, and wearing a fedora hat, the kind that was dead trendy around Soho. He was sighing, shifting around on his feet, obviously frustrated. She edged to the side some more and tried to get a look at his face, but she brushed against something dangling from the top of the dumpster, and a can clanged to the ground. *Fuck.*

The man turned, so fast that it took her by surprise. He took two paces towards her.

Their eyes met.

Her lungs were going to burst. She couldn't breathe. It was him, that guy from Dalbegie. She knew him. Didn't know his name, but he was one of the last people she saw in that place before she ran away. She'd been to his house, that white cottage, to do one of Roy's drop offs, a "free sample" to hand over. She'd hated doing Roy's dirty work for him, but didn't have a choice that terrible day. She remembered the smell of disinfectant in his house, the bareness of it. He'd slipped her a tenner for her trouble, but it had felt dirty. And now, the man from the cottage, from that first solo drop-off, was standing right in front of her. She could feel his stare on her skin, as well as underneath it, inside her.

She prayed that Roy wasn't here with him. What would happen then? He'd probably kill her. She looked up and down the alley, checking frantically for anything, an escape, help. Her feet seemed stuck fast to the ground.

The man spoke. "Don't worry, I'm not going to hurt you." He seemed agitated, and pulled at his hat so that it half-covered his eyes. "How did you find yourself here? Someone inside said they had a feeling they might have been tailed."

Her legs were trembling now; she could hardly speak. Everything in her was willing her to run, to get away, but she couldn't move. She held onto the corner of the dumpster, her fingers turning white. He had a distinct voice, posh-Scottish, educated. He'd given her the creeps at the time, and he was making her feel like fainting just now. Why was he here?

He came a bit closer, placing his phone in his jacket pocket. "There's no need to be scared, Lizzy." He was half-smiling now, and seemed calmer.

She shivered all over. "You know my name."

"I do know your name and where you're from. I've been looking out for you for some time now. I know you haven't had an easy time of it. Things are hard in this life, Lizzy, and so you have to help yourself as much as you can. Try and stay away from danger. Like this place."

He was smiling with his mouth, but his eyes were dead.

Lizzy managed to step out, and she folded her arms across her body, stood strong, as if this would protect her somehow, or at least give the impression that she wasn't scared of him. She fought back the tears. "I don't get it," she said. "What's going on? Are you something to do with Spinner? Or Roy? Just tell me."

He put his head back and laughed. It was slow and forced, like he was stalling for time. "I am," he said, "but not in the way you might think, Lizzy."

Her name again. She was sure she'd never told him what it was.

"Tell me what's going on," she said. "I want to know." If he was here, then he had something to do with Nat's horrible kidnapping. But she wasn't going to let on she knew the significance of the place. He might do the same to her that he did to Nat.

"I know everything about you. I know about Simon and about Roy." He clasped his hands together and held them against his chest. "But I can assure you, Roy will never find you. You needn't worry about him."

"How come?" Her voice came out as a whisper.

"Because, my dear, he is dead."

TWENTY

The Thrill of the Chase

When I turned to see you standing but five feet away, frightened yet defiant, I felt the blood rush to my temples. The alley behind The Audacious was the last place I'd expected to see you. Spinner was suspicious he was followed, but my thoughts of who it might be were of someone else entirely. Not much in this world can raise my heart rate, but the shock of seeing you in such close proximity threw me back to that day in Dalbegie, to the other time you appeared at my doorstep. You're older now and a little more streetwise, but the look on your face was the same as it was when you knocked on my door as a fragile thirteen-year-old.

I had been expecting Roy to arrive at my house, having hinted that I'd like to buy some of his despicable wares. I'd told him my address, setting the trap. Instead, here was his young runner, Lizzy, sent to deliver some kind of free sample. He thought, presumably, that this would lure me into his sordid world of desperate clients, ever eager to part with money in exchange for filth dealt out in plastic bags. I wondered at the time if he would have sent you had he known I was the one who killed your mother, that I'd captured and starved her to death, for the pleasure of my web subscribers, in that very house. But he wasn't exactly the sensitive type, having no qualms about sending a child to a single man's house, after all. And so there you were, beautifully naïve, but with attitude. I asked you in, and you stepped inside to complete the transaction in privacy, like you'd been told to do. I took the package, gave you some money as a tip, and resisted taking you right there and then. I was in turmoil; the idea of claiming a mother and then her daughter in succession was a temptation almost impossible to resist. I could have had you so easily. Fortunately my practical side reminded me that Roy, and possibly Simon, knew where you were, and I didn't want the police sniffing around again like confused labradors. So I let you go, my delicate bird, and vowed to take Roy out of your life forever so that you could fly more freely.

After you'd gone, I touched the floor where you had stood. I bent down and sniffed the wood, imagining the smell of your skin, the shampoo you used to wash your hair. There was a tiny smudge on one of the floorboards and I rubbed my finger across it, my own skin absorbing your mark.

That was the day you became a part of me.

The dumpsters in the alley are full of rotting food and the occasional, and I should say accidental, digital amputation. Or worse. The stench is unbearable. I prefer it that way, as it keeps prying passersby away from our entranceway, but I could never get used to it. You had been hiding behind one of them, too impatient to wait until I had gone to poke your head out, and half your body too. You were dressed in black, as you so often are, your nose half-buried in the sleeve of a rather thin cardigan. I could see your eyes were watering, and all that black kohl pencil was running down your face. Despite living rough for a long stretch, and now in some godforsaken halfway house, your skin is still fresh and youthful, and so the dark smudges are endearing rather than ugly to me.

I took one or two steps closer, my heart reaching out for you, my fingers trembling with the thought of touching the soft skin at the back of your neck, then slipping my hands around to squeeze it.

Then I stopped.

You were exposed, with nowhere to turn, so vulnerable. You were still that little bird I'd admired years ago. It didn't seem fair to close in on you that way. You recognized me, your mind obviously trying to understand what I was doing there, this figure from the past. I said your name out loud, which I hadn't done before, and it sounded harsh and final, like something had been decided. You didn't like it, me knowing your name, couldn't comprehend how this could be. I've been watching you for so long, it's easy to forget that you don't know me, have only met me once before. But you remembered our meeting, I could see it in your face. I'd made an impact on you, as you had on me. You seemed surprised at the news that Roy was no longer alive, and I realized then how afraid you must have been that he would ever find you.

We are the same creatures, you and I, made from the same god. We exist in the world and dance around its axis, with no real direction other than to be centred around each other. I decided then to pull you right into the core of me. The question was whether it was the right time. You were cornered and helpless, an isolated victim. Think: the predator doesn't always strike the prey that is tethered, but the one that is attracting his attention by running away.

TWENTY-ONE

Lizzy Keeps Schtum

Lizzy slumped to the ground. So Roy was dead. It was all too much to take in, and she had so many questions to ask. Could this man know the answers? And if so, how come? All the energy left her body and disappeared into the stench of the alley. Oliver crouched down, still at a distance, now at eye level. His stare was intense, like he knew what she was feeling, what had happened to her, everything about her as well as just her name. *Who was he?*

"I'm confused," she managed to whisper.

"That is understandable," he said. "We have only met once, and under questionable circumstances. My name is Oliver. Three years ago, when you knocked on my door, I was shocked that Roy had sent you. Do you remember coming to my house? A young girl, so vulnerable, standing there alone on my doorstep. A man's house. But you were so brave. I admired you, Lizzy. I remember seeing a tiny trickle of blood on one side of your nose and I wondered at the time whether he had done it. Had he?"

"Yes." She wanted to listen, to learn about the past, maybe. The life she had in Scotland was getting so far away. His voice was distinct, his mannerisms bringing back memories of the time she stepped inside his home and had felt so nervous but angry as well. Roy had forced her there, and she had hated him and everything about his world. There was that smell of hospitals or dentists, and the starkness of this man's living room. He'd spoken so posh, a private-school voice, not like everyone else in Dalbegie. At the time she'd felt uncomfortable, scared of his creepy stare. But now he seemed to really want to tell her something. Also, she reasoned, if he wanted to hurt her, he probably would have done by now.

"Well," he said, "Roy won't be hurting you like that again."

"Is it definite? That he's dead?"

"I saw him dead with my own two eyes, Lizzy. Take it from me, the man's in hell where he belongs."

"I thought he'd be looking for me all this time. So I'm free from him." She felt the relief bursting out of her heart, despite the terror of being in the alleyway from Nat's nightmares. "How did he die?"

"He was high, very agitated. There was a road accident. I saw the aftermath, his body being taken away, but never mind that. You're free of him. I don't want you to think that I've been following you, or anything," he said gently. "But I know where you work, that you're doing well. I don't want anyone to put you on the wrong tracks again."

"Like Spinner? I followed him here. I think he might have put my friend on the wrong track. You came out of the same door that he went in, so you must know him." Lizzy's heart was beating fast now. She was taking a risk, but she had to get to the bottom of this. For Natalie. She stood up and edged away from the dumpster, poised and ready to run. This Oliver guy could be part of Spinner's gang, and very dangerous. She wouldn't tell him about Nat's dreams. That would be even more stupid.

Oliver stayed crouched down where he was, unthreatening. He nodded. "Of course, I know of Spinner and I don't like the way he takes advantage of people." He smiled. "I'm sorry for what Roy did to you. But Spinner didn't do anything to your friend. I'd know if he had. I want to see you succeed in your life, and I wouldn't knowingly let him hurt a friend of yours."

"How come?"

"How do I know it wasn't Spinner? Because I look out for you and your friend."

Lizzy backed away. He'd misunderstood. "No. I meant how come you want to see me do well in my life? What's it to you? Who am I to you? I'm nobody, just some girl who delivered a package to you once. I don't get it." She was pushing him; she could see something waver in his face. None of this made any sense. There was a thin trickle of something reddish finding its way from under his hat and down the side of his face. His head was bleeding, just slightly. It seemed strange and out of place, a wound he was trying to keep hidden.

"I'm making sure you don't come to any harm, and have done since . . ." He faltered.

"Since what? Since I was on my own? Since my mum died and my dad didn't want me and my auntie Maureen forgot I was even around? Since I started to run drug messages for Roy back in Scotland? Since Simon threw himself under a train? Since Spinner took Natalie somewhere to do fuck knows what? Since I've been living in a hostel with junkies and murderers and women who look like they're just out of prison? Since when? Tell me." She couldn't help shouting. He wasn't being straight with her. Here he was in this alley, telling her he was looking out for her. Things weren't exactly going well because of it.

He looked away. "Since the day you walked into my house, full of bravado, but filled to the brim with sadness."

Lizzy felt the tears come. Her legs were trembling, but she didn't care that he might be dangerous. She needed to know things. "Who are you? How come you know so much about me?"

His stare bored into her once more. He paused, and she waited, wiping her face as the tears fell. She guessed that when he finally spoke, he would tell her something important, but wasn't expecting what came.

"I knew your mother."

His words nearly knocked her over. "You knew Mum? When?"

"I was new to Dalbegie and as you know, I lived in the cottage opposite the newsagents where she worked. I would go in every morning for *The Times*, and she was always so kind and friendly. I didn't know many people, but it didn't really matter because I'm a writer and like to keep a low profile. I worked from home, enjoyed the peace and quiet."

"But you talked to her." Lizzy touched her forehead, struggling to take it all in. "I suppose you must have done."

"A little. I wasn't exactly known for being outgoing. Her colleague tried to get me to the pub most days, but I was never very interested in socializing."

"Jessica. Aye, she would."

"But your mother, she was just a friendly person. And some mornings I needed a smile. That's all."

"So you liked my mum. So what?"

"I think she liked me back. She came to me in a dream. I know that sounds strange, ridiculous even, but it's true. I saw her in my sleep and she asked me to protect you. She said she could watch over you from where she was, but couldn't influence what was going on around you. It was hard for her to see you, while the people in your life were pressing the destruct button."

Lizzy couldn't stop the tears now, too many of them to wipe away, and this man, Oliver, was getting blurry. "She watches me."

"You know that, of course you do. She's your mother. But what you couldn't have known is that I've also been watching you for her, down here in the real world. A real-life guardian, of sorts."

"Jesus, I don't know about all this."

"I'm not watching you all the time, like a stalker. Please know that. I'm just making sure no one hurts you."

"Why would she pick you? It doesn't make sense. She hardly knew you."

"I'm not sure she had anyone better to ask. Who do you think she should have asked? Your aunt and uncle? A friend? Your dad? Who would it have been?"

Lizzy thought about it. He was right. If there had been anyone better, who would or could have supported her, then she'd most likely be with them now, back in Scotland. As it was, she was dumped on Auntie Maureen and all her boys and no one had time for her. That was why she ended up at Simon's place all the time, got in the deep end with Roy. Even her own dad didn't want her.

She decided to believe him, for now. What choice did she have? She swallowed. "She came to me in a half-dream as well. I felt her touching my face. That was a long time ago, when she first went. I always knew she was dead."

"I'll make sure Spinner doesn't hurt you or your friend." Oliver got up and brushed off his trousers. "That is a promise."

He stood up and held out a hand, motioning for her to walk ahead of him, back towards the main road. "Now let's get you back to safety. May I ask you never to come here again? It's very dangerous."

"Okay." She walked, her legs wobbling now. Oliver walked slightly ahead of her, as if constantly looking out for trouble. "You must also keep our liaison to yourself. If I'm to protect you, I need privacy and the freedom to go as I please. It wouldn't do to have people questioning our relationship, or suspecting the honour of my intentions. Do you understand?"

"I think so." It was a lot to take in. When they got to the road, the air changed, not exactly fresh, but the rancid smell faded. He called a black cab over and opened the back door for her. As she got inside, he handed the driver a twenty-pound note. "Take her where she wants to go, please."

"Will do, mate." The driver took the money and turned to face her. "Where to then, darlin'?"

She looked at him, resigned to the fact that she'd have to go back to the hostel. "Piccadilly, please. I'll show you where to go when we get there."

"Everything all right?" The driver frowned, looked into the alley where she'd just come from."

"Yes, I'm fine, thanks."

As the taxi started to pull away, she looked out of the window at Oliver. He had stepped back into the alley, standing just inside it, hands by his sides. He wasn't smiling but wasn't frowning either. He was just looking at her. A thought occurred to Lizzy and she tapped on the plastic partition between her and the driver. "Can you stop for a second, please?"

She wound down the window to shout at Oliver. "Why did you have to watch without me knowing?" But he was already gone, back into the shadows.

Shit. "It's okay, let's just get going," she said to the driver, slumping back in the seat, exhausted from the day. Why not talk to her before? It still didn't make sense. She'd get food from the corner shop, maybe some cans of lager, and take it back to the bedsit. Things might get a bit clearer when she'd eaten and had some time to herself. She had to think properly, and for once it was a good thing she'd be alone. All of this might be something she'd have to keep a secret, even from Natalie. Especially from Nat, she thought, or it would freak her out.

She was drunk. It didn't take much. Lizzy hadn't even finished all the cans and the room was moving around when she closed her eyes. There was a sour taste of mustard in her mouth after the hot dog, and she'd spilled a dollop of ketchup on her jeans. She smeared it into the black denim, to mix in with the rotten fruit and grime from the working day. There. You couldn't see it now. The Smiths had been playing on the CD player, and now The Psychedelic Furs were telling her she was pretty in pink, and she would be too, if she ever wore something that wasn't black or grey. Natalie looked good in pink, but Lizzy had always felt a bit self-conscious in anything bright, like she was drawing attention to herself.

She lay in the middle of the room, on the threadbare rug between the bed and the wee cupboard. Her feet were hot, but she couldn't be bothered to take her boots off. She tried to focus on the stains on the ceiling, on the cobweb that was dangling off the lightshade, grey on dirty yellow. It was late, probably the early hours of the morning now, and it should be quiet but it wasn't. Sirens, and banging like gunfire or car tires exploding, no one would know which. What was it like to wake up to the sound of birds singing? Was that a real thing or was it made up by folk in magazines?

Something had been niggling at her all night. Shortly before she disappeared, her mum had been acting a bit strange, happier than usual, taking a hot bath when she should have been making the tea, getting soppy with her at bedtimes. When she told her best pal Molly about it, they'd suspected her mum was in love. They were only half joking. Had she been in love, though? Did she have a crush on this Oliver guy? He'd said they often had some chats in the shop, so she could have fancied him. He wasn't bad looking for an older guy, except for the creepy eyes. Was he posh and precise in a weird way or in an acceptable way? The thing was, her mum didn't have a good track record with choosing men, and she might not have seen the kinds of warning signs that Lizzy could see. Like the trickle of blood, the intensity of Oliver's stare, the way he spoke without emotion. And the alleyway. He'd been there, and that was the place Nat had dreamed about.

If you're listening, Mum, I've something to say to you. I can't ask you any questions, because it's like sending them into space; they're never going to be answered. I could tell myself that I can hear your answers, but we both know that'd be a lie. I'm never going to hear your voice again, feel your hair, or watch you making the tea in the kitchen, spreading butter on the toast. There's so much I'd like to ask you. Where you went, who with, what happened to you, and lastly why you'd come to me and to some random guy, Oliver, in a half-dream. I just found out that you went to him—just the once—like you did with me. Why would you do that? I don't want to believe him, but it seems like too much of a coincidence for him to have made it up. Was he the one you were stuck on?

Anyway, the thing I want to say involves Oliver and my new friend Natalie and this other bad guy called Spinner. If you are watching over me, then you'll know what happened today. I wanted to let you know that I'm not going to say anything to anyone, not even Nat. I'm going to keep it all to myself, because Oliver asked me to, and I'm scared to go against what he asked, and also because I'm not sure anyone would really understand. Both you and I know that some things are best left. Wasn't that something Granny Mac used to say? Maybe it was your saying, blurring into all the other details I've kept in my head, all gradually fading away. I'm sorry about that.

When Lizzy woke up, she was lying in the same position as she had when she fell into sleep. She was still on her back on the floor, legs splayed out, her neck stiff. A few crushed cans of lager were lying next to her, stinking. She sat up and rubbed her eyes, itchy from left-over make-up. It was time to get back to the market and face Natalie, knowing that it was likely she'd been at the site of one of her nightmares. Would the power of it ever leave her?

As she changed her clothes, Lizzy thought about all the conflicting feelings from the night before, battling between wanting to believe that Oliver was some kind of guardian sent by her mum, yet feeling scared by his strangeness and the thought that he had been following her, watching her life unfold, from afar. Tying her hair back and wiping her face with a wet cloth, she had clarity, a realization that there was something not quite right about him. It was as simple as that. There was another thing Granny Mac used to say, and that was "never trust a man with eyes set too close together." She would go with Oliver's request for now, keep everything she knew to herself, but at the same time she wouldn't depend on him. There was only one person she could completely rely on, and that was herself.

TWENTY-TWO
Helen's Alternative

There was a spider on the bathroom floor. Helen stamped on it then flushed it down the toilet. She'd never been a fan of the card-under-the-glass way. She sniffed her armpits and decided it was time for a shower, possibly even wash her hair. Days, maybe weeks, had gone by since she had bathed. The hair on her legs had grown so long that it had become soft and downy. Time seemed to disappear of its own accord when she was feeling low.

Bad news had arrived. The familiar ping of Helen's email had got her out of bed; she hadn't received anything from The Circle in weeks and had been getting desperate for another viewing. She'd pounced on the mouse and double-clicked on the note, sent from an unfamiliar address with no subject line, as usual.

Apologies. The Audacious is officially closed due to a recent security risk at the location. There will be no more viewings or any communication from The Circle. Please delete all activity and addresses. Once opened, this message will disappear in one hour. Memorize the following URL and visit in six months' time for an announcement. www.spinaudacious666.com Use the usual password. ·

Six months? She wasn't going to survive that long without it, not even with the prospect of something new on the horizon. It was too long to wait. Helen let out a roar, which started from the bottom of her stomach and ended in the far corner of the bathroom ceiling. The woman below her thumped her own ceiling in protest. Turning the shower on at full heat, she threw her sweat-stained clothes in a heap on the floor. *Fuck you.* Steam filled the room and she climbed in, relishing the burning sensation on her skin. It was time for a fresh beginning. Perhaps the heat would wash away the tiredness, the reliance on other people for kicks. It might wake her senses up, along with her body. No point in wallowing when something could be done, if she put her own mind to it.

What to do?

As she scrubbed herself, she mulled over some ideas. Words and phrases, bad thoughts, jostled around in her mind. Online activity was too risky now, given what happened before with the web forum, and with media exposés of other secret clubs. Recently a young man had made a movie of himself killing his boyfriend with an ice pick, and it wasn't long before he was caught. It had been posted on a public site and taken down just as many times by the police, but she'd managed to watch it a couple of times. It had been somewhat gratifying, although the killer's narcissism had tainted her enjoyment. Helen avoided going out into the street when she didn't have to, shied away from the limelight to the extreme. She'd never seen the point of showing off; it only served to draw attention where it wasn't wanted. But aside from all that, the risk of digital had risen in the last year. It seemed the safest activity was face to face; flesh and bone, just like The Circle had been doing. If their group situation had temporarily disbanded, then she would have to act alone. It had been a while since she had been in the driver's seat, but there were some things you didn't forget. It was like riding a bike.

Back to basics, then. There was someone that interested her already: that girl from the market. But perhaps first she'd do a practice run, oil the cogs.

She needed the drug that would make a person drowsy, malleable. Oliver had always used straight Rohypnol, but Helen preferred a mix to include Temazepam or street morphine, because they were more accessible. She'd venture to the outside of the tube station, where men lurked in doorways, or leaned on walls outside. Dealers. It would be easy to replenish supplies, and she still had a stash of empty needles from another era. First, she'd visit the hardware store a couple of streets away. It was small and independent, an Aladdin's cave of tools and housewares, plastic pots and metal implements. Helen had walked past it many times, but had never been inside. She arrived a few minutes after opening, and the place was quiet. A man, most likely the owner, was reading a tabloid newspaper, his belly leaning against the countertop. Every so often he would look over the top of it, to see how she was doing.

"Shout if you need a hand with anything," he called over in a half-hearted way.

She nodded at him. She needed rope: fairly waxy, not too thin and not too thick, easy to tie. There was some yellow twine, used for fixing things to the roof of your car, which would do nicely. She picked up two packs and added them to the hammer and nails in the basket.

"I need gardening gloves," she said.

"What, love? Gloves?" The man yawned.

She nodded. "For gardening, the thick ones."

He pointed at the far corner. "They're over there, at the back, past the hoses. We got a few different ones. The green ones are for women."

She wondered if he ever got out of his seat, and what he'd do if she threw the hammer at him.

There were three sizes of green gloves and she chose the smallest so they'd be nice and tight and wouldn't fall off. There were five pairs left and she threw all of them into the basket. Then she was done. This first round would be expensive, but it would be worth it in the end, and some of these things she could keep and reuse.

The man put his paper down beside him and rang in the items, dropping everything haphazardly into a white plastic bag. "Doing a bit of gardening, are you? Looks like the weather's picking up. Making a fence, eh? That's a good hammer, that is. Packs a good punch." He held out his hand for the money, unaware that Helen hadn't answered any of his questions.

"I picked the heaviest hammer on the shelf," she said as she gave him some notes. "I thought it would be the most effective."

"Good lass," he said.

Hampstead Heath seemed almost a cliché, but there were so many places to hide, with lots of people trying to stay discoverable, yet out of sight. Potentials. It was well known as a playground for the devious and Helen was of the opinion that if you went there, you had to expect some trouble. It was your own fault if you got it bad.

It was now almost eight o'clock in the evening and light enough to see where she was going, but dark enough to keep to the shadows. The perfect time of day.

Face to face, flesh and bone.

She paused at the foot of the pathway. It wound up towards some large bushes on the east side. It was all here, ready and ripening, the beginning of something new.

It was a headline in the *Evening Standard*. She was a headline. Not on the front page, but on the first spread. The headline was a bomb scare on the London Underground. No one was killed or even hurt. It didn't seem quite right, that simple terror would overshadow a brutal murder, but it was all in the perspective, she supposed, the mass scale and the broader implications of bombs. It was a strange world.

Mutilated body found on Hampstead Heath

Apparently, police were investigating and treating it as homicide. Well, how perceptive of them. The short piece didn't include whether the body was a woman or a man, or any description of how it was found. It was probably because the police were keeping the details to themselves for now; it wasn't that the newspaper would be too sensitive to print such things. The British press did love a good gory story, preferably with some heartache and social depravity thrown in.

It felt good, that people knew what she had done, even though she would remain anonymous. Unlike some killers, she did not thrive on notoriety or wish to be found and glorified. The pleasure came from the act itself; the rest of it was satisfying, but definitely not the main thrill. Helen folded up the paper and set it on top of the bills and flyers on the kitchen table.

The clothes she had worn the night before were scrunched up in the laundry bag, ready to go. She'd had a hot shower straightaway, scrubbed her skin twice over. All the tools she'd used, her shoes and the gloves, were double bagged before leaving the Heath and thrown into a skip in an alley on the other side of town. She would leave no trail, clue, anything that would lead the investigation to her. Her intention to use some of it again seemed ridiculous once she had finished the act. It was easy to erase your tracks, if you knew how. London was a vast city, a place to hide. She put the bag over her shoulder and picked up her keys and some coins from the table. The clothes should be washed right away, so she could fully relax. The launderette most likely wouldn't be busy at this time of night.

When Helen got to the launderette, she was pleased to see only one other person. A middle-aged man in the far corner was pulling out white sheets from the dryer and folding them into a bag. Seemed like he was nearly done. She went to the middle of the other side, facing away from him, and went about preparing her washing powder and coins.

"Drag isn't it, all this," the man shouted over.

Helen ignored him, concentrating on counting out her money. She began to untie the laundry bag just as he walked past, his own bag slung over his shoulder. Half turning, she could see that he was watching her.

"You're the last one, enjoy the peace and quiet, love." He stopped just beside her and waited for her reply.

She gave none, could see no reason for entering a conversation with anyone, least of all in this godforsaken place.

"Just being friendly," he said as he walked away. "Some people."

The door clicked shut and he was gone. The physical presence of him had made the room heavy, but now it was nice and light again.

She pulled out the clothes from the bag and stuffed them into the washing machine. Most of the blood had dried now, the larger wet patches folded up and hidden on the inside of the pile. She inspected her hands, pleased there were no smears on her skin, and put the coins into the slot. The machine started to whir, the last of the evidence lost in the water, soapsuds, and industrial-strength spin.

Helen sat down on a chair opposite and stared into the churning laundry, like she always did. It was her life, her own circle, and it would go around and around and then start all over again when she needed it to.

The next morning, her Hampstead Heath killing was on *Breakfast TV*, just briefly. Helen sat on a chair at her small kitchenette bar, watching with interest as she sipped her tea with honey. The victim had been identified as a local woman, a prostitute, and the young presenter was telling everyone to be careful out there, as this "man" was very dangerous.

Helen smiled. Of course society would assume that a man had done this. How could a woman do such things to another woman? It wasn't unheard of, there had been plenty of violent female murderers over the years, but still, they couldn't think of it. They didn't want to think of it. This was fine by her, as it meant she was one of the least likely suspects.

The countertop was wiped clean, and the bed was made, pillows plumped and straight. Helen was dressed and had swept the carpet free of crumbs and picked up some of the dirty plates. She was getting stronger now, a renewed force driving everything forward. She had control of her life again, no longer relying on other people for dates or viewings or long-awaited anonymous messages. In fact, the laptop was switched off because she wasn't waiting for anything to happen any more, didn't even need the Internet to feed her mind. Since the news that The Circle had temporarily disbanded, she had gradually felt like a whole person again in quite an unexpected way. The energy had slowly crept through her until it had seeped into every cell. There was a clarity that had been missing these past few years, as if her drive had been lying dormant, waiting to be released. She could feel it vibrating out of her body, see its colours in the air around her. It was thick and viscous, a congealed emotion starting to run free.

Her buzzer went off. Someone was at the door.

Helen switched off the television and went to the window. The net curtains, she noticed, were yellow and stiff, like they hadn't been washed or even moved for years. Perhaps she'd wash them one of these days. She couldn't see who was on the doorstep because they were underneath the brick porch. The buzzer went again. She waited until eventually a tall, skinny man backed out and looked up at the window, as if he knew she was standing there. She kept still, hoping he wouldn't be able to see through the nets. Who could it be? He seemed agitated; he kept looking at his watch and checking a piece of paper in his jacket pocket. He was a bit scruffy, but had obviously made some sort of effort with his hair, which was wet and combed with a side parting. Was he a copper? Someone from the Benefits office checking on her situation? He wasn't carrying anything, so he wasn't selling anything. Whatever the reason, she wasn't about to answer the door to him.

He rang the buzzer for a third time. Perhaps he'd seen her. She moved away from the window and into the kitchenette again. After a few moments she heard his footsteps going up the pathway and onto the road. He was gone. She must check through her paperwork, see if she owed anyone some money, forms, or signatures. All her letters and bills from the last few weeks were piled up on the small table by the door. But not now; she'd done enough for one day. After so much time spent clearing up and getting ready, she would venture out, perhaps go to Dina's for a celebratory breakfast, relish her newfound lease on life. Perhaps the stall girl would be there, at the market. She could size her up for next time. The practice run had gone very well, after all.

Missy was in a bad mood, even more so than usual, which Helen found amusing.

"You asked for two eggs, sunny side up, and that's what you got in front of your face," she was saying to one of the workmen.

He shook his head. "I thought I said scrambled."

"Nope, it was them eggs, so enjoy 'em now they've been made for you." She walked away, mumbling under her breath so that everyone could hear. "Silly old sod."

Dina was half watching over her shoulder and called her over. "Missy come here, will you, I want to have a word."

Helen sat herself at one of the tables nearest to the kitchen and watched as Dina spoke to her daughter in a low voice, shaking her finger close to her face. Missy was pouting, hands on her hips. Dina handed her a plate of scrambled eggs and pointed at the workman. Missy snatched it and took it over to him, smiling in a fake way while she switched the plate carefully in front of him. He nodded in appreciation and gave Dina a wave.

It was hot in there, the small fan on the counter not quite reaching all corners of the café, with its low-blowing tepid air. Helen took off her coat and cardigan and turned to drape them on the back of the wooden chair. When she swiveled around again, Missy was standing in front of her, eyebrows raised.

"You having the usual, then?"

"Yes, and a cup of tea, please."

"No problem, I know what you're having and you won't be complaining about it. Not like some people." Missy looked pointedly at the workman, who was tucking into his scrambled eggs.

Helen was partial to this table as it afforded a view of almost all the other customers in the café and she could look all she liked without anyone noticing. There were the usual working crew, all hard boots and reflective jackets; a young family feeding their kids eggs and beans; and the usual smattering of singles and couples from around the market with heads down, enjoying their plates piled high to set them up for the rest of the day. She recognized the man with the tight, designer ripped jeans that she'd noticed before. He was eating quickly, his eyes shifting around the room as if he was worried about something or keeping a lookout. He was wearing a gold watch and three gold chains around his neck, too much jewellery for a man. It made him stand out and that was never a good thing when you were so obviously guilty. He was craning his neck to see out of the window, chewing fast, ketchup and grease on his chin.

Missy put a plate down in front of her. "There you go, eat up," she said. "I'll get your tea in a sec."

Helen looked down and surveyed the bacon and eggs and the white toast oozing with butter, her hands moving towards the knife and fork of their own accord. This was going to be even better than ever. Did she say thank you? She wasn't sure.

When she looked up, the man with the jeans was hurrying out the door, keys jangling on a chain hanging from his belt loop. Outside, someone was waiting for him, almost out of sight. He had a peaked hat pulled down over half his face and leaned on the window with his back to the café. The two men walked off together. Helen stood up, her cutlery still in her hands, straining to see the other man. It looked just like Oliver from the back. Could it have been him? Surely not. But that hat, the body shape, the clothes and shoes were all Oliver.

"Everything all right, there, Helen?" Dina called over.

She looked at Dina. Should she run out and check? "I'll be back in a sec," she called out.

Leaving her cardigan on the chair, she grabbed her bag and made for the door. Which way had they gone? She saw a flash of them down towards Wardour Street and hurried in that direction, wiping her mouth on her sleeve. She hoped her eggs would still be there when she got back. When she got to the corner, she slowed and creeped around it, and it was just as well because the two men had stopped just outside one of the other cafés, deep in conversation. In side profile, she could see the familiar outline of Oliver's face, his nose and those eyebrows.

He had his hand on the other man's lapel, but she couldn't tell if it was a threatening or a comforting gesture. She hoped it was a sign of aggression because the other man seemed like a lowlife. Curious, she watched for a few moments longer. The other man was nodding now, holding up his palms in agreement. They walked on, striding fast and with purpose.

Helen turned and trudged back to Dina's. Oliver and her used to be a team, the two of them against the world, and now he seemed to have so many people around. The Audacious, The Circle, someone from the market, and most likely others that she didn't even know about. He didn't need her any more. If he did, he would find her. He was good at that. She opened the café door to the glorious smell of bacon, and found her table.

"You're back. We weren't sure what to do," Missy said and fussed with the box of napkins.

"Forgot something," she said, and picked up her knife and fork.

Dina shouted over. "Want me to heat up the plate for you?"

"No, it's okay."

She scooped up some egg white and felt the sliminess of it in her mouth. If he didn't need her, then she wouldn't need him. It was each man for himself now. Six months to wait for some other group-viewing situation? *I don't think so.*

As she ate, she hardly noticed the café door opening and two young girls coming inside. It wasn't until one of them shouted over at Dina that she realized it was the girl from the market stall, the tall one that Oliver had been watching, all black clothes and black nails. The friend was a little smaller, more girlish, like the one they'd already seen at The Audacious. It could even be the same one. The one in black was young too, but had a defiant, street-wise air about her. They were giggling together, in that innocent and carefree way that only teenagers can get away with.

Helen's heart was beating faster than usual, just a little. She could feel it fluttering. Her face was burning too, although that could have been because of the heat from the cooking. Such a stirring of emotion; the girl was a definite candidate, especially as she was obviously one of Oliver's desires. Well, he could continue to circle around this girl, but soon he'd have to stand back and watch while she took his prey from him, like an eagle swooping, fast and premeditated. Unexpected. Would he be surprised, impressed even? Perhaps he'd want her back as a partner again. Helen scraped the last of the crumbs from her plate and sat back. It wouldn't take long to find out.

TWENTY-THREE

Steve's Lost Soul

He dialed the number, so familiar that it seemed strange to be ringing it. Him in London in a phone box, and Ma up in Scotland. Steve cleared his throat, nervous, but not sure why. The ringtone started and his heart began to beat faster. Christ, why was he so jumpy? He should have called her long before this.

She didn't answer. Of course, because she wasn't at home if she'd done what she was supposed to and gone to her sister's. It was a relief, in a way. He'd have left a message, but it had never occurred to Ma to get an answerphone or voicemail because she always said if it were important, they'd call back. And she was right.

Steve put the receiver back in the cradle and pulled out his notebook, bent and tatty from weeks of scribbling and pocketing and occasionally thumbing through it all. Next he'd call Ma at her sister's, Auntie Mary's, in Berwick. He flicked through the pages and found the number, glancing behind him to see if anyone was waiting for the phone. There was only a homeless guy on a mattress, so old he looked like he'd be away up to heaven soon. At least he might get a comfy place to stay up there. The street was getting dark, not many passersby at this time to throw their spare change in his wee pot. He decided he would chuck his pennies in there when he was done.

He dialed. Yes, it had been a while since he left, but he'd wanted to wait until he had proper news, something good to report. He had work now, and he was on the third part of the trail to find Helen. He had an actual address to try, or keep trying anyway.

Someone picked up at the other end. "Hello?"

"Hello, Auntie Mary? It's Steve here."

"Steve?" She shouted away from the receiver. "It's Steve on the phone!"

"Is Ma with you? Is everything okay?"

"Och, she's no' very well, Stevie. She's upstairs sleeping in her bed the now. Where are you? Where've you been, Stevie?"

He felt nauseated. "What's wrong with her?"

"There was an incident, back in Edinburgh at the flat. It was the day she was supposed to be coming to stay. It was terrible, so it was. Where are you, Stevie? Have you found your sister yet?"

"Oh my god, what happened? Is she hurt?" Steve put his forehead against the dirty plastic of the phone booth and his eyes rested on the old homeless guy, lying on the mattress.

"There was a man in the stair, pounced on her when she left the flat. Took her purse, so he did, and knocked her flying. She fell down the stairs, not all the way mind, but a fair way. Well. Someone called the police and they never caught up with him. They were amazed he didn't take anything from inside the flat."

"Who was he? Did she see who it was?"

"No, it was just some schemie out for what he could get. But Stevie, don't you worry yourself too much. She didn't break anything, just got a big fright and some bruises. She's just been ever so tired and stays in her bed a lot of the time, recovering from the shock I think. She talks about you all the time, told me all about you going away to fetch your long-lost sister. How lovely."

Auntie Mary obviously didn't know about D, that this "accident" was probably all Steve's fault. He tried to gather his thoughts. "Auntie Mary, tell Ma I'm in London the now. I've got work. I've been to two different foster parents and now I've got an address where Helen lived. She might even still be there. I'm going again tomorrow to try and find out. Tell her, okay?"

"Aye, of course I will. She'll be so pleased."

"Give her my love, Auntie Mary."

"I will, son."

Steve hung up and leaned back, eyes shut for a moment. It must have been D. He could just imagine what had kicked off when he realized Steve wasn't there. *Fuckin' bastard.* He'd get to that address in the morning and get all this sorted out quick so he could get back up to Scotland and make sure Ma was okay. In her bed all day? That didn't sound like just a fright. She was tougher than that.

D was going to pay for this.

He stepped out of the booth and remembered the homeless guy, felt in his trouser pocket for change. There was a decent handful of it. He went over and crouched down beside him. "I've got some change here, pal, if you want it. You still alive down there?"

The man didn't move. Was he even breathing? Shit, he'd been kidding about being still alive. Steve hesitated, then rolled him over onto his back, quick, just to make sure. His eyes were open, his tongue lolling out, dry and covered in a film of white. The smell of him was overpowering, and Steve staggered back a couple of feet. He took a quick look around, but there was no one who seemed remotely official. Back in the phone booth, he dialed emergency services.

"Police, please. Aye." He was put through. "I'm calling to report a dead guy on the street. No, I don't know him; he's a homeless guy. Aye, he's definitely dead."

When you see someone hurt, that's bad enough, especially when it's your own self, Steve thought. He was joking to himself, even though it wasn't funny. But he'd never seen a dead man, not close up like that. He couldn't shake the picture of the tongue, those filmy eyes, out of his mind. He needed to sleep, but couldn't seem to settle his brain. Even when Dad died, he never saw him, just the outside of the coffin. A few folk cried at the funeral, even though most were scared of his dad. That was a long time ago. He remembered Ma standing at the front, looking ahead of her at the space in between the priest and his uncle Joe. She never cried. He'd not thought too much about it at the time, but the image of her looking like that had always stayed with him. She'd hardly talked about Dad in all those years after his death. No one had. Was there something else he didn't know? Christ, his poor ma. She'd suffered enough without him making her life harder.

He screwed his eyes up but couldn't stop the tears escaping and soaking the lumpy pillow. He felt very small and lonely, like a kid who'd lost his parents. Curling up under the blanket, he hugged his knees and tried to stop the waterworks. Good old Stevie-boy didn't do this kind of thing. He'd let it all out, and that would be the end of it. He was trying to put things right, not go soft.

The street was typical of London, he decided. No trees, some scabby patches of grass next to the curb and rows and rows of terraced houses, crumbling and covered in a layer of black carbon. There were net curtains in some of the houses so yellow they'd probably been there since Victorian times. He wondered if they'd disintegrate if you touched them. Flutter away into dust.

A group of lads were blundering towards him on the pavement, bouncing a basketball between them and laughing and swearing. They were all wearing their hoods up, faces in shadows. It wasn't that part that feared him, but kids in London were unpredictable. Give him Leith kids any day; he'd be able to handle them. But these seemed bigger, some from faraway places that he'd never even heard of, talking in a city language that he didn't understand.

"Watch it, Grandad," one of them sniggered as he bounced the ball into Steve's leg.

"Yeah, don't nick our ball, man." Another one pushed up behind him, trying to intimidate.

Steve turned. "Get to fuck, you wee gubshite. I'm no' a grandad, but I'm old enough to give you a smack. Does your mammy sew? I hope she does, for the stitches when I'm finished wi' yous lot."

The kid backed off, hands up. "Keep it on, man."

"Fuck, he's a nutter. What'd he say?"

One of them grabbed the ball and darted off. "Let's go."

They disappeared, still bouncing and swearing, but not laughing this time. Steve watched them go, hands on hips, in case they turned, changed their minds. But they didn't; what a miracle. He must be harder than he thought. Or maybe they weren't used to his accent. Either way, he'd beaten off the little shites.

He had almost reached the address that was scribbled in his notebook. It was just like any other house on the street, dirty and faceless. Even though he'd been there the day before, he had a job recognizing which one it was.

Yesterday, when he'd found the right house, he'd discovered two names handwritten underneath tiny plastic covers, the place divided into flats. When he bent closer to review the names, he got a shock when the first one was "Stinson." He'd started at it. Stinson. Was she really still here? Had she really kept their surname? So she wasn't married, then. He'd stepped back, tried to look through the bay windows next to the front door. It was dark in there, and the nets hid what was inside.

And now, here he was again. Stinson. He couldn't believe it. He should have been ecstatic, but Steve just felt cold. He had that tingling feeling through him, the same one he got when he realized he'd done something very wrong, when someone was after him, or when he was about to get gubbed by D. It wasn't good. He looked up at the windows again. Maybe he'd see something other than a shadow this time. He crossed the road, took a few deep breaths and leaned against a lamp post. The upstairs windows were even dirtier than downstairs, thick curtains pulled right across, no lights on. He should press the buzzer. But who was he going to find? Someone who had been given away as a baby, who had been through two foster families who'd hated her, feared her even, and then left to fend for herself. Helen Stinson probably wasn't going to be easy.

Fuck's sake, just press the buzzer. She might be there this time.

He strode back across the road and pushed his thumb on it before he changed his mind. He could hear it, very faint, perhaps up the stair. He waited.

"Who you looking for?" A female voice behind him made him jump.

"Helen?" He spun around and saw that it was an older woman, perhaps in her sixties. Not Helen. "Oh sorry, I thought you were someone else."

She had her key in her hand. "I live here, on the ground floor. Who you after, then?"

Steve pointed at the buzzer. "Helen Stinson. Do you know her? I'm her brother."

"Oh, she got family, has she? That's nice. Didn't think she had anybody. 'Course, I'm talking about her upstairs, not that I know her name or nothing. Can't say I know her at all, and don't hardly ever see her, really. She keeps herself to herself, that one, funny old fruit."

"Don't suppose you know when she'll be in?"

"No idea, love. She might even be in now, but ain't answering the door. Does she know you're coming?"

"No."

"I can't let you in, just in case. You know how it is. If I see her, I'll tell her you was here. What's your name, dear?"

"Doesn't matter, she won't know my name." He stepped aside to let the woman to the door and stood in the front, looking up at the windows again. "I'll come back another time."

"What, she don't know her own brother's name?"

"Long story." He walked away, a bit relieved if he was being honest, stopping to take one last look at the place. It was depressing, even by his standards. As he turned, the curtain moved, twitched just a tiny bit. Was she watching him? He stared for a few moments, but there was no more movement. Once again, that feeling crept down his chest and inside. She was in there, he was sure of it. The trouble was, now he was scared of what he was going to find.

TWENTY-FOUR

Lizzy Gets Paranoid

The afternoon sun was glinting furiously, bouncing off something overhead and searing Lizzy's eyes. She put both hands to her forehead and squinted up at the buildings opposite the market stall. What was that? Maybe it was the glare from someone's watch.

"Dave, are you off just now? The rush has died down a bit." She flicked the end of her apron string at him. He should have left by now if he was to be back in time for the end of day clean up.

"Just now?" He grinned.

"Oh fuck it. I sounded Scottish, didn't I? I don't care because I found out that the person I've been hiding from all this time is actually dead. I can talk how I like *just now*."

"Dead? Are you sure? How did you work that one out, then?" Dave put on his filthy denim jacket, and then waited for his answer, one leg cocked up on a crate.

"Like I said, I found out from someone. I don't know why they'd be lying. I believe them, I really do. Roy's dead. He got run over when he was off his head."

"Who was he then, this Roy? S'pose you can tell us all your secrets now."

Lizzy leaned on a post, her back tired after standing and serving since her lunch break. Her hair felt damp and matted where she'd backcombed it at the front. She wiped her brow with the edge of the apron. "Remember my ex-boyfriend Simon, the junkie that was puking in the gutter a while back?"

"Yeah, how could I forget him?" Dave rolled his eyes.

"Well, Roy was his skanky old mum's boyfriend."

"That figures, dunnit. He didn't look exactly choice himself. Haven't seen him around since, which is just as well because if I had, I would have given him a good kicking." He stamped on the crate, as if it was Simon.

"Dave, he's dead as well. Simon jumped on the tracks on the tube. I suppose you didn't hear about it. I've been so upset for him, I haven't been able to talk about it."

"No, I never knew that. I mean, I read about it, but I didn't know it was him. Fuckin' hell, Lizzy. What the fuck's going on?" Dave rubbed his chin, like he did when he was getting twitchy, or ready for a ruck to kick off. "You ain't messed up in something really bad are you?"

"No, honest I'm not. I left all that behind when I came down to London, and Simon was the only link I had to back home. Now I know Roy's gone, I've nothing to worry about. Really, I haven't." She didn't look him in the eye.

A customer appeared, a middle-aged lady who always came to Lizzy and never to anyone else. She bought some strawberries and a bunch of bananas and tried to chat like she usually did, but Lizzy was distracted. Dave stared at her while she was serving, and it was unnerving. He was biting his top lip with one of his pointy teeth. Eventually, he jangled the keys to his van and went to move off. "You sure it's all sorted, Lizzy?"

"Yeah. I'm sure." Lizzy gave him a wave as he drove away. She worried that he thought she was bad news. It was good to have Dave on her side and she didn't want that to ever change.

There was that light glinting again. She screwed up her eyes and looked up at the window overhead, convinced it had come from the same place as earlier. There was a flash of metal and a hand, she was sure of it. Someone was up there, looking through binoculars or taking photos. Weird. After serving a couple more customers on automatic pilot, she waved at Nat, who was having a break and rubbing her ankles. She knew how Nat felt. Flip-flops weren't the best for being on your feet all day, not even the good ones they'd found for half price down Carnaby Street. Still, they were better than sweaty DM boots when it was hot. Nat opened her mouth and hung out her tongue, her way of saying "I'm knackered."

The beam of light had gone now, and Lizzy looked up just in time to see the shadow of a person come away from the window across the street. If she didn't know Roy was dead, she might have been paranoid it was him. But if it wasn't him, then who was it? Oliver? She turned her attention to a young guy in a knitted beanie, who wanted three bananas and a navel orange, all in separate paper bags. Some people were so particular. She gave him what he wanted without saying anything, and took his money with a smile. She was too exhausted to bother arguing.

Then she saw that woman.

She recognized her from around the market or the café, she wasn't sure exactly where. She was short and dumpy, with a funny hairdo and a vacant look. *Glaikit*, Granny Mac would have said. Now she was staring at Lizzy, or it looked that way, from the corner of the street. Lizzy stared back. What the hell did she want? The woman scratched at her face, then turned away, but stood there for a second before eventually plodding back down the road. Jesus, was she watching her as well as the person at the window?

"Boo!" A voice boomed out behind her.

Lizzy jumped and turned, a cold sweat breaking through her top as she instinctively brought up her hands in defense. It was Natalie. "Bloody hell, Nat, you nearly gave me a heart attack," she said, and clapped her hands down on her thighs. "I was freaked out by a weirdo staring at me. Did you see her?"

"No. Who was it?"

"I don't know but I think I've seen her before. She was just standing there, like a freak. See that window up there?" She pointed. "I thought I saw someone standing there with some binoculars or a camera earlier. I think we're being watched."

"Are you sure? Maybe it's the police keeping a look out for Spinner." Nat bit her thumbnail and put one foot on the other calf, like a yoga pose. "Shit, my ankles are killing me."

"Maybe you're right about the police. It's making me nervous though." Lizzy frowned and absently sifted through the coins in the pocket of her apron. "Maybe you should wear your trainers tomorrow, Nat."

"I know, but my feet get all sweaty, it's horrible." She rubbed her ankles again and dusted off the mark her foot had left on her leg.

"I'd better get back to the stall, now I've done what I came to do and scared the shit out of you."

"Yeah, thanks for that. See you later." Lizzy tried to act like she didn't care, but she did. She had goosebumps on her arms even though it was boiling. Something wasn't right. The police wouldn't have time to watch for Spinner like that, and there was no way that stump of a woman was anything to do with the law. Maybe it was Spinner himself up there, planning his next move.

Think. The market, all the people, the heat and the dusty buildings disappeared from her head, her being, and she was alone in her thoughts. An isolated bubble. There was Oliver in the picture now. His serious, angular face started as a pinprick in the distance, gradually zooming in towards her. She could see the trickle of blood oozing down the side of his face. He'd told her Roy was dead, that he would look out for her because her mum had asked him to. It wasn't the kind of thing a normal person would do: follow a teenage girl down to London to watch out for her, just because her mum had been kind. He was creepy. That woman was creepy. Nothing was adding up.

Had you been so desperate for company you decided that he was attractive? It doesn't make any sense, Mum. He's not bad looking for an old guy, but Oliver has an edge to him, maybe even insanity. He's looking out for me, and it must be because you asked him to, otherwise why would he bother? But I'm nothing to him. I'm just another girl.

"You got change for a tenner?"

Lizzy blinked and the bubble burst. She was back in the market again and one of the traders, Neil, was standing in front of her brandishing a grubby ten-pound note. He was nineteen or so, and acted like he fancied her, but she'd never be interested in someone like him. He wasn't going anywhere in life. Neil had dirty fingernails and greasy hair and wore battered white trainers all the time, not the cool ones but some skanky high-street brand.

"I'll have a look," she said, "hang on, Neil." She delved into her apron pocket and pulled out two fives. "There you go, your luck's in."

"Cheers, Lizzy." He grabbed them and put the tenner in her hand, a little too slowly. "What you doing after work today?"

178

"What? Uh . . . I dunno." She turned away to serve a customer, and when she'd finished she kept her back to him as she collected more apples from a crate. Eventually, Neil went back to his stall and she didn't have to pretend he wasn't there anymore.

After, she felt bad about ignoring him. For years she'd been invisible to a lot of people. When she was living on the street, grimy and tired, most of the time folk would look through her like she didn't count. If someone had looked her in the eye they would have seen a heart and feelings, a real person. A person who needed to be lifted from the shadows, looked after, and loved.

TWENTY-FIVE

Oliver holds back

I dream of killing you. I ache to protect you. The control I have, the intense feelings of power I hold over you, Lizzy, and of myself, are all-consuming now. Lately I've been watching you for hours at a time from the room above the market, my observatory. Today you had tiny beads of sweat adorning your neckline and a black smudge across the corner of your left eye. I began to think again, rather fondly, of your late mother. Some of your mannerisms remind me of her. The way you rub your fingers together and not your palms, is a habit you've acquired, quite unwittingly, from your mother's genes. You also blink twice in succession when you've finished speaking, and when I noticed that, it brought back a distinct memory of the dinner I had with Lauren, your mother, when I had started to seduce her.

I'd bought a decrepit stone cottage in that sleepy small town in the Scottish Highlands, and quickly found my first target in your mother. Dalbegie was full of victims, but Lauren was "a certain age" as they say, divorced and desperate, and an easy seduction. I remember I had been proud of myself because in the space of a few minutes of banal conversation on our date, I had established a no-ties family, a reason for being in Dalbegie, and the perception that I'd previously led a normal married life that had dissolved through no fault of my own. I'd been expecting her to ask me what I did for a living, and had rehearsed my answer. I told her that I was a freelance writer, working from home for knowledge-based web sites. She'd accepted this readily.

"*No romantic novels, then?*"

"*I'm afraid not. But I could give it a go in my spare time.*"

"*Maybe not, eh. But I get why you stay in your house so much. You'll be concentrating on all that writing.*"

"*Yes, yes, I need a lot of quiet. Sorry if I seemed a little reclusive at first.*"

"*No, away with you. Of course not.*"

Blink, blink. There it was.

I didn't take her that night, as I'd wanted to wait until the next time. I had to scrub myself in a scalding shower when I got home, scraping my body over and over until the thoughts and wants left the surface of me, and the inside of me. My scalp bled; my heart ached.

This is no different. After each day of watching you, I have to cleanse so that I can start fresh the next time, with new insights and perceptions. Sometimes my wounds open and my thoughts let themselves out, a release. It makes the waiting easier, as the outward flow calms the fire of desire.

All those years ago, it would have been impossible to predict the outcome of my first abduction in Dalbegie. After only a few weeks of easy flirtation, your mother entered my domain of her own will and suffered the consequences. I always liked to think she had done it to herself. The eighteenth subject of my online forum, Lauren satisfied a yearning of both my own and my subscribers to watch slow suffering. However, before long I battled an increasing desire to take you as well. A mother-daughter combination wasn't something I'd had the good fortune to make happen before, and the opportunity made me ache. It was only the danger of being caught by acting so quickly after the first disappearance that prevented me from going ahead.

Your mother died in my cellar. I starved her of food and water until she dried up like a leather bag and folded into oblivion. The length of time it took, her ongoing reactions and periods of panic versus acceptance, were fairly normal. She was an average subject, nothing to shout about, but she did keep us all captivated nonetheless.

Once I had got rid of her remains and the few personal belongings that Lauren had with her on the night of her seduction, my mind began to turn to you. However, something happened to my conscience, and my will, that was quite unexpected. In watching you over the following months, I enjoyed the ongoing repercussions of my previous abduction. The effects resounded throughout the town for much longer than it would have in a city and I enjoyed listening to the talk and theories about what had happened. Of course, people were suspicious of me, the loner and newcomer, but I left no trail, and there was a string of other suspects in my favour. The abusive ex-husband was the main one, taking the focus away from me.

I was left to observe you as you degenerated from a sweet twelve-year-old schoolgirl to an angry, forgotten teenager, taken advantage of by the scum of that oppressive town. You found solace in Simon, a bright lad from the wrong family, and as I began to despise them, the seed of protectiveness I felt for you grew.

And now here I am watching you at work in much the same way that I used to watch your mother in the newsagents. I do like the idea of this loop, Lizzy. I sometimes wonder if you'll ever work out that I killed your mother, and if you do, whether I will enjoy the feeling—or despise knowing that you hate me. But I can't worry about things that may not happen. You have the face of innocence and the heart of a much stronger woman and so it is not easy to predict your reactions.

There is one more thing that may be standing in our way. First Roy, then Simon, and now someone else.

Today I caught a glimpse of one of the members of my Circle in close proximity to the market. Helen has been a long-standing supporter of my ventures and we even worked together as partners many years ago. However, this does not mean I trust her. It was definitely her, standing on the corner, with her unmistakable bowl haircut and worn, flat shoes. My binoculars rested on her eyes. They were fixed on something. Was she staring at you, Lizzy? Did you feel her hateful eyes on you? I think you did. I felt anger rise to the surface, a growing hatred of this woman. Did she think she could take what's mine out from under my nose? Preposterous.

I put away my binoculars and made for the stairs but by the time I arrived outside, she had gone. I ran south towards Carnaby Street, but I had picked the wrong direction. I kicked a phone booth and swore shamelessly before giving up and coming home. Let me assure you, it's no coincidence that Helen has discovered you. Such a thing as random chance doesn't exist. She will have seen me looking, then followed me to the market, ideas forming in her head. She's been my follower for years, you see. Helen is nothing but a mutt sniffing around my ankles because she can't act for herself. Now she wants what I want, and thinks she can somehow get in on the act now that I've dismissed The Circle. She'll soon find out that I don't play nicely when I'm challenged. Don't worry, Lizzy, I have you covered.

TWENTY-SIX

The Twins Unite

He'd been to the house again, but still there was no answer. Steve was sure he'd seen someone in the top flat, same as last time, but they weren't coming to the door for some reason. Something told him that it was her, his sister, although he couldn't be sure of anything. It was just a feeling he got.

He shifted the gear lever and put his foot down. He was pretty much finished on the job site for today, him and Billy on the Cats for the whole afternoon, digging rubble and moving it up to the far end of the site. It seemed like a never-ending job, although seeing the pile they'd made at the end of each day felt really good. Billy had been brilliant, a true pal away from home, even if he was a Weegie. Folk from Glasgow weren't so bad when you got to know them, he thought to himself. They'd been regularly going for a couple of pints after work, sometimes with some of the other guys, then getting a burger or a slice of pizza for a quid on the way home. They'd watch a bit of telly with whoever was around in the house until they'd all finally fall into their beds, knackered from work and the beer and the sun. It was getting hot now, and Steve had a pink line running across the tops of his arms where his T-shirt sleeves ended. The other guys had been taking the piss out of his Scottish skin, turning from blue to white to pink. *Very bloody funny.*

He turned the engine off and leaned out the window. "Is that us?"

"Aye," shouted Billy. He motioned with his hand that he'd like a drink.

Steve gave him the thumbs up. He could murder a pint. He jumped down, and brushed off some of the dust on his trouser legs and on the hairs on his arms. Sometimes it felt like he'd never shake the stuff, even after a hundred hot showers. It was ingrained in the creases of his skin, stuck to every follicle after working on the site for a few weeks.

"Let's go, Billy-boy," he called out to his pal.

"We've to pick up our pay packets, don't forget," Billy patted his trouser pockets, feeling for his cigarettes. He shook one out and stuck it behind his ear, like he always did for the walk to the pub.

The two of them visited the foreman and got their wages, regulars on shift now and getting paid by the week and not just day to day, hand to mouth. Steve was putting a fair bit aside, saving up for when he went back home. He'd been thinking about Helen, about the strange flat, all through the afternoon while he was working in the pit. That was one thing about working the Cat, it gave a man a lot of thinking time. He'd made up his mind to ask Billy for some help.

"I was wondering if you'd give me a hand with something and I'll buy you a pint after."

Billy lit his cigarette and sucked hard. "What is it, Steve lad? Will it take long? I've a fuckin' thirst on, you know?"

"No, shouldn't take too long. Maybe an hour."

"An hour, eh? This had better be good and involve alcohol or girls or both."

"The booze will come later. It's about a girl, my twin sister actually. I've never met her, and I think I have her address. She won't answer the door, though."

"How've you never met her?"

"Long story, Billy-boy, I'll fill you in on the way. Will you come and help me get her out? When she finds out who I am, I don't know how she's going to be, you know?"

"Sounds interesting. I'm in."

The two of them walked to the tube station, Billy sucking on his cigarette, Steve trying to think of a strategy, but failing. He'd just have to see what happened, which was usually what he did in life. That way, things always went to plan.

The two of them looked up at the dirty bay window. Billy blew out the last of his third cigarette and stubbed it out on the pavement. "Jesus, is this it? Makes the fuckin' schemes look quite posh, eh?"

"This is it. I'll ring the bell and you keep looking up there, see if anything moves." Steve went to the front door, while Billy stayed by the gate. He rang, keeping his thumb on the buzzer for a few seconds, not really expecting anyone to come. He was more interested in what his pal might be able to see.

The door clicked after only a couple of seconds. It was opening, slow, and Steve felt his heart in his chest. *Oh Christ, was it her?*

"Oh, it's you again. I wondered what the racket was. You still looking for your sister, darlin'?" It was the older woman, the one lived in the flat on the ground floor.

"Sorry if I scared you," he said, stepping back.

"Nothing scares me, love, I've got a gun in there and I know how to use it an' all." She came out onto the front step, legs astride, and regarded the two men. "Any funny business and I'll shoot you in the kneecaps."

Billy laughed. "We'll bear that in mind."

"Her up there, who you've been looking for, she's been going out a lot more recently. She's out even now; I saw her go. She's looking a lot better an' all, less grubby."

"Charming." Steve ripped a page out of his notebook and scribbled his details on it. "If you see her, would you mind and give her this?" He offered it to the woman.

"Give it her yourself," she said, arms by her sides.

"Well, is there a place where her post goes?" Steve folded it in half.

"Yes, but what I mean is, you can give it her right now, 'cos she's coming up the street. I can see her funny little walk."

Fuck. He felt the cold again, travelling down from his heart into the pit of his stomach. It was her, and she was coming. He looked at Billy, who knew the full story now. He was sucking in his breath, pulling out another cigarette as if he was nervous. Shite, if Billy was nervous, it was a bad sign. He didn't know what to do with himself, and this old bag wasn't moving, obviously wanting to see all the action. He settled for walking out onto the pavement, away from the house a few strides. That way it would be less intimidating for Helen, and the nosy woman wouldn't hear so much from a distance.

She was taking her time getting down the road. She did have a funny walk, that woman was right. Steve could see that she'd cottoned on they were waiting for her; she was slowing down and nearly stopped a couple of times. If it really was her, his sister, she was a lot shorter than him, with brown hair and dumpy wee legs. They didn't look much like twins, from a distance anyway.

As she got nearer, he strained to see the details of her face, whether she had the same nose as him, a mole on her right cheek. That would be amazing. She was wearing too many clothes for this heat, socks and shoes and long sleeves. Soon she was just a few feet away.

"You Helen Stinson?" He tried to smile.

"Yes." She stopped walking and turned to face him.

"I'm Steve Stinson. Your brother from Edinburgh. This here is my pal Billy. I've been trying to get hold of you for a wee while. Is there somewhere we can talk?"

"My brother?" She looked confused, scratched at her forehead. Steve noticed her nails were bitten down to the quick. She did have a mole, but it was on the left side of her face, the opposite of his. It was hairy.

The woman at the front door shouted over. "He says he's your brother, darlin'. He's been here knocking on the door, god knows how many times before. Is he your brother, then?"

Helen ignored her, didn't even look over. She kept very still, regarding Steve's face. He felt conscious of his beaten-up jacket, and the dirty boots she was looking at.

"We're twins, believe it or not," Steve said and it sounded dead weird coming out of his mouth. "I've been to both your foster parents, trying to find you, one in Fife and one here in London. I said I'd bring you home to meet your real ma. I promised her. She's no' very well just now." He was blethering on, needed to slow down a bit. Hell, what must she be thinking? Two dodgy Scottish guys turning up on her doorstep.

She frowned. "I didn't know I had a brother."

"I never knew I had a sister, either, until recently. I only just heard about you. Ma was forced to give you up when we were born. She never wanted to, and always cried on our birthday and I never knew why. She's desperate to see you."

"Right."

Steve waited for a minute, but she made no signs of asking them inside, or even moving from the spot she appeared to have been glued to. He realized it was a lot to take in. "I've put my number and my address down for you, and you can call me when you're ready. I'm not saying you have to come back to Edinburgh, but it would be

186

good to at least talk to you properly, when there's no one else around, you know?" He motioned at the woman on the doorstep. "I've no mobile, but there's a phone at the house. I'm usually in at night, after eight." He held out the piece of paper he'd torn out of the notebook and nodded for her to take it.

She nodded her head back, just a fraction, and took the scrap of paper. She held the end of it between her thumb and forefinger as if it was on fire. Still she didn't move.

Steve turned to Billy, who was lighting yet another cigarette and leaning against the front porch near the old woman. They looked like they were plotting something together, both scowling as if they were disapproving. He jerked his head in the direction of the tube station and Billy jumped towards him.

"I'm glad I found you, Helen. Sorry if it's been a shock and that." Steve started to back away, Billy beside him now. "Get in touch, okay?"

They left Helen staring at the piece of paper Steve had given her. She didn't say a word or even look up as they left. The front door slammed shut as the woman from the flat below went back inside, now the show was over. Steve didn't speak himself, until they'd reached the end of the road, when he could no longer feel his sister's eyes on the back of his neck.

"Let's get to fuck down the pub and get blootered."

They went back to their side of town and straight into the Crown for a well-earned pint. No point going anywhere that wasn't stumbling distance from home. It was packed now, with the after-work crowd, mostly builders and tradesmen with a smattering of girlfriends here and there. Steve put his hand in his pocket and bought the first round. Star was on special, and it was a brain blower. They sat up at the bar where the drinks would come easiest.

"Cheers, Billy, thanks for coming with us, and that." Steve held up his pint and then sipped at it, the cold of it feeling good on his throat.

"Nae probs, any time. Thanks for the drink." Billy downed half of his in one gulp, then lit another cigarette. "Do you think she'll get in touch, then?"

Steve sniffed in the spiral of fresh smoke coming from Billy's cigarette and for the first time in ages felt desperate for a toke. "God knows. She looked like she needed a bit of time to get used to the idea, you know?"

"You could say that again, Stevie-boy. She didn't have a scooby you even existed, might not have even known she was from Edinburgh, the poor lass. Imagine finding out you're from the east coast."

"Fuck off, Weegie-boy."

"Aye, well, it's even worse than being from London."

Steve held up a twenty for the barman and got another couple of pints on their way. He had a thirst on. Helen wasn't quite was he was expecting, but then if he was honest, he never had much of a picture in his mind of what she was going to look like. He'd thought she might be tall and dark like him, but she was the opposite. She did have the mole and his eyes, and the thick eyebrows as well. They'd got them from Ma. It was definitely her, all right, like a squat version of him in the hall of mirrors at the fair.

They drank the next pints fast, talked about football and music, anything but the twin sister situation. Billy got a round in, then Steve got another. His head was spinning now, seeing as he'd not eaten.

"Let's get a kebab and chips," Billy downed the dregs in his glass.

"Aye, let's get going before I eat one of these beer mats." Steve nodded thanks at the barman, who was flexing his muscles while pretending to clean some glasses. He stood up and held onto a stool for a second while he steadied himself. Jesus, he was a lightweight.

Billy was already outside, lighting up again. Steve realized then how much he'd changed. He'd resisted his urge to smoke, had no interest in wasting his money on anything stronger, couldn't even drink four pints without getting shit-faced. He was earning proper cash, out doing a good deed for his ma, for himself. His life back in Edinburgh seemed distant all of a sudden, like a mad dream. He went and joined his new friend, a solid and reliable pal who reminded him of Ed sometimes.

"Let's get chili sauce in our faces and away home," said Billy, blowing a smoke ring above his head.

"Too right, I could eat a scabby horse. Can I ask you something, Billy-boy?"

"Aye, what?"

"Did you think my sister was weird? Did she give you the willies?"

"Naw. She'll be all right, when's she's warmed up a bit." Billy looked away, didn't offer anything else on the matter.

Steve wanted to like her, but he wasn't sure yet what he thought. Maybe he just needed to eat. Yeah, that was it.

Shredded lettuce on his chin, white sauce dripping down his hand, Steve had shoveled most of the kebab down his throat and had the chips wrapped in a bag for home. He'd eat them with a sneaky can of Pilsner.

They turned into their road just as Steve put the last bit of pita in his mouth. "Got a key handy, Billy? I've no spare hands just now, I'm covered in shite from the kebab."

"Aye, I've done with mine," Billy said, throwing the screwed-up wrapper on top of a pile of takeaway containers that were filling up a nearby bin. "Hey, is that someone outside the front door?"

There was an outline of a person there. Steve couldn't quite make them out, as the street lamp was a couple of doors down the road from their place and it was making shadows. "Yeah, there is some-one. Maybe Doug or Mike forgot their key."

As they got closer, they realized it wasn't Doug or Mike, but a woman.

"The answer is yes," she was saying. "I want to talk to you."

Steve took a deep breath in. "Helen."

"I made up my mind and came before I changed it." She wasn't smiling but didn't seem agitated either. She was just there, outside the house.

"I've had a few drinks, I'm afraid," he said, "but I'm happy to talk just now if you don't mind the smell of chips and beer."

She didn't answer, just stood there, looking at her hands. Billy opened the door and flew up the stair, mumbling about being tired and wanting his bed. Steve took Helen into the kitchen and pulled out a couple of stools at the breakfast bar. He grabbed two cans from the fridge and offered her one, relieved when she took it and actually opened it. And we're off, he thought. *Here we go.*

TWENTY-SEVEN

Lizzy the Protector

It was just by chance she saw him, the cheap gold of him, gleaming in the early morning sun. It was Spinner. What was he doing around there so early? Lizzy could only see him in outline, but would know him anywhere. The bandy legs in tight jeans, the greased-back hair, always leaning in too close. He had no idea of personal space. He had two hands up on the brick wall of the side street, straddling someone. Who was it? Lizzy was late for work, but couldn't move on knowing he might be trying it on with some poor soul.

She took a few steps closer. He was giving whoever it was a good talking-to. Then she saw the shoes: pink Converse. They were like Nat's.

Shit, it was Nat.

Lizzy ran towards them, shouting. "Nat? Is that you?"

Spinner looked up and revealed Nat's scared face, a flood of tears.

"Get the fuck off her!" Lizzy pushed his arm, punched it, and grabbed her friend. She pulled Natalie away, the two of them staggering backwards. "What's going on? Are you trying to take her away, again? I'll get the police on you!"

He watched them with a smirk on his face, smoothing down his hair. "You think you're something, don't you, Blondie? They can't touch me, I ain't done nothing wrong."

Natalie sobbed. "Mum was in a rush and had to drop me off here this morning. I said it'd be okay. We weren't too far from the market. Then he showed up."

Lizzy stared at Spinner. "It's okay, Nat. You weren't to know this scumbag would crawl out from under a stone. Disgusting creep."

"Hey, watch your mouth, little girl." Spinner came closer.

"I'm onto you. I'll tell Oliver to get rid of you," Lizzy blurted without thinking. She didn't trust Oliver, or even like him very much, but he did say he'd protect her.

"What'd you say?" Spinner took another step forward.

"I'll tell Oliver. Leave Nat alone or you'll be sorry." She kept backing away, pulling at Nat's hand.

Spinner darted forward and grabbed Lizzy by the jaw, then pushed her up against the wall in one fast move. Her throat was being crushed; she couldn't breathe. Natalie screamed. His face was close, sour breath warm on her face. She could smell something else on him, whisky maybe.

He whispered in her ear, the words tickling inside like spiders. "You don't know what the fuck you're talking about. Keep out of what you don't understand."

He released the pressure on her neck, but kept hold of it as she gasped for air. "Let me go you fucking bastard."

"I've got you now, haven't I." He pressed his mouth against hers, his tongue slipping inside, deep.

She tried to push him off, but he was too strong. His tongue was halfway down her throat and she gagged. Natalie was shouting and pulling on him but it was no use.

Lizzy bit down as hard as she could.

He jerked back and roared with the shock of it. Lizzy grabbed Nat's hand and they both ran in the direction of the market.

At the end of the road, they turned into Berwick Street and only then did Lizzy dare to stop and look back. She saw Spinner where they left him, at the opening of the side street. His fists were clenched, his legs spread apart like a gorilla's.

"Is he following us?" Natalie was panting and sweating.

"No, we're okay for now," said Lizzy. "Let's just get to the market to your uncle Keith, and figure out what to do."

Nat bent over to catch her breath, held onto her knees for a moment. "I wish I could remember who took me, what happened. I know it was him but I don't know how to prove it. You okay, Lizzy?"

"Yeah." Lizzy wiped her mouth with her sleeve. "His disgusting slobber's all over me."

They picked up a fast walk, Lizzy glancing behind every so often to make sure Spinner wasn't following. She linked her arm through Nat's. "We'll tell the police what he did, and they'll have to take him in again."

"Yeah, although a fat lot of good it did last time."

"Right enough." Lizzy looked at Nat's face, blue mascara and tear tracks on her red cheeks. "What was he saying to you, anyway? Anything that might give him away?"

"Just some creepy stuff about working for him at night, making good money. He said he knew I wanted it, could tell I would be good at it. He said I was a little whore deep down and I loved it."

"Scumbag."

Nat frowned. "Who's Oliver, then? You said you'd tell him about Spinner, and he got all funny about it. Who were you going on about?"

Shit. Lizzy had forgotten about that. "Just one of the market inspectors. Dave's always going on about how hard he is, and I just panicked and used his name. I think he got so angry because he doesn't like me talking back at him. I don't think it was because of who I was going to tell."

"Oh, right. Yeah, he thinks he's king dong, don't he."

They reached the market, twenty minutes late for the morning set up. Keith and Dave were busy unpacking, shouting and throwing boxes around, obviously agitated. They both stopped dead when they saw the two girls together, and everything went quiet.

Lizzy nudged her friend. "Tell them what happened, Nat."

Uncle Keith dropped a crate on the floor. "What is it? You look like you've been crying. Where's Karen?"

Natalie swallowed. "It was Spinner, he pushed me against a wall when I was walking down from where Mum dropped me off. Then Lizzy saw, and came over and he half strangled her."

"Fuck's sake." Keith kicked one of the posts of his stall and the whole thing wobbled. "I'll kill him."

"Lizzy bit him and got me out of there." Natalie punched the air.

"You did what?" Dave held onto his hair. "Are you mad?"

Lizzy shrugged. "I didn't really have time to think about it. Just needed to get her out of his greasy hands, didn't I?"

Nat picked up some courgettes that had rolled out onto the street from where Keith had dropped the crate. "I'm just going to get to work, if that's okay. Got to get my mind off it."

"If you're sure, darlin'. I'm going to call the police though. They need to get hold of the bastard and do that cunt." Keith started jabbing at his phone.

Lizzy started to help Dave. She was better than him at setting out the fruit, more thorough. His piles always toppled over. Her heart was still beating fast, but the routine calmed her down. Dave kept looking at her and then shaking his head. She could see him out the corner of her eye. It made her feel proud of herself, somehow, even though she knew it had been stupid to try and beat Spinner. She'd seen his type too many times, though, and it had felt good to stand up to him, even when it was just answering him back when he did the market rounds. A couple of regulars came and bought a few things before work, and she served them in automatic mode, their faces blurring, taking money and putting things in bags while she was thinking things through.

The guys decided to stay for the rest of the morning, in case anything kicked off. They'd take it in turns to grab something to eat at lunch, cover each other. Keith wasn't happy about either Lizzy or Nat being on their own, and called Nat's mum to say that Lizzy would be coming home with them both later. Lizzy was pleased, looked forward to a family dinner instead of another plastic hot dog she would have had on her own in the bedsit. It was nice, that the two men were so protective of them, when they would half kill someone else as soon as look at them. Including Spinner, she hoped, when he made his next appearance.

The police turned up and asked both girls a few questions, the usual stuff. They hadn't been able to find Spinner, but would find him, they said. They shouldn't worry. Everyone at the market said they'd look out for him and make the call straightaway if they saw him. There was a special number to phone, which made the whole thing feel important, even scarier. One of the police that came was a young woman, her hair tied up in a ponytail that sat just underneath her hat. Lizzy wondered what kind of home she came from, what made her want to see people right. Was it because she'd seen a lot of bad things or did she come from a good place and wanted to see everyone the same way?

After she'd quizzed her, Lizzy decided to question her back. "How old are you? Have you been in the police long?"

The woman sighed. "Old enough."

"Do you like being a policewoman?"

"Most of the time. Why, are you thinking of training when you get older?" You seem very young to be working here." She pointed at the stall with her thumb and frowned. "You like it here, do you?"

"I'm nearly seventeen." Lizzy had thought that was pretty grown up, but it sounded young, now. "I do like it. But I won't be working on a stall forever."

"Just be careful who you hang out with. But you know that. Good work with saving your friend from that creep." She touched the front of her hat in salute, and went to join her partner.

Lizzy realized that she hadn't really thought about how long she'd be on the stall. It was getting her by, keeping her straight. How could she think about the future, when she could barely make it through the now? She shifted around some apples, hiding the bruises and polishing some of them up. One day maybe she'd be doing something really exciting, like travelling or working with animals, or in one of those stylish advertising places, but this was okay. She looked over at Dave. Good old Banana Dave. This was her life just now, and it was better than what she had before. Folk actually cared about her at this place.

Natalie was tired out, especially after what happened that morning. Lizzy could tell by the look in her eyes and the way she was walking, even though her friend was denying it. They were nearly at Nat's house and they were all looking forward to pizza night.

Karen had been chattering all the way home. "I've got a good film for us to watch, and popcorn, and some of them cheezy things you like, Nat. We don't have to get up for work tomorrow, remember. It'll all be better in the morning, you'll see."

"Yeah right, Nat will be asleep in front of the telly by nine." Lizzy reached over and gave her a hug.

"No I won't. I'm fine." Nat shrugged her off.

"Hope you don't have any nightmares and keep me up all night. Maybe I'll sleep downstairs, like a pet dog."

They got to the house at last and Karen opened the front door for them. She kicked off her boots and reached for her furry slippers on the doormat. "Come on, then. I'll get the pizza in the oven; it'll be ready in fifteen minutes. Come here, you." She grabbed Natalie and held her close.

"I'm all right, Mum, really." Nat looked like she could hardly breathe.

"Can't believe that creep. Hope the police find him. He needs castrating, or put away somewhere." Karen sent her daughter into the house, then grabbed Lizzy and held her close. She whispered, "Well done, you. If it wasn't for you, Nat might have disappeared off again."

Lizzy patted her on the back. "I think he was just trying it on. The police are looking for him properly now, anyway."

"I don't know what we'd do without you, Lizzy." Karen pulled her inside and shut the door behind her. "Good to have the both of you safe at home. Now, let's get some grub going, and put our comfies on."

The house soon began to smell of popcorn and melting cheese. Lizzy shut her eyes and sniffed it all in, sinking into one of the armchairs.

Natalie ran upstairs. "I'll get two pairs of trackie bottoms, one for you, Lizzy."

"That's the girl," Karen called out.

The three of them eventually flocked together in the kitchen, grabbing slices of pizza and Cokes from the fridge. Darren burst through the front door and threw his work boots across the hallway. "I'm starving, who's going to feed me?"

"You're always starving, you are," said Karen.

"Dad, you're honking," said Natalie. "You need a shower."

He gave a mad laugh, and came towards her with his arms outstretched, sweaty armpits for them all to see. Lizzy giggled as Nat backed away, screaming and holding her nose. This was it, right here. What she wanted when she grew up. A family and laughing and being silly all the time.

"I'll have one in a sec, when I've stuffed my face full of pizza," he said, and grabbed a slice. He kissed Karen on the cheek, then turned to Lizzy. "How's my girl, then? I hear you've been a bit of a hero, today. Kicked that bloke Spinner in the nuts, did you? Whatever you did, he deserved it."

"I wish I had done him in the nuts, now."

"Probably too small to find," said Karen.

They all laughed. Then Darren frowned. "I don't think you two should be working the stalls no more. It's too dangerous." He looked at Karen. "I know what your Keith says, you can't wrap them in tissue paper all their lives, but I won't be happy until that creep has been put away."

"No, we like working the stalls, Dad. Uncle Keith and Dave, they look out for us, don't they Lizzy?" Nat was whining, her voice getting high-pitched. "I'm sixteen, now. You can't stop me."

He pulled out a beer from the fridge and sat down at the kitchen table. "You're still a kid; you're my little girl. I won't have some scumbag taking advantage. No, Nat, I'm putting my foot down this time."

Karen poured herself a glass of white wine and added two ice cubes. She took a big gulp. "It's not safe, darlin'. I don't know why we let you go back on the stall in the first place after what happened. It's all my fault, anyway. I was in such a rush this morning I didn't have time to take her all the way to the market. A few yards away, we was, Darren. So close, but not near enough. I feel terrible about it."

"It's not your fault. You didn't know he was there," Lizzy said. She could do with a beer or a cider, but didn't like to say anything. Nat was in a huff now, arms crossed and staring at the floor. It was all right for her, she could find something else to do, get a job in a shop maybe, but it wasn't easy for Lizzy. She didn't have a proper home, no papers or anything. She wondered if they even realized that about her. "I've got to stay on Dave's stall, I've no choice."

Everyone looked at her. Darren spoke, his mouth full of pizza. "You think you can look after yourself, darlin', but you're only sixteen yourself, look at you. Just a little girl, same as Nat. It ain't safe around there. You were lucky this time, but maybe next time you won't be."

She washed down the last mouthful of pizza with a gulp of Coke. "I'm nearly seventeen. It's my birthday soon. And apart from that, I have to work because I need the money. I've no family, don't forget. It's just me."

"Don't you have no one, then? Not even an auntie or a cousin?" Karen asked.

Lizzy was sure Nat would have told her. Maybe it hadn't registered with her. It was too far removed from what most people were used to. She'd have to spell it out for them. "I've some family back in Scotland. But no one wanted me there, which is why I left in the first place. My Dad is in Yorkshire, I don't know where exactly. He never wanted me either. My mum's dead. It's just me here in London, trying to make the best of things. I work for cash. I pay my rent on a bedsit. It's not brilliant, but it's a roof and a bed, two things I didn't have when I first moved down here. I was on the street for quite a while. I was basically a street kid."

"Blimey, I didn't realize it was that bad." Darren looked down at the table.

"It's not," she said. "Not now it isn't."

Karen decided things were getting too morose, and so put on a film for them all to "have a laugh." It was *Dirty Dancing*, which Lizzy had never seen, but the photo on the DVD box looked corny and funny. The music started and they all sat on the sofa, the two girls in the middle, a bowl of popcorn on the coffee table.

"Do we have to watch this great big poof?" Darren winked at Lizzy.

"Shut it, you." Karen laughed. "He was a bit of all right, was Patrick Swayze. Not half."

"Actually, you look a bit like him, Dad." Nat threw a piece of popcorn and it landed in his lap.

"Behave," he said. "I'm better looking than him."

"Yeah, and I'm Halle Berry," said Karen.

Natalie leaned into Lizzy. "Mum, can Lizzy stay the whole weekend?"

"'Course she can. You don't even have to ask. You want to stay, do you Lizzy?"

"I think I could just about cope with that," she said, grabbing a big handful of popcorn. "But say if you want me to go home. I wouldn't want to be in the way."

"That'll never happen." Karen leaned back to watch the film, plumped up a cushion and put it on her lap. "You're like one of the family."

Lizzy sat back and touched her throat lightly, felt the tender skin, her thumping pulse, and wondered if she'd be bruised tomorrow. People would think she'd been strangled. She had been, nearly. Spinner's breath was so rank; she could almost taste it, bitter and contaminated with something evil. The food and the fizzy drink were gradually taking the remnants away, but she would never forget how it felt, to be defenseless. Fear had been a part of her life for as long as she could remember, but those few moments of vulnerability, at the mercy of that man, were different. She'd been completely powerless, and she was left wondering if her mum had felt the same when she left this world. It was the most terrible feeling.

She looked over at Nat and hoped she would never get her memory back. It wasn't worth the trauma of it. Surely remembering what happened to her wouldn't bring anything but sadness and fear. They could all do without more of that.

TWENTY-EIGHT

Oliver and The Thames

Spinner, Spinner. Tut, tut, tut. He was threatening you, getting in my way, and I couldn't have it. Helen was one thing, but I would not for one second longer have someone as low as Spinner take any piece of you away from me. It seemed everyone wanted you, and it was making my skin burn.

He was already in my bad books. Mooching around Soho, leaving his rancid trail. He had boasted to me once about "working the market for potentials, being the main man there," and I had never fully trusted his promise that he wouldn't touch you. Admittedly there was a short period when he was sniffing around on my behalf, but since The Circle disbanded, I'd had little use for him.

Let me run through the details of that fateful morning, when he dared to touch what belongs to me. Before breakfast, I wandered down to Old Compton Street, keeping a lookout for his swagger, for I'd vowed to keep an eye on him. The stench of the café bins was already starting to seep into the morning air, the clack of office shoes filling the streets. The working doldrums of London is something I could never think of entering myself. All that false money and self-importance, the revolting rush of everyday life with no end in sight. I didn't pay too much attention to the plastic briefcases, the floral scarves, or worst of all, the suits worn with running shoes, to be changed upon arrival at the office, like in a terrible American movie.

When I got to Charing Cross Road, I saw him. He was coming out of a café, surprisingly early for him, takeaway cup in hand, and staring at that dreadful phone of his, thumb working away. Who could possibly be at the other end of his inane texting or emailing or whatever it is he did with that thing? Who would be interested?

I followed him towards Wardour Street, when he stopped outside the Duke of Wellington and stared like he'd seen something important. It was your young friend being dropped off by her mother. I had to watch from a distance while he pounced on her, and cornered her like a frightened animal. I don't care much about your friend, but it was a foolish move for many reasons, not least because we'd used her in The Audacious already. I didn't want her memory to be jogged by his spongy face, his odious presence.

Then you appeared and things entered a different realm.

I held back, furious, as he laid his greasy hands on you. I didn't want you or your friend to see me, but when he held you by the throat and put his lips against yours, I couldn't help but begin to step forward. But you got away, Lizzy, of your own accord. You were as feisty as ever, pulling your friend away, even using my name as a threat. I was impressed. You escaped, of course you did, and I didn't have to expose myself. I stayed in the shadows, and waited to make sure you were a safe distance away from that lowlife.

I spent the night thinking about his gold embellishments, the tightness of his jeans over his nauseating crotch bulge, and his ego, growing out of control. I drank my usual, The Macallan 12-year-old, from my favourite crystal glass, filtered ice cubes making that pleasing little clink as I made circles with it in my palm, as I pondered what to do with him.

My home in London looks out over the Thames, Lizzy. Sometimes I imagine you here with me, enjoying the view. I'm no entrepreneur, but I've made some wise real estate decisions over the years and although my apartment is a modest one, I can see St. Paul's Cathedral on the other side of the river. I can sit under a heated lamp on my deck and enjoy the feeling of being on top of the city, in rather a godlike position of power. From here, I like to think of you out there somewhere, and that I can swoop down when it takes my fancy, and pick you up. Nothing is in my way. I have two vantage points, and two settings on my inner lens. My home is the wide-angled lookout, where I can survey the bigger picture and make decisions. The flat above the market is the detail-oriented hawk's nest, where I can hone in.

From the big-picture position, I decided what I would do. It was that vulgar so-called kiss that did it—that was the tipping point.

It was the anguish he caused you when he put his hands on you. I resolved that he had to go.

This morning, I waited for him.

It didn't take long for him to "find" me, sipping tea outside one of the street cafés. You're the best person to help me, I told him. The only one who can handle a new project to replace The Circle. He was needed, for the most vital part in my plan. Flattery makes someone like him as malleable as putty, so easy to manipulate and knead into shape. I watched as he puffed out his chest and ruffled his feathers, thrilled with his own importance. Then he came with me down to the South Bank, to the deliciously dark tunnels, the disused skateboard park and the empty gardens at the top of the Festival Theatre. I told him I wanted to show him some new areas for abduction. What he didn't realize was that it was he who would be the victim. Locals are advised not to send children to the far end of the gardens alone. Tourists do not know the gardens are there, because they never look up, only down at their beige clothing and the pecking pigeons at their feet. There are tools, sandbags, mounds of earth. Have you ever wondered why it feels dangerous there? Because, my dear Lizzy, it is.

I've seen to it that his weighted body will never rise to the surface of the Thames. However, each night, as I sip my whisky, I can almost see the shadow of him rippling in the dark waters. And sometimes, to the discerning eye, there is a glint of gold.

TWENTY-NINE
Back to Edinburgh

The smell of the place hit her as soon as she stepped off the train at Waverley Station, so familiar, although she'd never lived in this city for very long. The first time Helen was in Edinburgh, she was fifteen and had just left her foster family in Fife. No one had cared enough to come and see her off. She remembered getting on the train and watching as folk stood and waved at other people in the carriage. No one looked at her.

Edinburgh. Here was the distinctive aroma of hops from the brewery, fresh sea air, and the sound of bagpipes floating over from the end of Waverley Bridge. It was tourist season and leaving the station on foot was like walking onto a film set, the castle towering majestic, and people in tartan milling around. She hadn't realized this was where she was originally from, but it felt like home, now that she was here. It was a strange feeling, nostalgia. Helen hadn't experienced many strong emotions in her life and now her eyes were watering, hot, and a tingling shudder was crawling its way down her back. She stood still, unsure how to deal with it.

Edinburgh was where she first met Oliver.

Steve turned to face her, weighed down with two large bags. Sweat was dripping down his face. "We'll go to Ma's flat first, stay the night, then I'll borrow Ed's car and we'll get ourselves down to Berwick in the morning to see her. How does that sound?"

Helen stopped and looked up at him. He'd been trying to talk to her all the way, but she wasn't exactly a conversationalist. She had tried to pay attention to him occasionally, but could tell he was disappointed with the way she spent most of the journey daydreaming and looking out the window. "Sounds okay," she said.

"We can walk there, if you're okay carrying your bag. I don't think I could carry three of these bastards."

"I'm fine," she said, and adjusted the strap on her rucksack so that it wasn't digging into her chest. It wasn't too heavy because she didn't bring much with her. A few changes of clothes and some basic toiletries would see her through the visit. Her emergency drug supply didn't take up any room either. She didn't intend to stay. Steve said he'd taken two weeks off work, with a view that he might not even need to go back, but she wasn't sure she'd last even that long—until now. This was a good city.

Steve led the way down Princes Street towards Leith Walk. "There's some fancy shops on this street. Nothing much for a guy like me in them, mind. And back over there is the Scott Monument. I'll take you up to the Castle and the Royal Mile another time. It's no' far to get to Ma's place, I promise. Are you thirsty? We could stop at an offy on the way."

She glanced at his face, shining with excitement. Of course he would assume that she'd never been here before. *Did he ever stop talking?* She shrugged and concentrated on walking without banging into the crowds. As soon as they were off Princes Street, there were fewer people and she felt a little more comfortable. Chip shops and workshops and boutique hotels. A seagull flew overhead in the blue sky. It wasn't meant to be like this. She didn't want to like it so much.

"Are you hungry? I'm going to get a few cans of beer and maybe a poke of chips to take back. I've been missing the salt 'n' soss like nobody's business." Steve stopped outside the off-license.

She pulled out her wallet, small and worn, and took out a ten-pound note. "I'll wait here with the bags. Can you get me however many beers that will buy?"

He took the money and dumped his bags at her feet. "Aye, I'll get you a six-pack and you'll have change for chips in the bargain."

While he was gone, Helen watched some girls on the other side of the road, on their way out somewhere, high-heeled shoes and no tights, even though it wasn't exactly hot. The Edinburgh sea wind never seemed to completely disappear, no matter what time of year it was, but still the girls were in their flimsy summer togs. They all piled into the pub, shouting and laughing, not seeming to have a worry about anything. Was it better to be like that in life, or was oblivion danger-ous? It hadn't been a good way to be for the woman on the Heath, she thought. The door of the pub shut and the shouting stopped ringing in her ears. She looked down Leith Walk, in the direction of the Docks, and Casselbank Street. There was a time when she was closer to her brother, and her mother, than any of them could have realized.

She was doing community service at the Edinburgh Cat Rescue

Society. It was ten years since she was last in Scotland and Helen had mixed feelings about being back. She'd returned out of curiosity, but wished she hadn't bothered after being caught robbing in Jenners. It was a stupid game she'd played, and now she was paying for it with a month's worth of volunteer work at that stinking cesspit of cat feces. It was enough to send anyone running back to London, where it was easier to get lost in the crowds, to hide.

She had to clean the cages each morning, sweep out the play area, and wipe off any kittens that had been sick on themselves, or worse. The stench was unbearable and she wore a bandana over her nose in an attempt to lessen the reek. There was a calendar on the office wall, and each day she marked a tiny "x" on the date as a personal count-down. There were volunteers there who'd been working at the centre for years. What kind of a person did that by choice?

On the third day she was assigned a working partner, a tall, well-spoken man roughly her own age. Everything changed. At first he seemed green around the gills, a naïve public-school type, but as they got to know each other, she realized that he might just be the only person she had ever met who yearned for the same things she did. Oliver had a charismatic smile for all to see, but he also had a dangerous glint in his eye that not everyone would notice. Helen saw it straightaway, and it lit up her heart. She wanted to ask him if he had taken a life, but decided to hold back until the time was right. The waiting hurt, because she knew what he was.

Oliver was one of her.

"Helen?" Steve was in front of her, leaning towards her face, frowning. "Are you okay? I've been calling your name."

Her eyes focussed on him. She must have been away again. "Yes, I'm fine. Let's go."

As they walked up the street, Steve kept sneaking sideways looks at her, always trying to get a read on her. She could see him doing it out the corner of her eye. It was so obvious. She wondered what he was looking for, if he was trying to find some glimmer of warmth inside her. Whatever it was, it wouldn't be there. He shouldn't bother.

They stopped off at the chippy and Steve bought two bags of grease, all wrapped up for when they got to the flat. The smell of them was good, there was no denying it, and she realized that she hadn't eaten since first thing that morning. The dull ache in her gut she'd put down to tension, but perhaps it was just hunger after all.

They turned off Leith Walk, navigated two or three cobbled streets and eventually got to the tenement. Steve pushed the main door open to reveal a large stone staircase winding up four floors. "We're all the way to the top," he said, blowing out his breath. "You forget how high it is, Jesus."

She followed closely behind, counting the steps for distraction. Her panting echoed down the stairwell, making it sound harder work than it really was. Steve was carrying his heavy load on his back, his hands full with the chips and the plastic bag full of cans from the offy. It would be so easy for her to pull him backwards and watch him bounce down onto the cold stone floor. A dark trickle of blood would start from his skull, gradually forming a pool around him.

The lost twin returns back home, as the other one goes to heaven.

"This is it. I'll just get my key out and we can have a sit down. Put the telly on, and crack one open." Steve put the plastic bag down and fumbled around in his jeans pocket.

He unlocked the door. Helen found that lump in her throat again, and swallowed it down. Why was it there? Here was Mother's home, open to them both for the very first time. She followed Steve inside and put her things in the hallway by the door. There was a faint smell of lingering cigarette smoke, bleach, and cheap perfume. The carpet had a pattern on it, swirling and faded. In the living room was a vase full of fake flowers sitting on top of a crumb-covered coffee table. Steve motioned for her to sit in one of the armchairs facing the telly, and handed her a can of beer. He grabbed the remote control, and turned on a documentary channel. Helen drank the beer and picked at the chips, noticing how Steve looked at home in this place, his shoes kicked off and his body moulded perfectly into the shiny fabric of the chair. She let her eyes glaze and retreated back into the world she knew best: the one inside her head.

At the end of their first week together, Oliver showed a strong interest in her. Helen could sense his admiration and respect after they'd spent only a few hours talking during lunch breaks, cigarette breaks, or periods when they could no longer clean without gagging. The way he looked at her was intense and she knew he wanted to ask her to partner with him in something delectably bad. She wanted it. They skirted around their desires, making references, hints and innuendos, none of them sexual but all of them erotic in their own way. It was Friday and so they would not see each other at work again until after the weekend. To Helen, it seemed like a long stretch and she didn't want to let him go.

They signed out and Helen marked her usual "x" on the calendar. Oliver brushed off his trousers and changed out of his work boots and into some leather shoes. They seemed out of place somehow, like they belonged to someone else, perhaps an older person. She slipped on her runners and they left together, the icy air of Casselbank Street welcome and refreshing after another day of stench and graft.

She walked slowly, not wanting to go too far ahead or in a different direction to him. There was a string between them, taut and straight, and she could feel the tension of it. She waited for him to make the first move.

"Where to now?" He stretched out his arms above his head, pretending to be nonchalant. He made a big show of the stretching.

"I need to get home for a shower first off," she said. "Then I'm not sure."

"I've no fixed plans but I was thinking of taking a drive later on. I'm picking up a hire car." He glanced at her, and she saw that glint flashing her way.

"Where will you go, do you think?"

"Around and about. It's supposed to rain hard tonight, and it'll be getting dark by the time I get going. They'll be plenty of folk that would love to get a lift home with that sort of weather."

She smiled. "No one in their right mind would get in a car with a strange man."

"No, that's true," he said. "But they might if there was a woman in there too."

"True enough." She paused. Let him want; let him wait. Eventually she spoke. "I tell you what. I will be that woman."

And so their partnership began. They were friends of sorts, working with the same purpose. At first, Helen was the apprentice and he the teacher. She helped him to ensnare the victims and he acted while she looked on. She enjoyed watching, but it wasn't long before she completed some masterful performances of her own. It was just the beginning.

Steve threw a screwed-up chip paper on the table, and the crackle gave her a start. Helen wished for tomorrow, so she could see her mother and get it over with. She was curious, to see herself in another woman's eyes, but yearned to get back to London. That was where Oliver's girl was, and she was going to take her. It might make him realize her potential, that he didn't have power over everyone like he thought. She wasn't a follower, but a partner, just as potent and formidable as him. Perhaps they would walk side by side once more, and the world would have to watch out.

THIRTY

Back to D

Steve banged on Ed's bedroom window. Ed lived in a ground-floor flat and so it was usually easy to get him up. He'd no doubt his pal would still be sleeping. Even when he was working, he left it to the last second to get up, the lazy sod. The curtains were heavy and dou-ble-lined, and he couldn't see inside, so Steve put his ear to the glass and listened. He thought he heard some kind of thud.

The curtains opened a bit and Ed's baggy face glared out. Steve held up a hand. "It's me, let me in," he shouted.

Ed opened his front door, rubbing the sleep out of his eyes and scratching his arse simultaneously. "What the fuck time is it? What you doing here? Where've you been, Stevie-boy?"

Steve pushed past him. "Time to get up, son. I'll put the kettle on. I've got a fair bit to tell you. Is the missus about?"

"No, she went off to work about an hour ago. It's my day off." Ed went back into his bedroom and reappeared wearing a beanie and a sweatshirt over the top of his jammies. "Bloody freezing the morn."

Steve switched on the kettle and rummaged in the bread bin. There were crumbs and clods of butter all around the counter. "Did you miss me, then? How's it all going? Will I make some toast?"

Ed sat at the kitchen table, yawning. "Like fuck did I miss you. Well, maybe just a bit. You're looking good, there, Stevie-boy, a bit of a tan going on there. Did you put on some weight?"

"Aye, maybe. I've been working outside mostly, on a site in Lon-don for a good few weeks, so I got the sun a bit. Good money. I found my sister Ed; I bloody found her. She's at Ma's just now, and we're going to get ourselves down to Berwick, to Auntie Mary's, to see them both. Can I borrow your car, pal? Just for the night? We'll bring it back tomorrow night. What do you reckon? I don't think I can face another train journey."

"Have you been in touch with your ma a lot?" Ed grabbed some juice out the fridge and drank it straight from the carton. Some of it slopped onto his chest.

"Aye, a bit. She fell and hurt herself, apparently. Auntie Mary said some guy took her purse and when he did a runner, he pushed her over. I bet you it was D. I'm going to sort it all out. I've got his cash and more, and I'm clean, Ed. Totally clean. I'll probably bring Ma back tomorrow. She'll want to be home, I should think."

Ed sighed. "You don't know, do you?"

"Know what?" Steve turned around, the toaster popping behind him.

"She didn't just take a fall. D beat her up, good and proper. She was in a state. She called me and I got Jake and we helped her get herself together. She's been recovering down at Mary's place, mentally as well as physically, if you know what I'm saying."

"Fuck." Steve held onto the sides of his head and slumped to the floor. "Fuckin' bastard. I'm going to get him."

"Don't do anything stupid. He's dangerous and he'll fuckin' kill you now, if you try anything."

"She's my ma. She's my fuckin' ma. How dare he?" Steve was shouting, his hands shaking, his face hot with anger.

Clearly he had some business to attend to before he went and got Ma back. He didn't care what Ed said. This was something he had to do. No one hurt his ma that bad and got away with it. He left the toast, the boiled kettle steaming, and Ed looking nervous as he ran from the flat.

This is war.

Steve clenched his fists, his eyes burning as he told his sister the details, tripping over his own words. "Auntie Mary told me that some guy had pushed Ma over, that she'd fallen down the stair. And I knew it was D, I just knew it. Ma obviously hadn't told her the full story, so Auntie Mary thought it was just some chancer, but of course it was fuckin' D. And now I've heard that he beat her up, completely had her. An old woman. What the fuck? How low can the man go? I can't fuckin' believe it. Although if I'm being honest, I can fuckin' believe it. I knew it, deep down. And that pisses me off even more, that I wasn't here to protect her. What kind of man am I?"

Helen looked deep in thought, her brow creased up and her stare intense, as Steve paced up and down the living room in front of her. She hadn't said much since they travelled to Edinburgh on the train together, but now she seemed almost fired up. She hit the arm of the chair with her fist. "Tell me when all of this first started. How D got on your back in the first place."

Her accent was all mixed up. It was London with a bit of Scottish and something else that he couldn't quite place. She was his sister, his family, and he'd have to tell her the full story. Too bad she'd find out he was a druggie, a waster, for years after his divorce, and a couple before that as well. He was better now, and that was the main thing. She'd get him warts and all, and have to deal with it. Christ knows she wasn't exactly perfect herself, from what he'd heard.

He took a deep breath, leaned forward on the back of the sofa. "D was my dealer. I got my drugs off him. Sometimes I didn't have the money and he'd let me off until payday. And the money I owed him seemed to pile up."

While he told her everything, he walked around the room; he couldn't bear to sit down and have her looking into him. She nodded occasionally; sometimes she'd look out the window. But even when she was distant, he knew she was listening, in her own funny way. When he finally stopped talking, he was exhausted. It felt strange, just the two of them in this flat, and no Ma here to seal them together. Helen the way she was.

"Right, then. So you want to get him back, this D?" She stood up.

"Too right. He's gone too far. I won't be stopped, either. He's going to pay for what he's done and I'm not going to wait a minute longer. I'm sorry if it puts off the trip to North Berwick. Shite, I forgot to get the car keys off Ed, I was that mad. We'll have to get the train later."

"I'm not going to stop you," she said. "I'm going to help you. But first we're going to need a few things."

They went to the Porty but there was no D; in fact there was nothing much happening in there at all. A couple of older guys were playing a game of checkers in the corner, sipping at their beers like only the retired can do. Nowhere much to go and all the time in the world. It was too early for anything to be happening.

Steve was glad to see Evelyn was working the afternoon shift. If anyone had seen D, it would be her. She was sitting behind the bar, reading a book, probably one of those rude ones.

"What you having there, Stevie-boy?" she asked, like he'd never left. She turned a page, then finally looked up at him.

"All right there, E?" he said. "I'm not in for a drink just now, just looking for D. You seen him?"

"No, I've not seen that man for a couple of days, but that's not to say he won't be in for a pint later the night. Folk have been talking about where you'd got to, yourself. And here you are, with a tan." She smiled, bright red lipstick cracking on her lips.

"Aye, salmon pink anyway. I got myself some work in London, been earning some proper cash, you know?"

"Oh, very good. Good for you, son." Evelyn kept looking between Steve and Helen, obviously wondering who he'd got with him.

Helen didn't open her mouth, as usual. Steve wondered if she even thought about talking or if she kept quiet on purpose. "So you've no idea where I might find D?"

"You sure you want to find him, Stevie-boy? Last time you were both in here, it didn't look like you were exactly pals."

"We're not. I owe him something. Might go down by the water, see if he's hanging about in any of the doorways."

"As good a bet as any, I suppose. If he's anywhere, it'll be under a fuckin' stone somewhere, with all the other grubs."

As they left the pub, Steve looked back and put Evelyn out of her misery, mouthing the words: "She's my sister."

Evelyn nodded in an exaggerated way, like she was saying *thanks for the information*. Steve wondered how long it would take for the whole of Leith to know he'd got his sister with him. And that she was a might peculiar. Well, he couldn't help that now, could he? It wasn't as if everyone else was exactly normal, anyway. This place was full of weird folk.

They were outside and on their way. He wasn't scared.

"Right then, let's get down to the water. I reckon our friend will be down there selling to the crack addicts, the ones who can't wait 'til it's dark to get a fix. There's a network of backstreets down there, most of them the police don't bother with if they know what's good for them. It'd be like trying to empty the world of ants." He led the way, didn't expect an answer from Helen and didn't get one. She had insisted on carrying all the stuff she'd bought earlier in her rucksack, and it was dead heavy; he'd felt the weight of the bag when they left the hardware shop.

She had picked up some funny things and wouldn't tell him why. Some three-inch nails, some tape, a wee clamp thing. Perhaps she was thinking of pulling D's toenails out, he chuckled to himself, aye right, like he'd sit still and let her do it. He shouldn't have agreed to have Helen along, but she'd seemed so keen on helping him he didn't have the heart to say no. Let her see for herself what D was like. He had everything he needed. The flick knife from out of Ma's secret cabinet drawer, sharp as a Samurai sword, was heavy in the front pocket of his jeans. He'd only used it once before. It could slice someone's throat, clean and deep, in a second. He'd never used it to kill someone, just to scare them, and once, to cut someone's hand to teach them a lesson.

They crossed Constitution Street and made their way down Tolbooth Wynd to the streets around the other side of The Raj. Expensive loft apartments and wine bars and a sculpture studio, mixed in with a couple of rank prostitutes to remind folk of the darker side of Leith. You can dress up a place, but you'll never get rid of its heart. Steve had seen plenty bad times down here, more than he wanted to remember. Helen was looking straight ahead, not really seeming to take any of it in. What was she thinking about?

As they turned down Henderson, the wind brought the smell of fish from The Shore, from restaurants and fishing boats both. Steve heard some heavy footsteps somewhere behind and he swivelled round on his heels to see a mess of hair and those boots. Turned out they didn't need to look too hard for D. He was coming up behind them, on his way somewhere, or on his way back from something, and he didn't look exactly happy.

Steve put his hand on Helen's shoulder and whispered. "It's him, D, he's right there."

She tensed, brushed off his hand. "There's an alley over the other side of the street. Let's aim for that."

Steve glanced over to the place she was talking about. It was a good twenty yards away. How was she thinking of getting him over there?

There was no one else around just now, just some folk in the bar across the street "lunching." She obviously didn't have a clue. "Just leave this to me. I'm going to knife him and run. Get behind me."

"I'm in this," she said. That was all. She stood back against the brick wall, hands in her coat pockets, her face set, blank and absent.

This was between him and D. He was getting closer, and now he'd seen Steve. He braced himself, turned to face his opponent; his legs wide and anchored to the ground, his arms folded. He could feel the end of the knife digging into his leg. He could open it fast, slice it across flesh even faster. He was going to get the bastard.

"The mighty fuckin' roadrunner returns, eh?" D sniggered as he slowed down to a cocky stroll.

"I was down in London, making some real money, so's I could pay you back." Steve stayed where he was, blocking the pavement. "Turns out while I was away, you visited my ma."

"So?" D was only a couple of feet away. Lunging distance.

"So you put her in hospital. An old lady. Proud of it, are you? What kind of fuckin' man are you? I knew you were scum, but I didn't realize you were a piece of shite stuck to the bottom of the scum. The worst." Steve put his hand in his pocket, wrapped his fingers around the knife. He was ready.

"Be careful, big man. You still owe me." D edged closer, his fists clenched. "Don't make me more fucked off than I am already. I've had enough today. Have you not learned anything from all this? I'll tell you a secret: don't mess with D." He looked over at Helen, who was still leaning against the wall, looking quite calm now. "Who's the fuckin' skank over there? Your pimp?" He laughed wildly, his head thrown back, hair bouncing on his forehead.

It all happened before Steve knew it had started. He pulled out the knife, flicked it open. It seemed as good a time as any to use it, while D was baring his throat like that. Before he could blink, Helen had jabbed something in D's leg, wrapped duct tape around his wrists behind his back and was marching him towards the alley. D's head was dropping, his eyes rolling back. "Take his other arm," she said, "and help me walk him over."

Steve skipped to attention and helped pull him to the opening of the alley, looking around for any witnesses, but there were none. Even if someone had been watching, he was sure they wouldn't have seen what had happened. It was so fast, incredible. D was dribbling and muttering a string of swear words.

"Let's put him behind that dumpster down there," Steve said. He could do the deed and they could even haul him in with the fish skins, the oyster shells, and the crates. Perfect.

They threw him down on the ground next to the dumpster. Helen started to pull it forward a little, as though she was thinking of dragging D behind it. "I'll take it from here," she said.

"What are you talking about? I need to finish him, Helen, or he'll finish me when he comes around. You can't do this to D and get away with it. You've got to understand how dangerous he is." Steve watched, scratching his head, as Helen pulled out the dumpster a fraction more and dragged D behind it, his body just fitting into the narrow gap. Christ, she was stronger than she looked.

Helen took off her rucksack and threw it on top of D, who was groaning quietly. "You can leave us now," she said. She was breathing heavily, a look of rapture on her face, her eyes shining. "I'm going to finish him, don't worry about that."

Steve stepped back. It was like she was getting off on this, and it was creeping him out. "What are you going to do?"

She smiled. "He won't come back, I promise." Waving him away, she jumped behind the stinking dumpster and disappeared from view.

Steve heard her unzipping her rucksack, the screech of duct tape. D went quiet. She must have wrapped it around his mouth. He moved off to the side and made sure they were out of sight from anyone coming through here, not that anyone in their right mind would. Certainly the lunch folk around the corner wouldn't be seen dead coming this way.

He waited a moment. There was a faint moan, a whimper. Jesus, he couldn't stand there. He shouted, "I'm off, then, back to the flat."

There was no answer. Of course there wasn't. A noise came from behind there, a strange sound that he could only describe as an inward scream. He turned and ran, had to get away from there. The thought of D suffering was kind of good. He felt guilty admitting that to himself, but any satisfaction he had was being overshadowed by a sick feeling that he had about his sister. He remembered the uneasiness he had felt when he first imagined her presence behind those curtains back in London. A sense of evil he'd got from her. At first he thought she was just a bit peculiar, but now he realized she was some kind of psycho. Having fun with D? She wasn't right in the head. She was his twin sister but she'd been abandoned and sent through a system and not properly loved. *What had it done to her?*

He was back on Constitution Street now, and he was still running, his breath in a rhythm like never before.

He could run forever.

THIRTY-ONE
Bedsit Hell

There had been a lot of noise in the corridor all night. It had started from the Indian woman's room. Lizzy had heard her voice a couple of times, going off. It was the early hours of the morning. At one point she had thought it was all over, but then it all kicked off again. She was too scared to leave the building, not sure who she'd bump into on the way. And in any case, where would she go? She couldn't turn up at Nat's at this hour.

She was curled up in bed, the covers pulled over her head even though it was hot in the room. She wore her old t-shirt with Robert Smith on it that she'd bought back in Scotland. Her and Molly had each got one from Dave's Discs. It was still long enough to be a nightie, even now. The window was open to the night air and the noises of the city. Sirens and traffic and intermittent shouting outside would occasionally drown out the noise inside the building. But it didn't help her sleep.

"Get back here," a man was growling somewhere outside her door.

"Fuck off, get away from me." A woman's voice was getting fainter as she walked away.

She didn't recognize either of the voices; they must be new people and not regulars. Could be anyone, in any state. Then came more banging against the wall, fists, growing more frequent now. There was some loud screaming from the woman; all of it was making her room vibrate, the walls so thin. More footsteps, and doors opening and then slamming again. Someone was shouting at them, at him, to stop. Lizzy was trembling now, pulling her pillow around the back of her head, holding it tight against her ears. The woman was being thrown against Lizzy's own door now, and she was scared it would fly open.

Someone make this end.

As if this someone had heard her silent plea, a final thud ended the woman's screams. Panting and deep growling came from the man. It was like an animal had finished his business, surveying the broken prey. A few minutes later, Lizzy heard an ambulance siren, lights flashing outside making strobes through the thin net curtains. She got out of bed and sat by the window, glad to feel the night air on her skin, a slight breeze blowing under her T-shirt. The police would be next, banging on everyone's door, asking for witnesses. What did you see? What did you hear? Did you know them?

She sighed, grabbed her watch. Two-forty a.m. She had to be up in four hours for the market. The ambulance paramedics were out in the corridor now, all bleeping and low voices. She resisted going out to look, to see the carnage. The stretcher was back out of the building in just a few minutes and she strained to see out the window, but didn't recognize the woman lying face up, both hands on her chest. She looked dead.

After filling a glass with lukewarm water from the tap, she returned to the chair by the window and watched as the back doors of the ambulance closed with a bang and the small crowd standing on the pavement dispersed. More voices started up in the corridor, probably just people talking about what had happened. Then the police siren outside finished the whole event with more drama.

Lizzy looked up at the sky, brightening already, bringing morning far too soon. Shining through the haze of never-quite-dark London, was a single star. It could be there, or it could be the one that lived in her imagination. It shone when she needed it to. It was always there for her to see, anyway.

Is that you up there, Mum? I've had a bad night; you might have seen. Remember when I had a nasty dream and used to come and sleep with you in bed? Well this is much worse, because it's real life and not just some nightmare, and I've no one to run to, to sleep in with. It's just me in here at night, stuck in this room. It's better than the life I had in Scotland, I think. I mean after you died. But sometimes I wonder if I did the right thing, leaving Dalbegie and Auntie Maureen, even though she didn't really want me. At least she was family. Someone. At the time I thought Simon was rescuing me, but really he was just taking me away from a bad place into another one. Now he's dead. He isn't a star though; it's just you up there and sometimes Granny Mac of course. Simon didn't care about me enough to be a star, watching from up there.

I've got to go now. The police are banging on my door. When I get back to my bed, I'll pretend you're in there and I'll cuddle up to your back, like I used to. Your hair will tickle my nose and I'll tuck it in underneath your neck. You'll take all the covers while we're asleep, and eventually, when it's not a dream anymore, I'll wake up cold.

She was actually early for work, because she hadn't had a chance to enter a deep sleep and had woken easily. It seemed like the alarm was going off as soon as Lizzy got under the covers again, but she might have been asleep for an hour once her brain had stopped turning over. She was wearing her fake Ray-Bans, even though it wasn't that bright out yet, because her eyes were stinging. The sun was hitting the streets, a new day, but one that was filled with a feeling of despair and exhaustion for Lizzy. She got off the bus and started the walk into Soho with heavy legs.

She'd worked it all out, in bed, after the police had been. They hadn't stayed with her long, because she'd not seen anything and didn't know the couple who'd been fighting. One of them had asked her how old she was, looked at her like she was a kid. It pissed her off and she'd got quiet. When they left, one of them said, "Look after yourself." Seemed a bit of a pointless thing to say. After, she lay close to her mother's memory and realized that actually there was someone who was looking out for her. She wasn't just looking after herself. There was Oliver. As she smelled her mum's hair, felt the wispiness of it on her face, she remembered again how she'd acted those last few weeks before she disappeared. In love. For some reason she'd asked Oliver to look out for her, and so he did, like some kind of guardian, a tiny part of her mum inside him. It was the only way to describe it. He had a piece of her past, something from before. She wasn't glad Simon had gone from the world, but if she dug deep into how she felt about it, she was the tiniest bit relieved he wasn't around to make her feel guilty anymore.

Now the market was in sight; she could see Dave pulling up in his van. He was early too. She held up her hand and he honked his horn at her. He jumped out and opened up the back, then pulled out a flask and two mugs from the cab up front.

"Oi, want a cuppa? We got time." He held up the mugs and smiled.

"Yeah, please. I'll need everything I can get today."

"Christ," he said, "you look like death warmed up."

"Do I look that bad?"

"Yes, you do. What the bloody hell happened to you?"

She slumped down and sat cross-legged on the ground, next to the van. "I didn't sleep last night. Something was kicking off in the building. A woman was killed. There was an ambulance and the police and then it was nearly time to get up."

"What's going on with that place, anyway? I don't think you should be living there anymore, darlin'. It doesn't sound safe no more."

"It's been all right until now. It's cheap and I get my own key and that. I don't know, Dave." She put her fingers up to her temples. "I just don't know anymore."

They sat and drank tea, while Dave talked to her about what was safe and what wasn't and what could happen to her. She knew all of it, but listened to him anyway. It was nice, him caring about her. Keith showed up, but no Nat, of course, who had been sent to her local High Street to look for other work. The two of them sat with her for a while, shocked because of the murder, cold and final. It occurred to Lizzy that she hadn't looked at the walls in the corridor when she left the building, partly because she had been half-asleep and partly because she didn't want to know what was there. Keith went on his phone, and the next thing she knew, she was being told she wasn't working that day.

"Of course I'm working," she said. "Where would I go, anyway?"

"You're going to see Karen," said Keith. "She wants to look after you for the day. She ain't working. You can sleep all day if you want, or watch telly."

Dave nodded his approval and pulled her to her feet. "Go and chill out, darlin', you need a bit of love today. Karen will enjoy feeding you up, it's her thing." He laughed.

"Thanks." She grinned at them both, already busy with unpacking and set-up. It was true, she was feeling sorry for herself and her bones were so tired she couldn't imagine being on her feet all day. "I'll be back tomorrow, all fresh and fattened up and super-human." Making her way to the bus stop, she turned and waved. It was like they were family, in a way. You just needed to look at what family meant. It was folk who were close to you, who cared about you.

Karen flung open her front door and came out onto the doorstep. She must have been watching out the window for her. "Here you are, darlin', come on in and I'll make you a nice cup of tea. Oh, just look at the state of you. You look terrible."

"Seems funny being here without Nat." Lizzy kicked off her boots and went through to the living room. It smelled of wood polish and she could see the fresh vacuum marks on the carpet.

"Don't be daft, you're like part of the furniture. Anyway, she'll be back in a couple of hours, once she's tried a few shoe shops. I told her to try the post office as well, because you never know. You put your feet up on that sofa and I'll go make the tea. Find us a soppy film to watch on the telly, will you, I fancy a good cry."

Karen went off into the kitchen and Lizzy grabbed the remote control. She lay back on the soft cushions and felt herself sinking into clouds. She'd shut her eyes, just for a second. It was so comfy, and safe and kind of floaty. She felt her body drift down, her mind emptying, the faint clinking of Karen in the kitchen. Everything was going to be all right.

THIRTY-TWO

Helen and Ma

Helen woke up in her mother's bed. Steve had taken the sofa, and there was nowhere else to sleep. It was a single, old and soft, a little too short, even for her. She hadn't bothered changing the sheets and they smelled faintly of lavender and old people. She sat up and found a white hair on the blanket, brushed it onto the floor. There was a wood dresser to one side, with a stool facing the mirror. On top were some talc and body cream that should probably be thrown away, the tubes squeezed thin.

A glorious feeling of calm had settled through her, following the attack. It was like an addiction satisfied, something resolved. Deep in the bottom of a dumpster, in an alley in Leith, was D and all his hair, wrapped up in plastic. Helen had made sure he was also well covered up with food scraps, fish heads, sodden cardboard, and egg shells. She'd ripped open some of the bigger bin bags, letting their contents spill. If anyone found him, it certainly wouldn't be because of the smell of his body, but because of some freak sighting of a foot or a hand. But even that wasn't likely. The contents of that thing stank and it wasn't exactly the kind of rubbish a homeless person would sift through. She hadn't spent that much time with D in the end, given the strange noises he was making. Worried that his squeals would echo down the alley, she had finished her business prematurely and spent the final few minutes making sure that he would never wake up. Still, it had been satisfying, working on an aggressive male with a personal link to her own life, her brother. That really made it. When she got back to the flat, it was very late, and Steve had been quiet, almost withdrawn. She'd seen fear in his eyes. "Don't worry," she'd said. "He's gone forever." But even that didn't seem to cheer him up.

Today was the day they would travel to North Berwick, to visit Mother and her sister. Steve had told them they were on their way and reported that she was still in her bed, sick, but excited to see them. Helen wasn't sure how to feel about the reunion. She should have a mix of emotions, presumably. There would be a touch of happiness to find her real family and a bit of resentment at being the discarded twin. Nothing of these had quite surfaced yet, but perhaps the physical presence of her mother would trigger something.

She got up, went to the bathroom and dressed. The telly was on in the living room, the news on full blast, so Steve must be up too. She put her head around the door. He was sat up in the armchair, fully clothed, his eyes bloodshot.

"Hello," she said.

He jumped. "Jesus, you gave me a fright. Did you sleep?"

"Yes, like a log. Doesn't look like you did, though." She might have said that in her head or out loud, she couldn't be sure. Either way, he just stared at her, blank, like he was expecting something else.

Helen went through to the kitchen, a tiny room with a hatch to the living room, presumably for serving food back in the day. She put the kettle on and looked in the fridge. There were some encrusted bottles of ketchup, salad cream, and relishes, nothing more. She looked through the hatch. "Is there a café near here?"

Steve jumped again. Was she talking too loud?

"I'm not hungry," he said.

She made two mugs of tea, found a jar of sugar in the cupboard, although there was no milk. Putting one of the mugs on the table next to Steve, she wondered when they would be leaving for North Berwick. That's if he was in the right frame of mind to go.

Steve switched off the telly, a sudden silence filling the room. "What did you do to him?"

"I hid him in the dumpster, like you were going to do. He's well buried." She sipped the tea. It was strong and bitter.

"I'm talking about what you did before he was dead. I heard some weird screaming from him, from inside, like you'd gagged him and were torturing him. Where did that come from? Done that kind of thing before, have you? It was sick, if you must know. I couldn't even stick around. I wanted to throw up." He clutched at the ends of the armchair, his knuckles stretched and pale.

"You wanted him dead. Does it matter that I wanted to play a bit?"

He put the tips of his forefingers to the corners of his eyes. "I don't care about D and I'm glad he's dead. He was a cunt. I'm just trying to understand you. I need you to talk to me properly, not just fob me off with the silent treatment. We shared the same fuckin' womb and so we should be able to tell each other anything. Never mind we spent forty years apart; we're from the same blood. You know about me. That I was an addict, that I fucked up, got divorced, that my life has been full of stupid mistakes. I even got my own ma beat up, for fuck's sake. So now I need to know what goes on in your head, and you need to tell me. Otherwise I'm not happy about taking you down to see Ma. You're making me very fuckin' nervous, Helen."

She had been listening, hadn't drifted. There was something about the way he spoke to her that she liked. He wasn't patronizing, didn't pander, nor did he dismiss her. There was an intangible bond between the two of them. He might even stick by her even when he found out that it was the pain of others that kept her feeling alive.

Gulping the rest of the tea down, she nodded. "I will tell you. I'm not one to prattle on, don't see the point. But I'll tell you the facts. Will that do?"

He looked at the ceiling. "That would be a start."

So she told him. She trusted that he wouldn't tell. It was the simplest of sibling rules, one that came naturally. He listened, silent, frowning and sometimes bog-eyed as she went through some of the pivotal moments in her life. Once she started to speak, she kept going, and unbelievably, found she couldn't stop. Forty years of containment and now she wanted to spout as much as she could remember.

Her earliest memory was of her first foster parents staring at her over the bars of her crib. She wasn't a baby, but a toddler perfectly capable of sleeping in a bed. Still, they liked to keep her in there, where she wasn't "in the way." She was put in the crib for long periods throughout the day as well as at night. Sometimes they would bring her food or books to look at. When she got old enough to climb over the bars, she would sit on the stairs and watch the rest of the family down below. They would say she was strange for watching them. One day, she threw one of the hardback books over the banister and it landed on another child's head, her foster brother Phil. The corner of it drew blood and she was excited to see it, a dirty red seeping through his hair. At that moment, even as a child, she discovered that hurting other people felt good.

From then on, it was an addiction, one that had to be kept hidden from the world. She couldn't ever talk about it, she knew.

School was something to get through, until she left as early as she was legally allowed. She wasn't exactly a popular kid, bullied until she stood up for herself one day and nearly scratched an older girl's eye out. Fifteen was the most difficult age, when she was rejected by her foster family in Fife and sent to London, to Kelly and Mick's. By the time she was seventeen, she had killed two boys. The first was the toddler in the family in Fife, and the second was her foster brother Kev at Kelly & Mick's. In both instances, they had been the centres of attention in the families, the annoying core of it all. They both deserved what they got.

Steve told her that he had met both sets of parents, that they had relayed their suspicions about her. Well, they were right. She explained to him that she had always covered her tracks impeccably, that if a killer didn't want to be found, they wouldn't be found.

She told Steve about the Cat Rescue, and her first encounter with Oliver. He seemed taken aback at how near she was to him and their mother all those years ago, that they could have walked past each other on the street like two magnets facing the wrong way. She told him how her friendship with Oliver eventually drew her back to London, to The Audacious, The Circle. She told him about her disappointment when it disbanded, albeit temporarily, and how it led to her venture on Hampstead Heath. She gave Steve everything, bared her soul and risked his rejection, but never doubted his loyalty. If he turned on her, she could turn on him harder.

When she finished speaking, her throat was sore, her voice unfamiliar and hoarse. It was the most she'd said in years, in the whole of her life probably. She found herself sitting upright, her back aching, fingernails stuck in her palms. Steve had gone pale. There was a much-needed pause, the enormity of her speech clawing at the faded wallpaper.

Steve eventually spoke. "How do you feel about me? About Ma? Do you resent being shoved out into the world, into the hands of folk that didn't really love you? Was it the reason you looked for something else to focus on? You've told me a lot, and thank you. But what are you feeling just now about all of this?"

She didn't know exactly. The past reared up in her thoughts and memories, of course it did, but it wasn't something that Helen wanted to bring to the forefront of her life. She felt how she felt, not because of what had been, but what was happening in the present, the touch of a victim's breath on her face, the feel of his terror in her heart. She pondered for a moment about how to answer him, how best to summarize. She had never had such a period of clarity, of conversing with someone with purpose. "I haven't ever blamed you or our mother for what's happened to me. How could I when I didn't even know you? All I knew growing up was what I had. I didn't know any different. I am how I am. That's it."

"Are you sure you want to meet your ma?"

"Yes, I'm sure. Are we still going down today?"

He released his hands from the arms of the chair and rubbed them together. "Promise me you won't do anything to her."

"I promise."

"Then I'll take you. And just so you know, I'm doing this for her. She's pined for you all these years and she's desperate to meet you. Don't disappoint her, okay? Talk to her."

"I will."

He paused, seemed to make a decision. "Then let's get cracking. I'm doing this for her. And I'll be watching you, Helen."

The two of them waited outside the station for Mary to pick them up. She had insisted, apparently. Helen had brushed her hair and checked her face in the toilet for mayonnaise and biscuit crumbs. She was wearing the grey coat, even though it was warm out, because she felt her most comfortable in it, less exposed.

"She said she's got a red Volkswagon Polo, bit fuckin' trendy for Auntie Mary, eh?" Steve was pacing up and down, biting the skin on the end of his fingers.

"She's my auntie as well, then." Helen realized only then that her family was going to grow by the day.

"Aye, she's really excited to meet you." He stopped dead in his tracks, as if he had realised something. "She's Ma's younger sister and she's a bit mental, talks a lot, and laughs all the time, but she's all right."

There was a honk, and there she was pulling up beside them, in her red Polo. She screamed and jumped out of the car, the engine still running. "Look at yous two together, oh my god, I can't believe it, so I can't."

Steve stepped forward to give her a hug, while she continued to talk with this high-pitched voice that Helen could barely tune into. Then she was coming towards her, arms outstretched, talking about chips and blocks, Little and Large. She bent forward briefly and Mary lunged in for a hug, their faces brushing together.

Then they were in the car, Helen in the back behind Steve, her knees against the back of his seat. She watched Mary while she drove, and was interested to see there was no physical resemblance between them. Mary continued to talk at them, occasionally laughing out loud, and driving very slowly, until they reached her cottage. It was white and surrounded by bright flowers, yellow and pinks and oranges all clashing together to create more noise.

"Come on in then, just put your wee bags in the hallway for now. You can put your shoes right there under the bench. Coats go on the hooks behind the door. That's it, make yourselves at home. I'll go up and see if your ma is awake or if she needs to loo or anything before she sees you. Get yourselves through to the conservatory, that's where I always relax myself."

Helen couldn't imagine the woman ever relaxing. She sat down on one of the lounge chairs in the glass bubble-shaped room at the back and rubbed her eyes. She had a headache.

Steve's legs were jiggling from side to side like he was getting impatient. "I know I said she talked a lot, but I'd forgotten just how much."

"It's a lot."

"Listen, I want to see Ma first, on my own. Okay?"

She nodded. He probably wanted to warn Mother about how her daughter was. That was fine; at least she wouldn't be too disappointed when they finally met. They sat and watched the trees blowing outside for a few minutes, waiting.

Mary came blustering back downstairs, and flapped at them with meaty hands. "She's sitting up and ready to see you. I've opened the curtains and I'll put the kettle on for everybody. I don't know, maybe now you're here she'll get out of her bed. I think she's had nothing to get up for in all these weeks, the poor wee lamb."

Steve got up. "I'm going up by myself first. Helen will wait down here with you." He widened his eyes at Helen, and smiled.

"Of course, of course, you get yourself up to your ma and tell her all about how you found your sister. It'll be too much if you both go together, all of a sudden, when she hasn't seen her son for weeks and her daughter . . . well, for a long time." She filled the kettle and crashed it down onto the stovetop and started opening and closing the kitchen cupboards.

Helen sat and waited, hands folded on her lap. Mary was talking to herself in the kitchen, occasionally making a loud noise with a cup and saucer or a tray or a cupboard. Was she searching for something in particular, or was she in the habit of looking through the contents of her cupboards in sequence, perusing, enjoying the business of it? She hoped she wouldn't ask her any questions, try and engage her in the whole parade, because she had switched off now, wouldn't hear the words coming towards her. The garden outside was soothing, green and wild looking, with some large trees at the back. She watched a sparrow flitting around the bird feeder just outside the window. It must be better for the soul to live outside of a city.

Eventually, some time later, Steve reappeared and sat down next to her. She realized there was a cup of tea on the side table next to her chair. She felt it and it was cold. Mary must have put it there; she hadn't noticed though. It was her turn to go up. Steve was offering to come with her and she told him she didn't mind either way. It didn't really matter. He followed her.

Then she was climbing the stair, slow, to meet the mother she never had.

The room was modest, just a single bed with a wooden chair next to it, but with lots of frills and bright colours on the curtains and bedspread. A small woman was sat up against the padded headboard, thin and wizened. Her hair was dull grey, her hands covered with liver spots. This, she supposed, was her mother. She was smiling at her, the tiny hands moving up under her chin to make a prayer. Helen tried to smile back, sat down on the chair.

"Are you cold, hen?" Mother pointed at her coat.

"No."

"Hold my hand, will you. Let's have a look at you."

Helen heard Steve shuffling away, back down the stair. Her mother's cold fingers wrapped themselves around hers. They felt like plastic, some substance that surely couldn't be real flesh and blood. Finally, she looked her in the eye and saw that Mother was crying, a few thin tears finding their way down the creases. She searched for the unfamiliar hotness in her own ducts, perhaps a tingle similar to the one she'd got when she first stepped off the train at Waverley, but found them empty.

THIRTY-THREE
Steve's Choice

The sun was out, but the wind was biting through Steve's jacket and he was freezing his nuts off. He rubbed his arms, wishing he owned a smart coat that he could have worn over his suit. Standing at the top of the hillock next to the church, he could see everyone arriving. They all seemed to come at once, some in their own cars plus a crowd of folk in a coach from Edinburgh that they'd hired a couple of days ago.

The church, the funeral, was held in North Berwick at the request of Auntie Mary, and who was Steve to argue? He was just the shite that had probably driven his own ma to her death. Carrying on in London while she was so ill and couldn't even get out of bed on her own. Of course Ma's sister should get her own way, and have her buried near the cottage and the sea.

It was all his fault.

There were Ed and Jake, head to toe in black, even their ties and their socks, which he could see quite clearly because their breeches were on the short side. Ed raised a hand and they began to climb up the hill towards him. He was wearing a black trilby to cover his baldy head and looked like one of the Blues Brothers. Steve spotted his two cousins, Auntie Mary's daughters, spilling out of a Mini. They must have left their kids behind, too young to be at a funeral probably.

Their heads were together as they walked towards the church, probably talking too loud, a genetic defect. Most of the folk appearing from the coach were oldies, greys or whites, Ma's friends from all these years passed. Who would come to his funeral if he died? Ed and Jake, Evelyn from the Porty? He had a sister now; maybe she'd come too. He looked over at Helen, at her small compact body over by the tree. She was wearing that coat again, the one she always wore. At least she was probably warm.

Ed and Jake were upon him and his thoughts were broken.

"Hey big man, how you doing?" Ed held out a hand to him, then put his other arm around him. It felt good, the big slap on the back he gave him.

"Not too bad, you know. Just want this bit over, so we can have a few bevs and remember her."

Jake was next, put both his hands on Steve's shoulders. His glasses were a bit steamed up. "Sorry about your ma, Stevie-boy."

"Thanks, boys. Glad you could make it. She always loved you both, for some unknown fuckin' reason." Steve straightened, put his hand in the inside pocket of his jacket, and pulled out two envelopes. "Here you go, boys, it's what I owe you, and some. Thanks for being good pals, eh?" He stuck his thumb out towards the church. "Shall we go inside?"

Jake nodded. "You're welcome." He looked across the grass and adjusted his glasses. "There's lots of folk here. Who's the weird wee gnome lady by the tree? Is she one of Mary's cronies?"

Steve spluttered. "That's my sister. You'll meet her later, although I'll warn you now, she doesn't say very much."

"Oh shite, is that her? Sorry, man. But she doesn't look much like you from here. I'm such an arse." Jake slapped himself on the forehead.

Ed chuckled. "You said it, pal."

The three of them walked down to the church, Steve in the middle. Their hands were thrust deep in their pockets, heads down. Out the corner of his eye, Steve could see Helen, still not moving, looking off into the distance. She could come in her own time. He was with his best pals now, dependable and long-standing. He felt solid with them. Helen he wasn't a hundred percent about, and didn't care if she knew it. Christ, he was only about fifty percent, and that was being generous.

The air was even colder inside than it was out there. They sat at the front, Steve next to Auntie Mary, who was already blubbing into a tissue. He put his arm around her shoulders and gave her a squeeze. He wanted Ed and Jake up front with him. They were closest to him. Helen would probably come inside at the last second and hide away at the back, and it was probably just as well.

When he went upstairs to see Ma only a week or so ago, he'd felt sick at what state he might find her in. She was known as a tough bird, but she was old now, and she'd fair shrunk the last few years. What had she told Auntie Mary? How was she in the head? He had so many questions and was feared to know what the answers were.

When he saw her there, so pale, her hair all stuck to her head, he felt he'd lost her already. His body shuddered and he put his hand to his mouth, at the very sight of her. She was sitting up, had made an effort to appear fine by plastering lipstick around her mouth. When she saw him, her face lit up in a smile, but the glow in her face was short lived. The pastiness and the pallor drew back to her cheeks in a second.

"I'm so glad to see you, Stevie-boy," she said, and put her cold hand to his cheek.

"Ma, what's going on? What did D do to you? Why are you not getting out of your bed?" He was falling over his words, couldn't seem to get them out fast enough.

"Oh, that. Well son, he did throw me around a bit, and it wasn't very pleasant, right enough. I got a fright. And a lot of bruising and a few cuts."

"I'm so sorry, Ma. I should never have left you there by yourself. What was I thinking? If I'd known you were in such a state, if Auntie Mary had told me, I would have come straight back, to hell with finding Helen."

She shook her head and patted his hand. "No, no, you mustn't think like that. I was pushing you out that door to find my baby girl and nothing was stopping me. You had to go and you had to stay away until you found her. And I was just about to get myself down here to Berwick, remember? We had it all sorted in our minds."

"I should have brought you down here myself and then gone on from there."

"Well it's done." She took a deep breath in. "And Steve, when I was at the hospital after, they found out that I'm ill. Not because of what D did, just because I'm old. I'm just ill, Stevie-boy, and it's nothing you did."

"Eh? Auntie Mary never said anything about any illness."

"That's because she doesn't know. What the point of telling a daftie like her, eh? It's late stage. The smokes got the better of me, son. You've done well to give them up. There's nothing they can do, and I'm comfortable here. She's so good at looking after me, so she is. She'll do anything, bless her heart. I think she likes me being here; she's been on her own since Uncle Charlie died."

He felt like he'd been kicked in the stomach. His ma was ill. How long did she have left? She seemed fine when he went away, but come to think of it, she had been getting tired all the time. He was such a selfish bastard, wouldn't have noticed if she was half-fuckin' dead, probably. She'd been looking after him, what with his leg and his ribs. They sat together for a while, and he told her about some of the journey he'd made to find his sister. She hung onto his every word, wanted to know all the details. He was building up to telling her about Helen, what she was like, but she beat him to it. She seemed to sense something was up, like she knew.

"Is she okay, my wee girl? Helen. Is she, you know, all there?" She pointed at the side of her head.

He couldn't believe she'd asked. What would he say to that? The truth, he supposed. "Not quite a hundred percent, now you've asked."

Ma paused, shut her eyes for a moment. "Can I tell you something? Seeing as I might not get the chance to tell you again."

"Aye, go on. You can tell me anything, Ma." He leaned forward.

Her voice lowered to a whisper. "When the two of yous were born, it broke my heart that I had to give one of you away, it really did.

You've got to believe that, Stevie-boy, it's important. I put you both on my lap, and I didn't know what to do. You opened your eyes and looked up at me, fuzzy and out of focus, and I swear you smiled. It was probably wind, but there you go. Then she opened her eyes, your sister. They were black and deep and empty. There was nothing there. She seemed strange to me, alien almost. I've read about mothers who struggle to bond with their wee 'uns in the early years, and I know what they're talking about. I felt that she was the one who had to go, no question. I know it's awful, but there's the truth."

"Ma." Steve lowered his head. "You did the right thing. I'll go and get her for you and you'll see for yourself."

The service had begun and the church was packed. He'd see everyone after, didn't want to turn around and wave at anyone, like it was some sort of social. Steve sat, looked straight ahead, and listened to the guy in the white gown. Was he a priest or a vicar? He could never get his head around all that. They'd asked if someone would like to do a reading, and it was decided that one of Auntie Mary's daughters would read part of Ma's favourite hymn. Steve couldn't do it himself, it was too much for him, and Auntie Mary said she wouldn't be able to stop crying, so his cousin Patricia it was. She stood up now, went to the front, with black stockings on her chunky legs and a black veil covering up her face. Probably wasn't a bad thing, he thought, seeing as she was a bit of a minger.

The hymn was "I Danced in the Morning." Patricia read it slow, pausing after every line. She started by telling everyone it was Ma's favourite, that she used to hum it sometimes while she was making the tea. Steve remembered that, although at the time he hadn't realized what she was humming. Then Patricia read.

> "*I danced on a Friday and the sky turned black;*
> *It's hard to dance with the devil on your back;*
> *They buried my body and they thought I'd gone,*
> *But I am the dance and I still go on.*"

She looked up briefly before finishing.

"They cut me down and I leapt up high,
I am the life that'll never, never, die;
I'll live in you if you'll live in me;
I am the Lord of the Dance, said he."

The congregation was silent. Steve wondered if they were supposed to clap, but then realized it wasn't a performance, it was a tribute. Patricia had chosen well after all; maybe she wasn't such a daft cow. He liked the idea of Ma living on. He nodded at his cousin when she came past him and she smiled back.

After the service, everyone went back to Auntie Mary's for the wake. She'd put on her best spread for everyone, plus Steve and all the lads had stocked the place up with booze. Beers, brandy, whisky, vodka, and all the mixers anyone could want, all paid for with some of the money that he'd owed to D. There was ice in cool boxes, and plastic cups stacked up in case they ran out of glasses. *Cheers, D.*

The place was full of folk talking or shouting, and drinking. The conservatory, as Auntie Mary called it, was crammed full of oldies drinking whisky and lemonade. They were eating all the sandwiches and talking about Ma as if she was the greatest woman that ever lived. She was great, thought Steve, never laid a finger on him even when he was a shite as a wee 'un, always supported him throughout his rocky life, the drugs, his dad's death, the divorce, more drugs. *She was a fuckin' saint.*

Ed and Jake were talking to Helen, both looking down with wrinkled foreheads, supping at their tins and whisky chasers frequently, like they needed it to get through it. What were they talking about? Who she'd tortured recently? Steve sighed. If they knew, they'd be running a mile.

Auntie Mary appeared in front of him, with a black shopping tote. "I've a few things here she would want you to have." She handed it to him. Her eyes were bloodshot, electric blue mascara smudged on both cheeks. "They were in a drawer, just some odds and ends she'd brought with her when she came down from Edinburgh to stay."

"Aw that's great, thanks Auntie Mary. This is a lovely wake you've done for us all here, by the way, it's going down well with everyone. Are you not having a drink?" He noticed she was empty-handed. "Can I get you one?"

"No, away with you. I need my wits about me the night. And if I have a few drinks, I'll just start blubbing away and make a right old fool of myself, as usual. You enjoy yourself, Stevie-boy, and stay as long as you like. Did you get a room at the B&B? If not, you can always stay with me. The sofa's dead comfy."

"Aye, all us lads plus Helen are at the B&B the night. We'll be fine, thanks."

Steve smiled politely and turned away, holding up the bag as if to say, "I'm going to put this somewhere." The bag wasn't heavy, couldn't have much in it. He found a quiet corner in the hallway and opened it up, pulling one or two things out and holding them up to the light. On the top was a shawl of some kind, made of cream wool. It was soft and smelled of Ma. Did she make it herself? He wasn't sure. Underneath that was a porcelain figurine of a woman shepherdess. It was protected with a couple of layers of bubble wrap, some tape wound around to keep it in place. He remembered it from the mantelpiece in Ma's living room, but not who had bought it for her. Then there was another wool thing, much smaller than the shawl. He held it up and his stomach churned. It was the yellow hat she'd knitted for him for his birthday. He'd left it behind, didn't want to draw attention to himself on his travels, not after Ed had called him a walking lemon. She must have found it behind the sofa or in-between the cushions, or wherever it was he'd stuffed it. What must she have thought? His birthday present and he'd not even bothered to put it in his bag. It didn't exactly take up much room. And he'd never sent her a post-card, had he? Not one.

He didn't look at the rest of the stuff, just put the hat and the figurine back, the shawl on top. There was no way he was going to greet just now, not here with this lot. He was right beside the front door, able to leave without anyone seeing. He walked out the door, still clutching the bag, and ran towards the end of the road. His eyes were pricking, threatening to spill. There was a small wood down the end, with a pathway leading into some sort of clearing. There it was, lit by a street lamp. He ran inside a short distance and found a bench overlooking a pond, glassy and still, with the moon reflected in the middle of it.

He sat.

The tears came and flooded down his face. He needed it.

A few minutes passed, the light changing as his eyes got used to the dark. He wiped his face with the sleeve of his jacket and shivered. There was a crack of twigs, some footsteps, he was sure of it. Someone was coming out from behind the trees. At this time of night?

"Hello?" he called out, half scared and half curious.

"It's me."

Helen. *What was she doing here?*

She sat down on the bench next to him and looked out to the pond, where he'd just been staring. "I followed you."

"What? How did you notice I'd even left? I was fast, like a ninja, stealthy like a fuckin' tiger. Were you watching me from behind those trees? That's creepy, you know."

"I know," she said. "Back in London, there's a pond near where I live. Sometimes I go down there and sit on a bench, just like this, and watch the ducks. I lose myself there."

"Sort of calms you down, doesn't it?"

"Sort of, yes. Sometimes I wake up to myself and realize I've been there for hours."

He looked at her face, half shining in the moonlight, and saw his own reflection there, just for a second, the lost helplessness of him. "I saw you talking to Ed and Jake in there. How did you do?"

"Not too bad. They'll probably tell you different." She smiled faintly. "And you? Are you doing okay?"

"Aye, just needed to greet a bit. Didn't want anyone seeing. But you did, you wee creep."

"Sorry." Then, still looking at the moon, she said, "I would never hurt you, you know."

"Aye, I know," he said.

Ma was gone now and he felt empty for it, like there was no one to better himself for, to feel proud of him. A fresh start is what he'd wanted, some kind of direction in his life. He'd been hoping these past few months to feel whole once he'd found his twin, that somehow things would take a turn for the best. Well, he was clean for one. For another, she'd got rid of D for him. Who knows what would have happened if she'd not been there. Would he have stabbed him with the knife, or would he have copped out? He'd never killed a man before, and D was one of the hardest guys he knew. He could easily have fucked it up, and ended up dead himself.

"I'm going back to London day after tomorrow. I've some unfinished business." Helen slid the black bag closer to her and pulled out the shawl. "I'm freezing. Can I put this on?"

He shrugged. "Aye, all right. It was your ma's."

"Oh." She put it on her shoulders, pulled it in close.

He put his hand in the bag and pulled out the yellow hat. "I've been cold all day, I don't mind saying." He put on the hat, a perfect fit. It felt warm the second he put it on, a fleecy lining around the rim just covering the tips of his ears. Neither of them said anything more, didn't need to. Steve didn't want to go back to the wake, to the shouting, and he was pretty sure Helen didn't either. No. They'd sit here for a bit in the dark, and watch the pond. It was amazing what a tiny chink of light could do for the soul.

THIRTY-FOUR

The Final Game of Chance

I see you're packing up your things, Lizzy, ready to finish work for the week. Of course you're oblivious to what I've planned for you and me. Your face is shining with perspiration and you look a little tired, as you often do at the end of the day. You've painted your nails a ghastly purple, but at least it hides those bitten ends, and the flaky skin underneath. I've been watching you all afternoon from my window above you, aching with anticipation, desperate to execute my latest idea. But you know it has never been my style to rush things, especially at the last moment.

What have I been doing? First I wanted to rid you of your other admirer, the last one standing. Through my resourceful contacts, I learned Helen's address, and I went to her filthy abode with the intention of eliminating her. She has always been a trusted ally, her vitality renewed of late, however I will not allow her to take what's mine. And as you know, history doesn't count. Her current interest in you is not something we should entertain. When I arrived, I could sense that she wasn't in the building. The weight of her presence, that familiar smell, were elsewhere. I picked the lock and went inside, found her bedsit upstairs. I removed my shoes so as not to alarm anyone living underneath, although it probably wasn't necessary.

My instincts were correct. She had gone. There was a half-full laundry bag in the middle of the room, two mugs growing mould on the kitchen countertop. Her bed wasn't made, the duvet thrown aside, revealing a yellow-stained sheet. She repulses me now more than ever before. There is something grotesque about entering the living space of an acquaintance. Suddenly every characteristic that you believed about them goes out the window to be replaced by a new set of traits. She is no longer an interesting and strong woman with convictions worthy of admiration, but a stinking, lazy slob with no self-respect.

It turns out that Helen posed no immediate threat to you, Lizzy. After sifting through her paperwork and perusing her computer desktop, I found out that she'd in fact taken off to Edinburgh. It's the place where she and I met, many years ago, when I was fresh faced and a touch more forgiving than I am these days. Perhaps now that The Audacious is temporarily out of the picture, she's servicing her needs somewhere familiar to her. Not that her motivations are any concern of mine. All that matters for now is that she isn't around and in the way of our special liaison. There will be plenty of time to get rid of her for good when she reappears from the abyss of Scotland—but perhaps by then I won't need to bother.

Back to the point, to the now. I've got a plan for us.

Russian Roulette, as you know, is a game that interests me. But it's a fascination for many reasons, one of which being that someone is always in control of the participants. No one wants to pull that trigger, unless they're clinically insane, but the pressure to do so overcomes the fear of it. They pull it because if they don't, the consequences are worse.

In this, I am the controller; you are the passive participant.

I'm going to load the bullets, and I'm going to pull the trigger when I think it's appropriate. It's my game. And of course you may have realized that I speak metaphorically, Lizzy. We are not going to play with guns.

On Friday, you will take the bus from Charing Cross Road alone like you always do these days, as your friend seems to have given up on the market job. You will walk from the bus stop at the other end to stay at Natalie's house for the weekend. It seems to have become a habit on Fridays, and I believe that it's making you happy as you seem to have a spring in your step at the end of every week. This time, I'll be waiting for you somewhere along your journey, and will surprise you, dear Lizzy, with an offer you may refuse or accept.

It could go either way, and will come down to how you feel at the time. If you accept my offer, you're instantly mine. You will have chosen a bullet, as it were. If you choose to reject my offer, then I will leave you be—for now. You will have made a wise choice, because you will have picked an empty chamber, that you will be able to enjoy some respite. Let's face it; if you remain on this earth, the next few years will undoubtedly be your best.

One more thing.

We both know that it will always be there: my terrible, conflicting desire for you. Even if you earn some reprieve, I shall most likely track you down again one day, review your small life and once again alight the deep yearning to claim your soul. And the waiting will make it all the more sweet. Something to savour. So you see, Lizzy, whether you choose a bullet or not, I win.

THIRTY-FIVE
Helen's Life Shifts

Her bedsit stank of dust and wet cardboard, as if she had been gone for a year. Had it always had that smell? Helen stepped inside and threw her backpack on the floor with a thud. What a dump. She pulled back the net curtains to let more light in, and pulled her finger across the glass, the trail leaving a line through the grime.

When she looked back into the room, she noticed the empty laundry bag, folded neatly on the bed. Her duvet was straight, tucked in on both sides. She'd been tidier of late, but had she really left it that way? She moved into the kitchenette and saw the pile of clothes on the countertop, folded and clean. She picked up the T-shirt on the top of the pile and sniffed. It had been washed using the detergent they had at the launderette, she was sure of it. That she definitely hadn't done, otherwise these clothes would have travelled with her to Edinburgh. She distinctly remembered discarding the laundry bag on the floor, half-full of stinking clothes, after she'd picked out one or two must-have items to take on her journey.

Someone had been in here.

Surveying the rest of the space, she realized that everything else was intact; her laptop was still on the bedside table, admittedly straight and parallel to the wall, and the kettle and dirty mugs and other odd items were where they should be. It was a mystery. Why would someone come in, launder her clothes, and then bring them back, without robbing anything? She sighed. Most things were unfathomable to her.

Tired of it all, Helen climbed into her pristine bed. Perhaps after a long sleep, things would seem clearer. She would need strength and mental agility to get through what she wanted to do the next day. First she must retrieve the girl from the market, take her for her own before Oliver or anyone else did, then pack up her things, ready to go back to Edinburgh where she belonged. She'd be away from here very soon.

Tomorrow was Friday. She would go to the market towards the end of the day and follow the girl home. It would be both sad and pleasurable to take a victim inside her own domain. She'd been thinking about it throughout the trip, even during Mother's funeral. Your own home was somehow impenetrable, safe, so when it is violated, the act itself seems much worse. For the victim, that is.

Had her space been compromised? She thought of all the people she'd encountered over the past few months. There was Lou, and she was as dangerous as anyone else. Was she playing a game with her? There was Oliver, and games were his thing.

She pulled the corner of the duvet around her ears and shut her eyes. Tomorrow would come.

Sunlight was pouring into the room. Helen screwed up her eyes and felt for the clock. It was almost noon. She slumped back under the cover and dozed in the thick heat, wrapped in the damp aroma of her body.

When had she last eaten? On the train, she had an egg sandwich, some cheese and onion crisps. Hours and hours ago. Her stomach was aching, an empty pit. She could go to Berwick Street, eat at Dina's, and still have plenty of time before the girl at the market would be packing up and leaving for home. She would follow her, and complete her final triumph in London before she up and left this sprawling, faceless city. She'd lived in this place for so long, it felt a part of her, but it was time to move on to fresher air.

Her eyes closed again, her body relaxing.

Then it was two o'clock.

She must get up. Helen pulled herself out of bed, ventured into the shower and washed herself briefly before changing into a clean T-shirt and jeans from the pile on the countertop. It felt strange, as if they weren't really hers, but she couldn't worry about that now. There wasn't anything she could do about the intrusion, especially as she hadn't been robbed. It could even have been the landlord, come to check on the premises, but she knew that wasn't true. She must focus on her own contravention, which was much more interesting now than any other.

The girl in the market would be hers tonight.

Oliver would be livid, then no doubt full of admiration. Then she would be gone, perhaps leaving him with yearning for her collaboration. She took one last look around before leaving, and stepped out the door. Everything felt different now, her surroundings sharply in focus, every sound ringing with clarity. There was a brand new corner to turn.

THIRTY-SIX

Lizzy's Room

It was her favourite part of the week. Lizzy loved Fridays, because now she always went to Nat's for the weekend. Normally there'd be an hour or two to go until packing up, but Dave had decided to finish early because of the heat. It had been a long day, busier than ever. Where did all the people come from? She tied her hair up in a loose ponytail and dabbed at her forehead with a tissue.

Dave winked at her and dusted off his jeans. "You off to Nat's, then, love?"

She nodded. "Don't you ever wear summer gear, Dave? You must be boiling in them jeans."

"Nah, jeans are fine for me. What d'you want me to wear? Manpris? Meggings? Fucking shorts? I'm not a poof." He stood with his legs apart, the apparent stance of a real man.

"What about them Lycra cut-offs that Tom sells down the other end?" She grinned.

Dave threw a rotten apple at her and it hit her on the shoulder blade.

"Hey! That hurt." She laughed. "They'd show off your knobbly knees."

He belched. "You can talk, Dark Witch of the West. Get the fuck out of here, will you. I'll see you Monday, bright and early. Don't forget your broomstick."

"Charming." Lizzy tightened the strap on her bag and slung it over her head and one arm. "See you Dave. Have a good one."

It was a bit of a laugh, just what she needed after getting the heebie-jeebies again that afternoon. Dave seemed to have stopped worrying about Simon and Roy and all the deaths and was back to being his usual rough-and-tumble self. But she hadn't forgotten about them, and still felt there was something funny going on: people watching, or conspiring. She'd had an ache in her belly all day.

There had been one or two of those flashes of light, the hands at that window opposite, and once she thought she'd seen Spinner in the crowd. There was a vision of black leather, greased hair, gold glinting in the distance. She'd frozen while the figure came towards her, partially hidden by the crowd and the stalls, but then it wasn't him, just some other creep who looked like a pimp. Maybe she was just being paranoid.

As she started to walk off, Dave called her back. "Oi Lizzy, I nearly forgot. I got something for you."

She turned. "Not another rotten apple. I can't take any more."

"Nah, it's for your birthday. Nat told us you was seventeen today. Are you?"

She rolled her eyes. "Yeah, but I didn't want anyone to know."

"Well I do," he said, "and I got you this. Have a good night, and don't do nothing I wouldn't do." He messed up her hair, rubbing the top of her head, like she was a dog.

She looked down at what he'd put in the palm of her hand. It was a silver pin. It said "The Smiths" and had their faces above the letters. "Brilliant, Dave, thanks." She pushed it into the flap of her bag and fixed on the underside. "Looks pretty cool."

He shrugged. "You're a good girl, Lizzy. Don't forget what's best."

"I won't." She made for Charing Cross Road, walking as fast as she could without getting too hot. Her flip-flops were slapping against her heels, flap-flap, as she dodged around the commuters and the folk already drinking beer outside the pubs. She could murder a pint, but avoided the bars as always, especially on the way to Nat's, as she didn't want Karen and Darren to think she had a drink problem. Not that she could afford to drink in a pub, even with wages in her pocket. They'd have to last her. Nat wouldn't be home yet; she was going job-hunting that afternoon with her dad, but said she'd got something for Lizzy and would give it to her later. When was the last time someone gave her a birthday present? She couldn't think.

The bus was packed, people stuffed along both decks, between the seats, and even standing on the stairs, which you weren't supposed to do. It smelled of hot bodies. Lizzy edged her way to the back. It was strange, but she still felt eyes on her, like someone was staring. Once or twice she thought she'd caught a glimpse of someone looking her way, but couldn't see through all the people. Was it her imagination? She'd been getting the willies recently, that was for sure, and she needed to calm down. In the end, she shut her eyes, pulling her hair forward over her face so no one would see.

No one was watching her right now, were they? They couldn't be. A trickle of sweat ran down her neck, and it made her shiver.

When her stop came, she barged through so she could jump off first, and waited partway up the pavement so she could see who got off after her. She pretended to look in her bag, hair still dangling over her face, but she could see through it. First came a woman in a suit, then a couple of old men with a walking stick between them, then two kids laughing and pushing and nearly bumping into her. Then, just as the doors were about to shut, a short, middle-aged woman hopped out. Lizzy lurched further forwards as if digging deep in her bag, her fingers suddenly seizing up and not working properly. It was that bloody woman: the woman who stared at her in the market that day. She was wearing that same coat, too hot for a summer's day.

Shit. Was she following her? Who was she?

The woman seemed a bit confused, looking all around her. She had a black rucksack on her back, which didn't seem to go with the rest of her. It was too outdoorsy or sporty, and pulling heavily on her shoulders. Lizzy stood up straight and made a decision. She tied her hair back again with an elastic band she had spare in her pocket. Here she was, right here. If this woman wanted something, she should just say. There'd been enough crap recently and she didn't want any more uncertainty.

But the woman wandered past.

Lizzy shrugged. Maybe she'd got it all wrong. It was the heat. She walked down the street towards Swan Road, grey-terraced houses on both sides, with rows of closed doors, and grimy stucco. They all looked the same, except some had hedges out front, evergreen and faceless, empty crisp packets and fag ends stuck in the bottom thickets. No one seemed to be around; most of the working folk were not back from town yet. She came up with a plan: at the end of the block, she'd turn to face where she'd come from. If the woman was following then she'd confront her. If she wasn't, then Lizzy was obviously imagining things. It wasn't far to Nat's house, so if things got weird, she'd just run all the way there. That woman looked like she wouldn't be able to run more than a few steps before she passed out.

Here was the end of the street, coming up fast. Lizzy took a deep breath, didn't slow down or give any hint that she might spin around. Then she turned on one heel, wishing to hell she wasn't wearing flip-flops.

Oh my god. The woman was there, perhaps ten metres behind. She stopped walking and they stared at each other. The woman didn't move.

"Are you following me?" Lizzy shouted, put her hands on her hips, and waited for an answer.

The woman said nothing, but took a few steps forward.

"What do you want? Are you a friend of Spinner's? Because if you are, you can get the fuck out of my face. I'm done with you lot. I've had enough." Lizzy stepped back, just one step. She wasn't getting a good feeling. A drop of sweat ran down her forehead and into her eyes.

Shaking her head, the woman came forward again, but still said nothing. Lizzy got a shiver, goose bumps on her arms despite the heat, and bent to take off her flip-flops. She was going to run. As she took off the second one, the woman launched herself forwards and grabbed her by the shoulders. There was a sharp pain in the side of her neck. It all happened so fast. She was off-balance, and her head started to get fuzzy.

"What you doing, get off me, you fucking freak," she said, trying to pull away, but the grip on her shoulders was like a vice. She could hear her own voice, getting distant, deeper with every word. Every-thing slowed.

She was pulled, or pushed, down towards the narrow passageway at the end of one of the terraces. Her head felt heavy, her body all soft and limp. There must have been a drug in that thing in her neck; what had she done to her? Her mouth was dry and slow and it was like one of those nightmares where you want to call for help but can't, like that time Natalie was groaning in her sleep. *Fuck.*

More steps, down the passageway.

She was lying down, now.

The woman's face looked down at her, smiling. Why was she smiling?

Another face, partially covered with a cotton scarf and low-peaked hat, loomed overhead. Who was that?

The woman's face stopped smiling. Then the grey sky overhead came nearer, clouds looming. The face was gone, out of the picture. Lizzy was sinking, then rising, couldn't feel her arms.

After a time, minutes, or seconds, or hours, Lizzy couldn't tell, the second face came back and helped her sit up. It was Oliver. He leaned her back against the brick wall, unravelled his scarf and crouched down in front of her. The woman was gone.

"Are you coming back, Lizzy?" He tilted his head to one side, studying her, his eyes intense.

She shook her head, scratched at the place in her neck where she'd been pricked with something. "I don't know. I feel funny still. Where's that woman?"

"Don't worry about her. I'll make sure she doesn't bother you again. You don't have to even think about her." He cleared his throat, then wiped a trickle of red from his face.

Was he bleeding again? Was that his own blood or someone else's? It didn't appear to be coming from anywhere this time, but smeared on one cheek. Lizzy tried to get up, but her legs gave way. She wasn't ready to stand up yet, but wanted to get to Nat's so badly. No one would know she was here. What time was it? It was her birthday.

"Who is she? What does she want?"

Oliver shrugged. "No one of any significance."

"Were you following me too?" She rubbed her ankles, saw her flip-flops discarded on the ground a few feet away. They were covered in brown dust from the road. Her feet were filthy too. She didn't have much choice but wait until she felt ready to walk. Or run.

"I was. Because I've got an important question for you. And I want you to think carefully before you answer. I'll wait until you feel better." He rubbed at the smear on his face again, his eyes boring into hers.

"Okay." She could feel the world breaking up into pieces, then coming together again inside her head, a surreal mess with Oliver's face at the centre of it all. His eyes were black. They didn't end. What was he going to ask her? What did he want with her? Her head was clearing, but she didn't like the clarity that came with it. She wanted to be in Nat's house, safe. Not here with him.

Oliver stood up, shuffled his feet around, and cleared his throat again. "Listen to me. Are you feeling up to the question? Or do you need more time to recover from whatever that woman gave you?"

"Just ask the question," she said. "I can think now. But I want to go."

"Take yourself back a few years, to when you were living in Dalbegie with your mum. You lived in that house with the green door and you had a friend, a girl, who you would meet to walk down to the High Street. You went to school. You were good, looked after your mum. You were happy." He nodded as if agreeing with himself.

"Yes," she said. "I remember. I would never forget how it was then."

"Of course not. The question is, if you had the choice, would you want to find out what happened to your mum? I mean, what exactly happened, every detail, every feeling, every anguish. Would you want to know?"

She screwed her eyes shut, tried not to cry. He was making it sound like her mum had been tortured. "Why are you asking me that? Do you know what happened to her?"

"I could find out," he said. "I could make enquiries. It wouldn't be easy, but I'm making you an offer. I can give you the chance to find out what happened to your mother. But if you accept my offer, you must be absolutely sure you'd want to know. Because if you do, you can't erase the details and go back. So my question is: do you want to? You need to think carefully about it."

Lizzy could feel a dull ache in her heart, where her mum was. She was gone from the world, dead, never to come back. Did she really need to know if she'd been killed, hurt, raped, discarded, how much pain she'd felt? Did it make a difference to things? She'd already decided it would be a disaster if Nat ever fully remembered what had happened to her. She tried to stand up again, and this time her legs were more stable. The feeling was coming back throughout her body and her mind was less fuzzy.

She felt a bit like a newborn foal, knees wobbling. But her head was seventeen years old and it had already seen too much. "No, I don't want to know. I can't handle it."

Oliver nodded, rubbing his hands around and around. "Are you sure?"

"Yes, I'm sure."

"Good answer," he said.

Later she would regret that she hadn't asked more questions, but for now she just wanted to get away from him. She shuffled to the street, slipping on her flip-flops on the way, feeling Oliver's eyes on her. They burned.

She woke up on Nat's bed. The room was much darker than it was when she'd come up here for a lie down. *Shit.* What time was it? Lizzy turned the alarm clock; it was nearly six-thirty, which meant she'd been asleep for two hours. She stretched out and yawned, listened to the voices downstairs for a minute, muffled and broken up by occasional giggling. Natalie must be home now. The pillow was so soft, the bed like cotton wool compared with the lumpy mattress she had at the bedsit. Her eyes were closing again.

She shouldn't fall back asleep.

Lizzy sat up. She didn't want to lie there any longer, make them all wait for their dinner, if they hadn't started already. The drug she'd been given by that woman had worn off and now she felt more normal. Nat's mum had been so kind to her when she got to the house, shaken up and drowsy all at once, but trying not to show it. Karen could tell something was wrong and sent her upstairs, even brought her some snacks on a tray. There was a sandwich cut into wee squares, crisps, chopped cucumber, and a Penguin biscuit, all arranged on a big white plate. She almost didn't want to eat any of it, as it would ruin the display. She rubbed her eyes and smoothed down her hair, checking in the mirror on the wall for mascara smudges. Her face was less blotchy now, the dark circles faded.

The smell of lasagna drifted up and she imagined biting into the pasta, melted cheese filling her mouth, the tomato sauce tangy in the middle of it all. Lizzy stomped downstairs, not wanting to surprise them by suddenly appearing in the middle of their time together in the kitchen. They all went quiet when she opened the door; or was it her imagination?

Eventually Darren spoke. "There she is, our very own Sleeping Beauty." He was sitting on a bar stool, drinking a can of Heineken. He held it up in salute. "Happy Birthday, Lizzy."

"Hello, darlin'. You had a good nap, then, didn't you? Happy Birthday again, love." Karen was holding the lasagna, flowery oven gloves up to her elbows. She put the dish down on the counter and shut the oven door with her foot.

"Sorry I slept so long." Still feeling a bit groggy, Lizzy sat next to Natalie at the table and smiled at her.

"Hope you didn't dribble on my pillow." Natalie cracked open a can of Heineken and gave it to her. "You have this one and I'll get another one out the fridge."

"We're having beer?" Lizzy held the can up to her head and sighed as the cold of it seeped inside. Things were getting better and better.

Darren crushed his can. "'Course we're all having beer, it's your birthday. Can't have you missing out, can we? Nat, get us another will you, I've guzzled this one."

Karen clapped her hands together. "Right, the lasagna's ready and I've cut the garlic bread. Shall we all sit around the table? I'll pass some knives and forks to you, Nat, and put out the salt and chili sauce, will you?"

Lizzy was grateful that no one mentioned having to wait for her, that to eat later seemed a natural thing. That to drink beer with dinner was normal. They all fussed around, grabbing plates and drinks and scraping the chairs back on the lino, until they were sat down. Karen dished up the food, and put the bread in the middle, and everyone grabbed a piece.

Karen cleared her throat. "We were all talking about some things while you were upstairs, Lizzy. Just before you appeared, we were going to come and wake you up."

Lizzy had just taken a big bite of bread, and found she couldn't chew it properly. Her heart had stopped beating for a moment, her stomach clenched into a knot. "Oh," she said through her food.

Karen looked at Darren, and Natalie was shifting her head from side to side, as if she was trying to look at both of them at the same time. Something was wrong. Maybe they thought she was on drugs, the way she'd showed up at the door.

"Anyway," Karen continued, "we wanted to ask you about this bed-sit of yours."

"I know I shouldn't be staying here so much. I'll go as soon as we've finished eating. I honestly didn't mean to sleep for so long. It's just that I was so, so, tired and I just died." Lizzy kept her eyes on the plate, couldn't bear to look at anyone now. "And you all had to wait for me."

"No. You can't go back there. It's no place for a young girl." Darren pointed his fork at Lizzy, and went back to his dinner as if he had settled an argument.

Lizzy frowned. "We've talked about it before. It's where I live. It's cheap. I can't help what goes on there. I don't get mixed up in any of it, honest. I know I'm young, but I've been there and done that already, and I won't do it again. I won't, honest."

"Of course you can't help it, darlin', and it ain't your fault." Karen pursed her lips. "But what with the other night's to-do, well, you can't go on like that. We want you to come and live with us, here. Nat'd love it, like having a sister. The two of you can look out for each other, save me and Darren a few worry lines. Have you seen my forehead? Covered in them. Nat could even go back to the market, if you stick together. No one seems to want any staff down the High Street, do they Nat?"

Nat shook her head and shrugged.

Karen continued. "You're a good girl, ain't you, Lizzy. Don't give us any lip. Look at you, pale and skinny as a rake. You better have second helpings of that lasagna."

"Watch it. I want the rest of that," said Darren. He winked at Lizzy.

"Go on, Lizzy." Natalie nudged her arm. "We'll go and get your stuff tomorrow, bring it all back here. I bet you haven't got much, anyway."

They were asking her to live with them—in this house of laughing and telly and comfy beds. She didn't have to go back to that place, suffer the noise, live in fear of someone bursting in with a knife or a gun. Lizzy looked at each of them in turn, and studied their faces. They were all waiting for her to speak, forks held midway to their plates, like she'd paused them with the remote control. It seemed like they were all wondering what her answer would be, that they genuinely wanted it to be "yes."

She desperately wanted to belong somewhere, to feel warm again, to stop having to be on edge. "I hope this is real, that I'm not still upstairs dreaming."

"Hang on, I'll give you a pinch." Darren reached over and tweaked her arm, tickling her and laughing. Some melted cheese was dribbling down his chin.

"Dad, what are you like!" Natalie rolled her eyes and stabbed her fork into her food.

"Okay, okay, you're real," Lizzy giggled. "I can't think of anywhere else I'd rather be than here, with you lot of freaks."

"Welcome to The Munsters," said Karen. She was grinning.

Her eyes locked with Karen's, just for a second. They were shining bright with something. Was it love? Lizzy couldn't be sure of it, but the last time she'd seen that look, it was on the face of her mother.

I'm okay now, Mum. Can you see me down here, in this house? It's the one with the funny picket fence at the front, and the red brick doorstep. You know the one.

I think you'd like everyone in this place, even Darren who's pure mad.

I haven't dared to say "pure mad" for such a long time, but I can now. Sometimes I forget how I'm supposed to talk, like I'm halfway between Scotland and London.

Karen made me a birthday cake. It was chocolate with chocolate buttons all over it, and they put seventeen black candles on it. That bit was Nat's idea. Nat also gave me a new poster of The Smiths, which is just as well because my old one was getting scabby around the edges. She also got me some metallic nail varnish. We saw it in a magazine and it was dead cool. Well, I've got some of my own now.

The best present of all was being asked to live here. They've made up the box room for me, so I can have my own space. It's tiny but it's mine and I love it. I can do whatever I want with the walls, even paint them, but for now my posters are up and I have to say, The Smiths are looking good up there. Dave was right; they're great, even though they're from the old days. Anyway, I like how my bed faces the wee window, so if I keep the curtains open, I can lie here and see the stars at night. It's a bit cloudy just now, but I know you're out there somewhere, glowing bright, all the way through to the other side. To me.

I don't wake up cold any more; I'm all warm and cozy in the mornings. I just wanted you to know that. As for all the weird stuff that's happened recently, I'm still not sure what to think. I feel bad that I haven't told Nat's family about the alleyway, about what Oliver said and the protection he's giving me. No one has seen Spinner since he tried it on with Nat again, and I just know he's gone for good. I have a feeling Oliver has had his guts for garters, as Granny Mac used to say. He's probably scared away that weird woman as well. I'll never find out who she was, but I'm guessing something to do with Spinner.

I don't know what happened to you. I hope I never know. Oliver offered to help me find out, but I think it would upset me even more. I don't see the point. You're gone and there's nothing I can do about it. All these things I feel like I need to keep inside. It's too intimate, stuff that no one else would understand, to do with me and you. I'm going to keep it that way so we'll always have a secret between us, and never let each other go.

I don't feel like the secret is wrong, but it's something that makes me feel safe. Somehow, it's protecting the memory of you.

I'm falling asleep now, Mum, so I'll talk to you soon.

Sweet dreams, my wee angel.

ABOUT THE AUTHOR

Jackie Bateman grew up in Kenya, and lived in London and Edinburgh for many years before settling in Vancouver with her husband and two children. Her first novel *Nondescript Rambunctious* won a national First Book Competition in Canada, sponsored by Simon Fraser University. *Savour* continues the dark story of Lizzy and her obsessive nemesis Oliver. Jackie has also published many award-winning short stories, some of which can be found at **www.jacbateman.com**